THE GUNPOWDER CHRONICLES

THE REBELLION ENGINES

USA TODAY BESTSELLING AUTHOR

JEANNIE LIN

THE REBELLION ENGINES

Print: ISBN: 978-0-9909462-9-8

Cover design by Deranged Doctor Design (www.derangeddoctordesign.com).

For inquiries, please contact Jeannie Lin via the e-mail contact form at www.jeannielin.com.

LIST OF CHARACTERS

Note: The family name comes first for characters who have both given and family names listed. I.e. Jin Soling has a given name of Soling and a family name of Jin.

Jin Soling - Daughter of the former imperial Chief Engineer. Trained in traditional medicine and acupuncture, she struggles with securing her family's future in amidst threats of rebellion and colonization.

Jin Zhi-fu - Soling's father and former Chief Imperial Engineer who was blamed for the empire's loss in the first Opium War.

Jin Tian - Soling's studious younger brother who shows hints of his father's ingenuity.

Shi Anlei - Soling and Tian's mother. A talented mathematician who is struggling with opium addiction.

Crown Prince Yizhu - Heir to the throne who seeks to strengthen his empire against the *Yingguo* (British) invaders.

Chen Chang-wei - Engineer and member of the Ministry of Science who was formerly betrothed to Soling before her father's execution.

Yang Hanzhu - Rogue chemist and former member of the Ministry of Science during the first Opium War. Defector and traitor to the Chinese empire.

Dean Burton - American merchant living in the foreign concession of Shanghai. An ally of Chen Chang-wei.

Sagara Satomi - Daughter of Sagara Shintarō, a renowned inventor and scientist of the samurai class. Satomi is an expert in crafting firearms.

Makoto - Disgraced samurai and ronin. A sword-for-hire.

PART I

THE FACTORIES

PROLOGUE

Qing Dynasty, 1853 A.D.

C hang-wei and I made the journey by river in a towering ship built like a fortress, to a final destination even we didn't know.

I had in my possession the imperial decree notifying me of my new appointment. Jin Soling, daughter of Jin Zhi-fu, is granted the title of Physician at the Imperial Factories.

Chang-wei's decree didn't name him as anyone's son. It simply read that Chen Chang-wei was assigned as head engineer at the Factories.

I'd been relieved we were being sent to the same place, even though I had other doubts. I'd petitioned to be reassigned from my previous position as physician in the Emperor's harem, a place filled with perfume and intrigue. I was happy to be free of the palace — even though it meant leaving Mother and my brother Tian in Peking for a time. It was dangerous to hover in the circle of court politics. I didn't have the talent or stomach for it.

As the son of a military official from the north, my father

had thrived in those circles of power and influence. He had risen through the ranks of the bureaucracy to become head of the Ministry of Science — only to be condemned to death after we'd lost the war against Yingguo, known as England, and their armored steamships.

I should be grateful the imperial appointment saw fit to include Father's name. I should be happy he had any mention at all. Maybe it meant the Jin family name was no longer held in disgrace.

The current Emperor on the throne was not the one who had sentenced my father to death. Prince Yizhu, now styled Emperor Xianfeng, had been tutored by my father. He had recruited men like Chen Chang-wei to build up the Qing army using their knowledge of technology and science — even if it meant adopting the ways of the West.

The Emperor's bold plan was the reason I'd been summoned before the imperial court after living in exile for years. Yizhu had given me a chance to gain protection for my family and restore our standing, but for every task I completed for the imperial court, there was always another, more difficult one to follow.

For now, the Emperor was far away. The foreigners who had taken over our ports were far away. We floated through a corridor of vast mountains rising high above, along the Yangtze River which seemed as wide as an ocean.

I was nothing more than a grain of sand. The smallest seed. I liked that feeling. The dark mountains shielded us from the world beyond and there was nothing but rock and wind and water. I couldn't remember ever feeling such peace.

Chang-wei appeared to feel the same way. The worry lines that frequently hung over his brow had smoothed out. He wrote in that little notebook of his every day while we stood on the deck of the ship. Observations, he told me. Reflections. I suppose it was his engineer's version of poetry — committing details to his impressive memory.

Between writing, whenever he glanced up, his dark, thoughtful eyes would search for me. My heart leapt at each contact.

Chang-wei was graced with high cheekbones and a squared, well-formed chin that spoke of steadiness and loyalty. I secretly found him handsome. Secret because we never spoke about things like that. Trivial things. Things that would make him laugh at me when Chang-wei rarely laughed.

There was a dark cloud looming over us despite the gentle river. Soon, the idyllic part of the journey would come to an end. The Factories had been a source of fear and dread in me for years now. There were imperial factories throughout the mainland. Where we were going was understood to be one complex among many, but the exact location of this one was kept secret.

After the Qing empire had suffered defeat against the foreign warships in the Opium War, we had become determined to never be caught so ill-equipped again. Foundries and factories were raised quickly, using the same system of conscription and mass labor that had built the Great Wall and shaped the Grand Canal.

I had lived in fear that my younger brother, Tian, would be conscripted into the Factories. I'd done everything in my power to protect him and my mother, even agreeing to work for the same imperial authorities that had executed my father. The empire had suffered a humiliating defeat and Father had been Chief Imperial Engineer. Someone had to take the blame.

The factory conscripts were paid for their labor, but they had little choice in the matter. I'd known of men in our village who had been marched off to never return. Yet I was going to the hidden and hated Factories now to serve as physician.

To live in these times, in the shadow of the Factories and beneath the haze of opium smoke, was to learn to take what oxygen I could from every breath, no matter how corrupted the air might be.

At night, we retired below into the hold. Chang-wei and I had separate sleeping compartments, but there was no one on the ship to serve as chaperon. We were the only true passengers - the rest being crew and imperial guards overseeing the monthly shipment of supplies to the Factories. It was a bountiful shipment, which was why it had to be guarded by a floating fortress. Pirates and bandits stalked the waterways.

That night, I lingered in Chang-wei's berth, sensing that the journey was coming to an end. I rested my head on his shoulder as he told a story.

"Over a thousand years ago, in the Zhou Dynasty, there was an artificer named Yan Shi," he began.

"What's an artificer?"

"Like an inventor." Chang-wei's arm circled around me as if it was the most natural thing in the world.

I settled in closer, warm and sleepy.

"The artificer appeared before King Mu, the fifth king of Zhou," he continued. "He presented a life-sized machine with a man's body. The invention looked just like a living person from the outside, able to move and walk."

"What was it made of?"

"The records say it was leather, wood and lacquer."

"Like a puppet."

"Yes. But without sticks or strings."

My eyelids grew heavy as I listened. My palm rested against his chest feeling his heart beat just beneath my fingertips. When had I ever had Chang-wei completely to myself?

He went on, his fingertips trailing absently over my hair. "While the king watched in astonishment, Yan Shi had the automaton walk and nod. If he touched the automaton's chin, its mouth would drop open and it would start singing. If he touched his hand, it would react. Then the automaton turned to the king's concubines and started flirting."

"How would a machine flirt?"

"With lewd and naughty gestures too scandalous to re-enact." I laughed.

"The king became outraged at the insult and started to call for his guards to have Yan Shi executed. Thinking quickly, Yan Shi opened up his invention like a cabinet to show the king that it was merely a construction painted to look like a man on the outside. Inside was a fully connected set of artificial bones, joints and muscles. Even a full set of organs. The king was delighted and spared Yan Shi's life."

"That's an interesting story," I murmured.

"It's in the dynasty records," Chang-wei mused. "We've been envisioning these designs for hundreds of years."

Boastful engineers and impulsive kings. A time-honored tradition.

He shifted positions to lay down beside me and I curled up against him. A year ago, I would have thought such actions too bold, too familiar, but we'd been through so much. We'd faced life and death together.

Chang-wei was quiet for so long that I thought he had fallen asleep. His breathing slowed, deep and steady. I listened with my ear pressed to his chest and started to drift as well, when he spoke again.

"This will be an opportunity to establish a name for myself."

"You have a name," I insisted drowsily.

"I can redeem myself in the eyes of the Ministry." His arm tightened around me. "And then, perhaps I can finally—"

He didn't finish. I started to ask him what sort of redemption could he possibly require? He was Chen Chang-wei, eternally faithful servant to the imperial court.

There was something else I wanted to tell him, but the

7

words slipped from my grasp as I sank into dreams, lulled by the sway of the water. I was safe and warm in Chang-wei's arms, as content as I could ever remember being.

Right before sleep took over, I remembered what I'd try to say. I wanted to tell him not to be like the artificer Yan Shi.

Barely clever enough not to get himself killed.

CHAPTER 1

Qing Dynasty, 1854 A.D. - One year later.

I stood in the workroom with a large bowl before me. Inside was a combination of ginseng and zicao root mixed with beeswax and ground into a paste. I added drops of sesame oil and stirred until the pale-colored ointment became smooth. The salve would be applied to wounds and cuts to aid healing.

Even though I was on my feet, the routine task of measuring and mixing felt like a respite. There was little time for rest in the year since I'd arrived at the Factories in Hubei.

When I was satisfied with the consistency of the ointment, I scooped it into ceramic jars. The supply in the infirmary needed to be replenished as well as the stashes directly at each facility. Most of the cuts and lacerations that the workmen suffered on a day-to-day basis never made it to the infirmary.

As I wiped my hands clean, an explosion thundered through the outpost.

I held my breath, every muscle coiled for what would happen next. Silence followed, interrupted by the clang of the gong. I rushed for the door, nearly colliding into Kai, an ox-shaped, ox-sized man dressed in the same dove-gray uniform that I wore. He met my eyes briefly, exchanging a look of quiet dread. All around us there was the echo of footsteps. The infirmary crew spilled out into the front of the administrative section to stare toward the factories.

The insistent beating of the gong told me the damage this time was serious. A signal flare shot into the sky, trailing green smoke.

"Tai Shan." I reported the name of the facility for the benefit of anyone new to the medical team who wasn't yet familiar with the signal code. "Everyone. Now."

The Factories consisted of five main facilities, each named after one of the five sacred mountains, along with an array of supporting storehouses and workshops.

The sedan was already loaded with supplies. I gestured for Kai and the errand boy Po. Kai was the resident bone-setter. I had chosen Po for the simple trait that he didn't faint at the sight of blood.

My heart was still pounding as I slid the beads of the abacus control to set the coordinates. Tai Shan was the largest facility at our outpost. Over a thousand workers toiled within the walls. One thousand lives in possible danger.

The gunpowder engine in the sedan awoke with a low rumble just as Kai settled his large frame into the carriage. He pulled Po in beside him. The vehicle could carry more, but we needed to move quickly. We were speeding away even before I seated myself.

"How many days since the last one?" Kai muttered.

I stared straight ahead as we sped past the staff quarters toward the factory grounds. "Focus."

Black smoke rose into the sky in the distance.

"Twenty days," Kai said beneath his breath in answer to his own question. "If the Directorate cared to pay any mind to our well-being."

"*Focus.*"

I knew it had been twenty days. I knew how long it had been to the hour. I knew it by the tightness that had grown in my chest with each passing day as I waited for the next tragedy to strike. And now the tightness was replaced by this pounding, pounding of my heart inside me which was, guiltily, almost a relief. Because now action could replace fear.

The factory appeared before us. It was a dark tower that on normal days spewed a stream of smoke and gunpowder residue from venting pipes. A billowing cloud, bitter with ash surrounded it. My stomach dropped. A fire inside had to be the source of the smoke. The whir of the pumps indicated the irrigation system had engaged. Water was being funneled from the cisterns underground into the facility.

Chen Chang-wei had the system built months ago. He'd enlisted a hundred men and the ire of the imperial inspectors for the project. At the moment, I laid my hopes on his invention.

As we neared, workers streamed out of the factory gates. With the aid of the mechanical sedan, we had arrived before the rest of the medical crew. There was a resident yishi assigned to each of the five factories to see to injuries that happened on the lines, but altogether that meant there was only a handful of trained physicians to care for the thousands conscripted to work in the factories.

When I'd first arrived, Zhuzhi yishi, the appointed chief physician, would only assign me to the care of the women who worked the Factories as well as the ones who had come with their families to live in the adjacent village. That number was few in comparison to the rest of the workforce and the need for a physician's care was too great. Soon, propriety became a second or third thought. I was being sent wherever I was needed.

Then Zhuzhi yishi was killed during a scaffolding collapse at the Hua Shan facility. Of the physicians that remained, many were apprentices and village doctors. Though I was in essence a village doctor as well, I had been appointed by imperial decree from Peking. This left me as the acting chief physician.

I don't think anyone else wanted the job.

The sedan came to a halt just beyond the gathering crowd. There were no section leaders or foremen to direct the evacuated workers, but I couldn't worry about that. I had my own job to tend to. During a crisis, it was of utmost importance to remember that and only that. Do your job. Don't get overwhelmed.

"We must get inside," I said.

Kai moved in front of me and started clearing a path. He was a large man, with thick arms and hands that looked as capable of breaking bones as setting them. The crowd parted easily for him. As we passed through, I heard scattered reports.

"The main furnace—"

"All around me, men hurt—"

It was tempting to stop and ask questions, but my questions would be answered once I surveyed how much damage had occurred and how many were injured. How many were killed. I took a deep breath, clenching my teeth as I stepped through the doors.

The interior was hazy with smoke, but I sensed it was bad in there.

"Find the foreman," I ordered and the boy Po started running, weaving through the crowd.

Black smoke filled the interior and workers shoved against one another as they tried to find a way out. They were like ants in a frenzy. There was movement overhead as the workers climbed down from the scaffolding around the upper levels. A few of the section leaders had gathered their wits enough to direct their people to the exits.

Kai and I made our way to the central furnace. The smoke was thickest here, and I pressed my scarf over nose and mouth as we ventured into the haze. Water rained down from the bamboo pipes above. What had been a fire was reduced to a trace of soot and ash. I could make out several figures scattered about the factory floor.

"Who's hurt?" I called into the smoke. "Is Yishi Lao there?"

We followed the muffled reply to find the elder physician crouching over one of the fallen workers. The infirmary's gray uniform was both meant to be nondescript and to stand out from the darker clothing of the work crews. At the moment, the pale cloth made it easier to pick Lao out through the haze.

Lao was a man of fifty years of age and had been assigned to Tai Shan for several years. Enough to see several rounds of workers come and go.

"Broken lower leg, right side," Lao reported.

Kai crouched next to the injured man. "Can he be moved?"

Overhead, I heard the creak of wood and glanced up as Kai assessed the limb. The explosion in the furnace had damaged one of the main rafters. Part of the upper deck had fallen, trapping several workers underneath.

"We have to get everyone outside," I warned.

Kai followed my gaze up to the factory roof. "I'll get help."

"Sound the drums," I called out after him.

I didn't know if the bone-setter had heard me, but he would know what had to be done. Outside, the rest of the medical staff had hopefully arrived to set up the infirmary tent. The incidents of the past year had given us ample opportunity to refine a process. My eyes teared up from the acrid smoke as a knot of fear tightened in my chest. Of all the accidents, this was the worst.

I turned back to the fallen worker who would have to be

carried. There were others still in the area. Anyone who hadn't staggered up and out by now was probably unable.

"Go to the next one," I told Lao, dispensing with any semblance of courtesy. There was another man nearby being dragged out of the rubble. His cry of pain told me he was at least alive.

I knelt by the worker before me, placing what I hoped was a comforting hand upon his chest. His pulse beat frantically beneath my fingertips. His teeth were gritted in pain.

Retrieving a vial from my jacket, I jabbed the attached needle into his thigh. The prick would be nothing compared to the pain of the broken bone. "We'll get you out of here soon," I told him, hoping it was the truth.

Then I left him to move on to the next worker. There was no time to be nursemaid.

I moved through the next few as quickly as I could. The evacuation gong had sounded, sending workers streaming for the doors. I enlisted as many as I could to help take out the wounded. For those who could not be moved, I administered the needle for pain. For the one man who lay unmoving, there was nothing I could do but close his eyes.

Swallowing past a lump in my throat, I kept going. The worst thing to do in a disaster was freeze.

Kai had returned with a team bearing stretchers. He began his work of stabilizing broken limbs and instructing the carriers. The next fallen worker was deep in the boiler complex and still partially buried. A section of the piping had collapsed. One of the others knelt over him, speaking to him. As I approached, I could see blood flowing from the injured man's mouth. I prayed it wasn't from a punctured lung.

I took my place at the fallen man's side, shouldering pushing aside his companions without apology.

"Can you hear me?" I asked.

The young man opened his eyes to stare up at me. His face was covered in soot, but he appeared fifteen or sixteen at most.

"We'll get you out, Little Brother."

It was merely an honorific, but I couldn't help but see my brother Tian in him. I saw my brother in all the young men who were conscripted from the surrounding provinces to work in the Factories. I had succeeded in having my family relocated to Peking to avoid this fate, but so many other families in the villages had not.

He groaned as I felt his pulse. No blood bubbled up from his throat with the sound. A hopeful sign, despite being pinned down by falling debris.

"He was working in the boiler room," the man kneeling beside him said. He scrutinized my imperial jacket, his reaction obscured by the soot covering his face.

"Are you the section head?" I asked him.

He had an authoritative air about him, but he shook his head. "Just another peasant."

The sharpness of his response raised the hairs on the back of my neck. I looked down at the injured youth. His eyes had closed again, but his fists were clenched in pain. "Jiang Wen. Help me."

Jiang took his friend's hand and leaned down once more. "Don't be afraid, Guo."

I scanned the debris pinning the injured worker down as the rafters creaked above. "We need to get him out of here."

The irrigation system had doused the area, reducing the likelihood of a secondary explosion, but the area was still unstable. I tried to lift the wooden beam to no avail.

"I already tried that," Jiang said through his teeth.

Guo's voice started to fade as he begged once more for help. I considered going to seek aid when another voice cut in.

"You need leverage."

I looked up to see Chang-wei. He was dressed formally in

the black embroidered engineer's jacket, his hair braided into a tight queue. The look was stiffly out of place, but immediately signaled authority. He met my eyes for a long moment, his expression unreadable other than the deep crease cutting across his brow. Over the last year, the worry lines had come back stronger than ever.

He searched about the area before gesturing to the workmen behind him. They went to retrieve planks from the scaffolding against a nearby wall.

"Be ready to move him." Chang-wei shoved his queue away from his face before turning to position the levers.

"It's going to hurt," I warned Jiang as he took hold of his friend's shoulders. There was no time for me to administer the needle for the pain. The bone beneath was likely broken if not shattered, and Guo was rigid with shock. The sudden movement would jar the injury mercilessly, but it couldn't be helped until we had moved him and ourselves away from the accident.

"On three." Chang-wei and his crew had wedged the planks, angling them against stone blocks for leverage.

He began his count and Jiang's muscles tensed as he prepared himself.

"Three."

Chang-wei's voice interrupted my thoughts as the workmen lifted the broken beam. Jiang Wen dragged his friend clear of the rubble as Guo let out a scream. His hand grabbed onto my sleeve. The sudden move made me stagger before I caught myself.

Gently, I uncurled his fingers from my jacket. "You're free, Brother Guo," I soothed. "We'll take care of you."

With his eyes squeezed shut, Guo managed a nod. I administered a needle of opium and then another when the first one didn't take as quickly as I'd like.

Kai had returned with a stretcher and more of our medical crew. The other injured were being moved out around us.

"Get everyone out," Chang-wei commanded. "Tai Shan Facility is being locked down."

I didn't thank him for his assistance and he didn't thank me for mine. This was routine for us now, communicating with nothing more than a few passing glances when our paths happened to cross. There were always another hundred things to tend to. When we'd both been assigned to the Five Factories, I'd been grateful we weren't separated. Lately we might as well have been at opposite corners of the world.

We exchanged another silent glance now. For a moment he looked like he wanted to say something more, but Kai was calling for me. The factory foreman came to prostrate himself at Chang-wei's feet. He begged for forgiveness with his forehead pressed to the floor.

I didn't want to think of what would happen to him. Whenever there was an accident, someone had to be held responsible and punished. It was protocol.

The steadfast Jiang Wen remained by his friend as he was carried outside to the medical tents. I followed closely behind. As we neared the doors, armed guardsman streamed into the factory, forming a perimeter around the inside. Immediately following them was Inspector General Hala flanked by his guards.

The inspector presented an imposing figure, not so much in stature but in his demeanor. His face was thin, his cheeks lacking, and his nose sharp. He wore an expression that perhaps was meant to be piercing, but it more simply appeared unpleasant.

I quickly ducked away from his gaze, head bowed. I had nothing to fear from the inspector other than the fact that everyone always had something to fear from him. He was the one who reported back to the Emperor and his war council.

As we moved past the heavy iron doors, I forced the black smoke and the inner politics of Peking aside. I needed to focus my energy on fulfilling my duties — tending to the injured.

~

THE MEDICAL TENT was a structure made of a folding bamboo frame draped with canvas. The severely wounded were set up inside on cots. Those with more moderate injuries were relegated to the benches immediately outside.

I bypassed the rows, ignoring the questions, the pleas, the expressions of pain. They would be seen to in time. The moment I passed under the shade of the tent, a different energy emerged. Physicians bent over the injured, hands pressed against wounds that were bleeding too quickly. Bone-setters righted shattered limbs as best they could. Runners darted in and out with bandages, liniment, and opium. For the pain.

I became another pair of hands, doing what I could to patch things together. Gritting my teeth to keep on going.

"Yishi Jin." It was Po. The boy was flushed from running supplies and out of breath when he reached me. "Kai is asking for you."

I followed the boy to the back quadrant of the tent. The place where the most serious injuries were placed.

Jiang was still there. Guo's body lay slack while his friend stood over him, head bowed. My stomach dropped as my heart hammered in my chest. I'd just seen him, spoken to him—

My view was suddenly blocked by a broad chest. Kai.

"They had to remove it," he said grimly. "His left leg."

I swallowed. "At least he's alive."

"Let's hope the next person is as well."

Kai was plainspoken. He'd come from a small village in Anhui, the same province my mother was from. We'd befriended each other on that shared connection, but had grown closer over the last year working side-by-side. I'd come to trust his honest perspective.

There was no time to check on Guo myself and there was

little I could do for him now anyway, but I made a silent vow to not forget. Losing a limb was in itself a small death.

As Kai and I started down rows of cots, something caught my eye. Chang-wei had entered the tent along with the Inspector General. They surveyed the injured laid out with grim expressions. I intercepted them as they began to move down the row.

"Inspector," I greeted. Then, after a brief glance at Chang-wei. "Engineer Chen."

"Miss Jin." The Inspector's gaze slid past me to rake coldly over the injured workers.

I'd been assigned to the Factories for over a year, yet the inspector still refused to address me by my title. "If there's anything I can assist you with, Inspector?" I refused to yield when he took a step forward. "These workers are badly hurt and need immediate attention—"

"Then you should go about your duties," the senior official interrupted. "If we require anything from you, you'll be summoned."

He swept past me disdainfully. A hush had fallen over the tent. The assistants who were caring for the injured paused in their duties to glance furtively over at the exchange. Everyone became more guarded.

I stopped Chang-wei as he started past. "What is this about?"

He glanced at the inspector's back before turning to me. "This is the second incident this month," he said under his breath.

"Because you're pushing the production lines too hard," I hissed, not as quietly as I probably should have.

It was unfair to put the blame entirely on Chang-wei, but the orders to increase production came from the Citadel and the Directorate.

Chang-wei looked away guiltily. "Inspector Hala suspects

sabotage. All of the workers in this factory are being detained for questioning."

He fell in line behind the inspector, leaving me to trail after them both.

"You can talk to them after we've treated their injuries," I insisted.

"They could be dead by then," the Inspector tossed coldly over his shoulder. "The workers closest to the explosion are likely to have seen something. They're also the ones who may realize now there's no value to harboring traitors."

He deliberately spoke loudly enough so that all in the tent could hear. I gritted my teeth and started forward. He held higher rank than me, but this was my domain. Chang-wei took hold of my arm.

"The quicker this is done, the sooner he'll be out of your way," he said. "Go see to the injured. I'll keep watch over Hala. Make sure he doesn't overstep his boundaries."

"What boundaries?" I demanded bitterly.

"Soling," Chang-wei began gently. He looked into my eyes while holding onto me.

He was still Chen Chang-wei and I was still Jin Soling. We had come here together, with a similar purpose, but Chang-wei's idea of duty was different than mine. My responsibility was to those immediately in my care. He worked from the Citadel, effecting changes that would be felt far and wide.

I closed my eyes and took a breath. He was exhausted. I was exhausted as well. Everyone and everything in the Factories was strained to the breaking point to try to meet the orders coming from Peking, and it was hard to remember why any of us were working ourselves to the bone.

When I opened my eyes again, Chang-wei gave me a small nod. I returned it, telling myself at least he was trying to help, but I was far from completely reassured.

"Later," he promised in low tones.

"Later," I echoed.

He left to join Inspector Hala who had been watching our exchange. I didn't care.

Kai returned to my side wordlessly. "Let's go," I told him.

We moved through the more serious injuries first. I administered medicine; salves and ointments, and opium when needed. Kai set what fractures he could. Out of the corner of my eye, I could see the Inspector stopping at one cot after another, asking questions. I braced myself — if he were to try to remove any of the workers, I'd have another battle to fight. About half an hour in, a messenger came into the tent to speak to him. Whatever it was, the matter was urgent enough that the official left immediately, leaving behind only two of his agents to continue the interrogation.

I watched as Chang-wei exited the tent on the Inspector's heels. He spared one glance back, searching. I looked down, focusing on the needle dose of opium I was administering to someone who had a shattered arm. There was an endless line of injuries and after an hour, I could no longer see the faces behind them. They all blurred together in the endless cycle of need, surrounded by the smell of ash and blood and fear. Perhaps I needed them to.

This accident was worse than the last. It would be a long time before any of us could rest.

When I finally returned to check on Guo, the worker who'd lost his leg, I was happy to see that his bleeding was controlled. He was still unconscious, which was probably best. His friend Jiang had remained and was helping others by bringing water and doing what he could.

Now that Guo was sleeping and his face cleaned of soot, he appeared even younger. My guess was still fifteen, with a slight roundness still to his cheeks and a prominent forehead that signaled cleverness. Boys and girls as young as twelve could get conscripted to the Factories. My brother, Tian, was eleven. He

21

was in the capital now, studying for entry into the Academy. When we'd lived in exile, it had been my constant worry that he'd be sent to the Factories, or, if not there, to the army, conscripted to fight the rebels.

Was one fate any better than the other?

Guo shifted then, a look of pain marring his expression in sleep. I smoothed a hand over his forehead, even though it likely provided little comfort. That's when I saw something slip out from the fold of his tunic. It was some sort of wooden token or charm tied around his neck with a length of cord. Curious, I lifted it to look over the design carved onto the face. It appeared to be a kind of wheel with a central point and spokes radiating out from the center.

"Yishi?"

Jiang had returned. I dropped the charm and turned to him. "I wanted to see how your friend was doing."

"Not well, as you can see," he replied, his expression grim.

I glanced at the stub where his leg had been and quickly looked away. Jiang was watching me through narrowed eyes. His features were rougher than the boy's. The thin line of his mouth appeared wary and unwelcoming.

"It's best if he's not moved for a few days," I advised. "This is a critical time. He needs to be watched for fever or chills. Any signs of infection."

"I'll stay with him," Jiang declared.

I started to remind him that there was no space to rest in the tent. That his section was likely to be called back to work if not the next day, then the one after. Even if the line wasn't operational, there would be cleanup and repairs.

"Was he close to you?" I asked instead.

There was something in his eyes that said it didn't matter what the rules dictated.

"I'm responsible for him," Jiang replied simply.

I considered asking him whether he'd seen anything suspicious but decided against it. Inspector Hala was certain to interrogate him about the accident. That was the inspector's responsibility, not mine. I was only there to help the injured and sick.

As I moved on, I turned back to see Jiang tucking the necklace back into Guo's tunic and folding the edges of the cloth securely over it.

CHAPTER 2

C hang-wei was waiting for me at the dormitories. He was seated on one of the benches outside. There was a lantern hung from the pole beside him.

"I didn't think you'd be here," I said.

He rose to come toward me. "We promised we'd speak later," he said, matter-of-fact.

That was before I knew it would be midnight before I was able to return to my sleeping quarter. After I'd left the medical tent, the Inspector General had sent word that he wanted an accounting of all the workers who'd been assigned to the Tai Shan facility, who'd been injured, and the nature and seriousness of their injuries. The workers who hadn't needed to remain in the medical tent were also detained while the Inspector and his men questioned them, taking down a written account in each case.

I'd stayed to make sure they were brought food and water until they were released to the factory village.

Those were all things I could have told Chang-wei, but lately our conversations had become stripped down to logistical details about the Factories.

"It's late," I said.

"I can go," Chang-wei offered.

I shook my head tiredly. Even though I didn't know what we had left to talk about, I didn't want him to leave.

Chang-wei came closer. "Today was difficult."

I nodded, feeling the weight of the day's events dragging through every bone. It had been a long time since we'd been alone, able to speak like this.

"Sometimes I forget how orders from the Directorate affect every single person here," he admitted.

I took a deep breath and let it out slowly, trying to expel the fire, ash and pain from my lungs. "It's gotten worse. The facilities are running all day, every day."

He stiffened defensively. "The rebel army is growing stronger by the day. Nanking is impenetrable. Our task here is more important than ever."

Nanking was the main stronghold of the Heavenly Peace rebellion, the so-called Taiping army. The rebels had captured the city a year ago and declared it their capital. Other cities had followed, falling one after another to the growing insurrection.

When we'd first come to the compound, Chang-wei and I had been of one mind. Serve the Emperor as best as we could and keep each other safe. Chang-wei had confided to me when we'd escaped Nagasaki that he wanted for us to be together, but he'd spoken of it just the once and then nothing.

We'd been betrothed when I was a child, with the understanding that the wedding wouldn't occur for another decade. Though at the time I hadn't met Chen Chang-wei, it was my father's wish that we would be wed. The arrangement fell apart when the war came. My father was sent to his death and my family exiled. Chang-wei was taken prisoner by the Yingguoren.

During those dark years, Chen Chang-wei remained only a name to me. A ghost from a lost past. When I finally did meet him, we were strangers and the empire was at the brink of another war.

Chang-wei had helped me bring my family back to Peking. More important than that, I had come to know what sort of character he possessed. He was intelligent, steadfast, loyal. He continued to honor my father as his mentor when others in the Ministry acted as if my father had never existed.

If Chang-wei had one fault, it was that he was too trusting, just as my father had been. If he had two faults — the second one was that he could be distant. He would close himself off like a silkworm spinning a cocoon.

I knew he was keeping things from me. There was only one reason he would do so—loyalty to the Emperor. To Greater Qing.

In that, he also reminded me frighteningly of my father.

"We don't have to talk about this if you don't want," I relented.

He shook his head. "You should know. Inspector Hala is convinced the string of accidents have been due to sabotage. He wants the perpetrators caught and punished."

"As I see it, Hala is under pressure to name someone, anyone as the culprit."

Chang-wei didn't respond, but he was visibly troubled at my outspokenness. It was dangerous to challenge someone like Inspector Hala.

"These incidents are threatening the cause," Chang-wei continued. "You're closer to the workers. If you see or hear anything—"

"I haven't heard anything," I protested, too quick.

Chang-wei eyes were unreadable in the lantern light. I wanted to tell him it wasn't only the work crews who would suffer if we failed. Chang-wei was the one who had brought his vision of the fearsome automaton army before the imperial throne. He'd promised armored warriors made of rods and gears that could be wired to march on the enemy without risking any lives.

But that was an illusion. How many lives had we lost over the past year in the Factories? Even for those who hadn't suffered injury, they had been taken away from their homes to be brought here.

"Do you regret coming here?" he asked quietly. *With me,* were the unspoken words.

"No." But was he starting to regret it?

"Head Engineer Chen," a voice called from down the path. The messenger stopped a respectful distance away.

Chang-wei took a step back from me. "Yes?"

"You're needed at the Citadel."

"Now? It's past midnight," I protested.

Chang-wei regarded me for a long moment, his eyes dark and thoughtful. He looked as if he wanted to say more, but he turned away to reply. "I'll be there right away."

The messenger stood rooted where he was, looking on impassively. We weren't going to be given any privacy.

"Try to get some sleep," Chang-wei said finally, disappointment showing on his face.

"You as well."

He nodded, but I knew there would be no rest for him. Chang-wei was Head Engineer. If the work crews were being run into the ground, I could only imagine what the Directorate was demanding of him.

THE NEXT MORNING, families came from the factory village to set up a cook stand outside the infirmary tent. I arrived to the sight of a large pot of odds-and-ends stew simmering over a fire.

Conscripted labor for the Factories were typically young

men and women. In rare cases, some of them came with families, feeding into the broken-down settlement that had sprouted up outside the factory complex. The presence of the so-called factory village wasn't officially sanctioned by the Directorate, but the villagers intermingled with the workforce and had become interwoven into factory life.

The ongoing skirmish with the rebels had displaced many families in the surrounding provinces. Those stragglers had also found their way to the village. It was a fragile and ever-changing community. One I had only experienced in small glimpses during brief visits.

I entered the infirmary tent and found the numbers inside had thinned. Kai was already at work but paused to come to me with a report. More than half had been well enough to return to the dormitories and only serious injuries remained. One man had died overnight.

"One," I echoed, feeling sick to my stomach. "The boy who lost his leg?"

"Little Guo?"

I regarded Kai curiously. "You know him?"

"I heard some of them using the nickname. He's fine. Still here, asleep." He gestured toward the center of the tent.

The factory authority would hardly care about one life lost. More conscripts would be brought in to replace him and anyone deemed too injured to continue work. The cycle would continue.

I went to Guo's cot and was surprised to find his friend, Jiang, crouched beside him. He appeared to have slept on the ground. His usually rough look was even rougher with the dark circles under his eyes.

"Yishi," he greeted, looking up at me somberly.

I bent to feel for Guo's pulse. It was faint, but stronger than yesterday. "His pulse is steady," I said to Jiang as he watched me with his hawkish gaze.

"Guo hasn't woken," he said.

"That may be a good sign. As long as there's no fever."

The boy had enough opium in his system to keep the pain at bay so he could rest. That was what he needed most.

"Have you not been summoned back to the line?" I asked.

"Tai Shan is shut down."

"Still?"

I wasn't knowledgeable about the factory schedules and quotas, but yesterday's fire had been extinguished and by now the smoke would have cleared. Only part of the building was damaged while the rest had appeared stable. With the aggressive schedule set by the Directorate, I would have assumed everyone would be ordered back to work as soon as possible. That's what had always happened in the past.

"Perhaps that's for the best at the moment." I looked down at Guo, my heart aching for him. "Once Guo has recovered, he'll be transported back to the main infirmary and arrangements will be made for his discharge."

"Discharge?" Jiang frowned. "Won't he be put back on the line?"

I was shocked at the suggestion. "His injury is very serious."

"He can be fitted with a mechanical leg. I've seen injured workers put back on the line in a matter of weeks." His mouth twisted. "Isn't that what's important to the Directorate? Productivity?"

"It may be better for Guo to be sent home."

"As a cripple?" Jiang spat. His anger hit me harder than a physical blow.

"It's not my decision," I told him.

"Guo would want to return to work," Jiang insisted. "The term of his conscription isn't done," he explained, seeing my look of doubt. "He has a younger brother at home who will be brought in to take his place."

I thought of the carving young Guo wore around his neck. I

didn't recognize the symbol, but there were numerous cohorts and brotherhoods among the factory workers. It would explain Jiang's protectiveness.

"Your friend was close to the explosion. Inspector Hala will insist on interrogating him," I warned.

It was too easy to be branded a traitor. I didn't want to see that happen to Guo after all he'd suffered.

"You're Manchu, aren't you?" Jiang challenged.

I braced myself. "I am."

My father was Manchurian, directly descended from the banner armies that helped found the dynasty. My mother was Han. It didn't matter that Manchu and Han lived among one another or that a Manchu emperor had been on the throne for hundreds of years. There were Han loyalists who still considered the Manchu barbaric foreigners. I was used to the insults.

"You wouldn't understand," Jiang said, his tone cold.

"What wouldn't I understand?" I asked carefully.

He looked directly at me with a gaze that was weighted, dragged down by time and experience. "We're all the same to you. We're all expendable."

THE TAI SHAN facility had been cordoned off. Armed guards stationed at the entrance moved to block my path as I approached. I argued that I was there to inspect the safety conditions, but the guards refused to move.

The door opened after one of the guardsmen had raised his voice.

It was Chang-wei. "Let her in."

For him, the guards moved aside easily. I slipped through the door and Chang-wei pushed it shut behind us.

"Tai Shan is closed for the day?" I began.

Chang-wei cast a pointed look at me, cutting my inquiry

short. He directed me farther into the building. There was a small cleanup crew inside, but no one I recognized.

"We are completing a thorough inspection for safety purposes," Chang-wei explained. "Starting tomorrow, the factory authority will rotate new workers onto the lines at Tai Shan."

"Won't the new crew need to be retrained?"

Each of the facilities was outfitted with a unique set of machinery.

"It will be a minor delay. An argument was made that the old rotation was overworked. Many of them were injured in the explosion or witnessed it close at hand. They might be nervous to come back."

"Is *everyone* who was assigned at Tai Shan being treated as suspect?" I asked, lowering my voice.

"We need the assembly lines functional as soon as possible. Production is critical to our success."

Chang-wei's use of *we* and *our* when talking about the Directorate made my head throb.

We had reached the furnace, a massive structure with an outer wall of stone and mortar. It took up half of the facility. Chang-wei ducked beside the hearth and gestured for me to follow. I hesitated in front of the cavernous hollow. The walls were charred black and the supports around it were warped and torn. The surrounding debris had been cleared away, but the smell of sulfur and ash permeated the air.

"It's safe," Chang-wei assured, holding out his hand.

Letting out a breath, I placed my hand into his and allowed myself to be drawn into the alcove.

"The gauges were tampered with," he said, tapping against an instrument panel. "Heat and pressure inside built up unchecked."

"Have you told Inspector Hala?"

"Not yet."

No one from the cleaning crew was nearby. Chang-wei kept

his voice low, making me wonder the reason for the sudden secrecy. Surely Chang-wei wasn't the only one who suspected sabotage.

"This is going to cause a major disruption. Hala will have everyone interrogated. I fear he'll demand all of the workers replaced and dismantle the factory village, but that's not the worst of it." He paused, considering his next words. "I don't think it was the conscripts," he said finally.

"Who else could it be?"

He hushed me as footsteps passed by outside. We waited until the sounds faded.

"I think someone with detailed knowledge of this machinery tampered with the configuration."

"You always tell me it's easier to break something than build it," I said.

He shook his head. "Whoever did this was more than an operator. The changes were subtle, hard to detect."

I realized then why he was being so secretive.

"Do you suspect it could be one of your engineers?" I asked, incredulous.

Jaw clenched, he stared at the instrument panel, as if the answer could be read in the needles and dials. His mouth formed a hard line. "There's been some talk in the Citadel that I'm the one deliberately delaying production."

"You? Who would think that?"

As Head Engineer, Chang-wei's reputation was tied to the success of the project.

"I have deliberately caused delays," he admitted.

I frowned at him. "Why?"

Chang-wei had dedicated himself night and day to the creation of the Emperor's automatons.

"The prototype isn't ready," he said. "The imperial court has demanded an army large enough to march on several fronts while all I have are worthless hunks of metal." He stared at the scorch marks singed over the panel. "If I tell Inspector Hala my suspicion, he'll bring everything to a halt. Including the engineering work in the Citadel. And right now, that's all it is—a suspicion."

I held out hope there wasn't deliberate sabotage. The facilities were well-guarded and I didn't like the thought of Inspector Hala exerting his full authority over the entire compound.

"At the very least, I have to assume all the facilities could be compromised," Chang-wei ran a hand roughly over his face. "I'll need to check the equipment myself if there's a chance the culprit is someone from the engineering corps."

"That's madness, Chang-wei." He couldn't do it all himself.

"I have to go."

But he didn't. Not yet. Instead, he lowered his forehead to rest it against mine. I could feel the weight of mountains pressing down on him and wished I could do something to lighten the burden. I reached up to touch his cheek and he closed his eyes. We stayed like that for a long time, the moments flowing by.

"There's so much I want to say to you, Soling, but it never seems to be the right time."

My pulse skipped. "I feel the same."

I could hear Chang-wei exhaling slowly, as if coming to some decision. Then he opened his eyes and left to carry out his new task, knowing it would mean further delays and more pressure from Peking.

I watched him go, wishing I had said more to him. It was the last I saw of Chang-wei for months.

CHAPTER 3

s Chang-wei feared, Inspector Hala tore through the
assembly lines after the incident at Tai Shan,
removing conscripts. Every day, I would receive a list
of names purged from our records with no other explanation.
Chang-wei was incorrect about one thing, however. Work did
not stop at the Factories. The Directorate pushed for production to continue.

By the end of the month, all of the facilities were at least
operational, if not at full capacity. There were guards stationed
at each site, and a guard even accompanied me whenever I
visited the factory village to check on the residents. Inspector
Hala became more insufferable in his requests for reports.

Every week, Hala and his crew rounded up and expelled
people marked as undesirables. Half the village was either
forcibly removed or pushed to leave on their own.

The workers at the factory compound became quieter, more
guarded. They kept their heads down to avoid being singled out.
Work in the Factories involved long hours and dangerous
conditions, but no one wanted to become one of the
disappeared.

"They're just taken away," Kai remarked in a hushed voice one day as we mixed a batch of ointments. "Where do they go?"

"I don't know. No one knows," I replied.

"It's not right." Kai glanced toward the door, assuring himself we were alone. "We may be peasants, but we have families. Our lives are worth something."

Kai rarely voiced such an objection. Like me, he was practical by nature. When it came to dealing with imperial politics, it was best to observe and stay out of harm's way.

"I'll try to find out more," I promised.

I had been trying to solve the mystery, but so far had little to show for it. It was a long way from where we were to the nearest village. Anyone transported to or from the Factories would need to go by river, but the waterway was too far away from the compound for me to track.

Before long, it was my turn to go before Hala. I was brought into a room without windows where I sat on a bare wooden bench across from the inspector. I folded my hands in my lap to keep them still while he asked about the accident, about the workers stationed closest to the explosion. What did I know about this person or that one?

"I only know what's in the records. What afflictions they've been treated for. Any physical complaints," I replied calmly, my gaze sliding over Little Guo's name on the list.

He shocked me with his next statement.

"Your father is Jin Zhi-fu."

I straightened and returned his steely look, saying nothing.

"He's well-known," Hala intoned.

Only someone with connections to the bureaucracy in Peking would know of my father.

"It's surprising, given Jin Zhi-fu's history, that his daughter would be approved for assignment at our most critical factory complex. And for one of Jin's disciples to be promoted to Head Engineer."

He flipped slowly through documents that I assumed contained more information about me and perhaps Chang-wei as well. I hadn't realized I warranted such a thick stack of papers.

"You and Engineer Chen are acquaintances," Hala said slowly.

"Yes."

My heart thudded in my chest. It wasn't a secret that we had come to the Factories together, but what was Hala trying to uncover?

"He's Han," he said. "And he's spent several years with the Yingguoren."

I was tempted to insist that Chang-wei hadn't gone by choice. He'd been captured, but that knowledge might be seen as even more damaging.

"Engineer Chen has proven himself to the Emperor many times," I protested.

"So, it seems." The Inspector rifled through the papers in some thick report. "The two of you have made some advantageous connections. Your last appointment was to the Imperial Court of Physicians."

I didn't tell him I had been assigned to see to the well-being of the imperial concubines in the Emperor's harem. I didn't want to tell the inspector anything. When dealing with people like Hala, everything was cause for suspicion.

"It's good to have associates," he went on. "But one must be careful of who they call friend."

I frowned at him, not comprehending.

"Do you know when the rebels took Nanking, they slaughtered the Manchu in the city? The garrison surrendered but were executed anyway. The women they burned alive. Tens of thousands."

I paled. "Not every Han is a rebel—"

"Of course not," Hala replied in clipped tones. "But every

Han likely thinks of us as demons. They hate us, Miss Jin. As much, if not more, than they hate the foreign devils."

I started to protest but bit back my reply. *Give him nothing.*

"Be careful, Jin Soling. Loyalty to your country must always come before personal friendships. If you see or hear anything, from anyone, you know your duty is to report it to me."

I nodded, but it wasn't enough for him.

"Yes, Inspector," I said aloud. Only then was I allowed to leave.

I walked away from Hala's office twice as quickly as I'd come, grateful to resume my rounds at the infirmary. I only wish the infirmary was farther away so I could put more distance between myself and the inspector's paranoia.

Guo was one of the more serious injuries and he remained in the infirmary even though most of the other workers from Tai Shan had been released. I assumed the boy had had his own visit from Hala.

Guo was young and his body was healing well, but his manner was subdued as I tested his leg for responses. It was only after I'd set an array of needles around the knee joint that he spoke.

"It's strange, I still feel my leg is there."

"That's common after losing a limb." I focused on fixing an acupuncture needle into the meridian that ran along the upper thigh. "The nerves are still active." I looked up at him between needles. "Does it hurt?"

"Not right now. The worst is the itching."

"It will be another month before engineering can fit you for a mechanical leg."

The Directory had approved for Guo's procedure as well as his eventual return to the line. I'd submitted a recommendation on his behalf and had tried to write to Chang-wei as well, though I never knew if he'd received my communication. He'd been walled off in the Citadel for the last month.

"They say I'll be able to control the leg like it's my own," he said.

"There will be needles, similar to these ones, to connect your pressure points."

"The nerve impulses will be transmitted through the steel wires to the artificial joints," he concluded. "The gears must be very intricate."

"You seem very knowledgeable."

He looked embarrassed. "Just a passing interest."

"Did you work with machinery at home?" It occurred to me that this was the first time I'd been able to speak to Guo on his own, without Jiang hovering protectively nearby. Many of the workmen had adopted Guo as a younger brother, which was heartening to see.

"My family are but simple farmers," Guo said before withdrawing.

He remained silent for the rest of our session while I set the rest of the needles. Stimulating the proper pulse points would aid in this recovery as well as treat the phantom pain.

I tried once more to engage in him conversation, but a wall had gone up around him. It was understandable. My father had lost his arm in a gunpowder experiment. Mother said he'd lost it when I was still very young, so I had no memory of my father without the steel replacement. Mother once told me how he'd suffered a period of grief after the accident.

"Your father didn't seem like himself afterward," she'd confided.

Sometimes Mother spoke of her life with my father as if it had happened to someone else, far away. Losing him had been worse for her than losing an arm or a leg. Her eyes had gone listless and void of light. She'd lost herself for a long time.

After an hour had gone by, I returned to remove the needles from Guo to return them to my case. I saw him watching out of the corner of his eye as I worked.

"I'll be back to see how you're recovering in a few days."

He gave a small nod.

As I left, I resolved to find out more about Guo's assignment at Tai Shan Facility. What had brought him so close to the blast? And why was his protector Jiang so intent on keeping the boy here, despite the seriousness of his injury?

I spent an hour searching the records room for information on Guo and Jiang. They had both arrived on the same transport and had been at Hubei for six months now.

The number of accidents had increased within the last few months, but so had the production quotas. Before that, accidents had been uncommon.

The rest of the records had been requisitioned by Inspector Hala. I couldn't ask for them without arousing suspicion, so I decided on a more direct approach.

Women were conscripted to work at the Factories as well as men, but their numbers were far smaller. Most of them were employed in a large workroom at the Song Shan facility. I stocked up my carrying case with common remedies and an assortment of herbs with both cooling and warming properties to balance yin and yang.

Unlike the general population, the women were much more familiar in how they addressed me. I was greeted by a chorus of voices the moment I entered the workroom.

"Yishi Jin!" they called. "Why has it been so long, Jie-jie?"

Some of them were younger than I was, though most were older. Every one of them referred to me as an elder sister out of respect and, as one girl had told me, I carried myself as someone who had seen something of the world.

The girl was trying to be kind. She'd come from a region where women only bound their feet until they were married.

With my natural feet and non-pleasing disposition, she of course assumed I was old and unsuitable for marriage.

The women sat in rows before contraptions that looked like textile looms. Instead of thread, the machines were loaded with an array of copper wire stretched taut over the rollers.

The workers were tasked with weaving the wires into a specific pattern over steel plates. Chang-wei had explained to me that the different pathways would determine the machine's actions.

It reminded me of the story he'd told of the artificer, Yan Shi. When Yan touched his invention's hand, it could respond.

The work in the weaving room was scrutinized closer than any other part of the production. This net of wires would connect inside the automatons and provide the means to control its limbs. The women were meticulous about every detail, even if they didn't understand the nature of the design.

"She's too important to come see us now!" Sister Yan teased. She rose to smooth out the wire pathways on her loom, standing on tiny feet bound into the prescribed lotus shape.

I saw to the women's feet and to any other complaints, moving down the line and providing supplies to be used once the day's work was done. It gave me a chance to speak to everyone and each of them wanted to be the one with something new and interesting to share.

The wire room was aware of the recent accidents. One woman's husband worked at the foundry at Tai Shan. He'd narrowly missed being caught in the explosion. Rumors began to circulate about what had happened even before the last of the fires had been extinguished.

It didn't take long for me to bring up news of Little Guo who'd lost a leg.

"The clever orphan from Sichuan," Yan remarked. "How very sad."

"Orphan?"

Jiang had told me that Guo had a younger brother. The wire weavers insisted, however, that Little Guo was without family. Of course, rumors were just rumors.

I also learned that Guo had earned a reputation for cleverness by fixing the ramshackle devices that churned along in the factory village. Materials were scarce and the hovels there had been erected haphazardly. The village machinery buckled due to exposure to wind and rain and frequently broke down. Guo had a knack for keeping things running.

When I tried to ask about the wheel carving, the women merely shook their heads. They'd never seen anything like that. After several hours, I was confident I'd uncovered everything I could and politely took my leave.

"Be careful, Big Sister!" they warned by way of farewell. "Don't forget us now that you're Zhuzhi yishi and all that."

As I walked back from the facility, I considered how it might be useful to pass some knowledge of remedies and treatments to one of the girls from the workroom. It was how I'd come to learn my trade. Our village physician had needed help so I became his apprentice. The closest person I had to being a pupil was perhaps Kai, but it wouldn't be appropriate to send him to the women's quarters.

These were the sorts of concerns I should have been occupying myself with. I was making too much of young Guo's predicament. It wasn't that peculiar he was curious and even excited about machinery.

My brother Tian was like that. He took after our father, inheriting a talent for engineering. And then there was Changwei. Whenever something bothered him, he threw himself into some complex mechanical project. My mother was mathematically-minded and numbers provided her with a sense of order.

There was something comforting in the thought of interlocking parts and systems. It was akin to meditation.

The last thing I wanted to do was point my finger at

someone who was innocent. Guo's only failing was he was too bright to escape notice.

By the time I returned to the infirmary, half the day was gone and I had a long list of tasks to complete. Kai might complain he was doing my work as well as his own, except he never complained.

As I approached, I was nearly knocked over by a blur of skinny arms and legs. It was Po, the errand boy.

"Yishi!" he exclaimed, out of breath. "They need help. At the Citadel."

A knot formed in my stomach. "What happened?"

"They need someone strong. And right away."

Another accident? There was no alarm sounding, but the citadel wasn't set up with the same warning system.

Kai was already coming down the stairs when I waved him over. He gathered two others and Po led the way, breaking into a run. I did the same, struggling to keep up with the men's longer strides. I still carried my medical case though I prayed it wouldn't be needed.

Po yelled something over his shoulder. All I could catch was "Engineer Chen" and my blood ran cold.

We approached the towering stone structure. It was the seat of the factory Directorate as well as engineering and munitions. The bureaucrats who ran the Factories were housed there, literally looking down over the rest of the compound.

I was out of breath by the time we reached the front gate. Kai and the two men he had gathered darted in first. Po and I followed. Oddly, there was no one at the gate to stop us. Inside, the place was in disarray. We searched down the corridors for someone who could help us and finally happened upon an attendant.

"In the yard," he directed, his voice shaking.

I'd been at the Factories for a year, but I'd never been summoned to the citadel. It was a fortress connected to a perimeter of stone walls and guard towers. As we neared the inner bailey, I heard a sound that stopped me cold. It was the heavy thud of footsteps, each movement accompanied by the grind of metal gears. I had heard that sound once before.

My heart raced as I peered into the wall-enclosed area. A massive automaton tore through the yard, its limbs crashing wildly against the walls in a cloud of shattered rock and dust.

The thing resembled one of the battle-suited assassins who had attacked us in Nagasaki. It was covered in overlapping armored plates. Behind its helmet loomed a black void where a face should have been.

It was my nightmare come to life. The machine stood head and shoulders above the tallest of the men. Chang-wei's creation was mindless and more destructive than the clockwork assassins we had faced. And he had lost control of it.

In the far corner, two men from the engineering corps crouched inside a steel cage. The automaton's massive arms struck at the bars with enough force to dent the cage.

Frantically, I searched the yard for Chang-wei. He was stationed at the opposite end with a unit of armed guards. Someone lay on the ground at their feet. The guardsmen had rifles aimed at the automaton, but Chang-wei held them back with a raised arm. His eyes trained on to the raging automaton.

My first glimpse of Chang-wei after so long was a shock. He was so thin. The sculpted lines of his face appeared taut and ragged. Eventually, he turned and saw us as we hovered at the entrance to the yard. Chang-wei met my eyes only briefly. The look I saw there could only be described as desolate.

"You'll have to pry them out!" Chang-wei shouted across the yard, indicating the men trapped in the corner.

The protective cage had been badly damaged. The door wouldn't open without force.

"We need tools," Kai said.

Our small crew slipped back inside the citadel. We went

searching through the corridors until we found a series of workrooms. Inside were some potentially helpful implements.

"What is that thing?" Kai asked, turning to me as he took up something that looked like an iron pickaxe in one hand and a long, thin rod in the other.

Hitokiri was the name that came to mind. It was a word I'd learned in Japan.

"It's a machine," I told him. "A killing machine."

THE CRACK of rifle fire split the air as we hurried back through the corridors. I looked over at Kai in alarm. His jaw was set in a hard line as his pace quickened.

"They're shooting," Po said breathlessly. The boy had grabbed an iron bar as well.

We emerged out into the yard to see that the automaton was no longer intent on bashing in the safety cage. The thing was rampaging through the walled enclosure, bouncing and crashing into the walls as it chased after the guardsmen on the other side. They took aim with their rifles and fired directly at the machine's torso, but the shots glanced harmlessly off the metal hull to deflect into the surrounding wall.

"Stop shooting," Chang-wei ordered. He and the guardsmen scattered as the machine crashed through their ranks.

The automaton was outfitted with a helmet. Though the face was an empty void, it had the illusion of being human. One might imagine the thing could somehow use sight to direct its attacks, but that was impossible. It only had the shape of a man, albeit a giant one. The machine had to be operating by responding to pressure and impact to direct itself. Maybe even sound? Chang-wei was using the firearms to draw the automaton away from the engineers in the cage.

"Go quickly. It can't see you," I shouted to Kai as the machine charged toward the guard unit.

Kai barked orders to the two men who'd come with us. The three of them ran along the wall to reach the cage where they wedged their tools against the bars of the door, working to pry it open. I grabbed Po by the shoulder when he tried to run into the melee. He shot me a rueful glare but obeyed.

With no other inputs, the machine had started to circle, turning when it struck against the stone walls. It thrashed around wildly, whipping and striking its arms. Even blind, the thing was dangerous.

I tried to recall what I knew about the automatons we'd encountered in the island empire of Japan. There had been one programmed to act as a bodyguard. Its behavior was so controlled that I'd mistaken it as human for a long time. Nothing like this machine smashing through the courtyard. A guardsman ducked under a swinging arm and I caught glimpse of the orange glow in the center of the machine's torso.

The automaton was powered by an elekiter device. Maybe if someone could break it...

Chang-wei must have been thinking the same. He retrieved a spear from the dirt, aimed it at the glowing heart, then charged. The tip of the spear stabbed into the device, sending sparks raining from it. The automaton went still. I held my breath. In the corner, Kai and the others had managed to wedge the cage door partially open.

Suddenly, the automaton whirred back to life. It struck the spear aside and charged after Chang-wei. I gasped as he disappeared from sight, trapped against the corner as the hulking machine advanced on him.

The guardsmen had scrambled to a safe distance and were attempting to reload their firearms. Desperate, I picked up a fallen brick and hurled it at the automaton's back. My aim being as poor as it was, the brick barely glanced off the automaton's shoulder.

Po was inspired to pick up his own brick. He ran into the fray before I could stop him.

"*Ay!*" the boy yelled, winding his arm back and throwing his brick at the back of the machine's head. The metal ping could be heard through the yard.

The automaton paused, then turned around. I ran forward to grab Po and pull him aside as the metal arm swept overhead, narrowly missing me as I dropped to the ground. There was movement behind me. Glancing over, I saw that Kai and his crew had managed to free the engineers from the cage. The entire group ran back to the shelter of the citadel, but Kai broke away when he saw Po and I crouched in the dirt.

I shouted for him to stay back. The machine was swinging its arms blindly, searching for a target. All we needed to do was get out of its path, and we would be out of danger, but Kai didn't know that. He ran forward and aimed the pickaxe at the automaton's shoulder. The machine countered with a back-handed sweep that threw Kai halfway across the bailey. Kai thudded into the dirt. My stomach plummeted when he lay there, unmoving.

The commotion provided enough cover for Chang-wei to retrieve his spear. Gritting his teeth, he jammed the tip of the weapon into the socket at the automaton's knee. The joint locked up, gears whirring as the machine lurched sideways. The entire thing toppled to the ground in a clang of metal. Chang-wei then scrambled for the pickaxe and swung it at the glowing elekiter in the center of the machine's chest. He struck home once, twice, shouting in desperate rage with each blow until the device cracked in a shower of sparks. Finally, the orange light dimmed.

The whir of the gears cased. The smell of hot grease and

burnt oil filled the air as the machine slumped onto the ground, now little more than a lifeless heap of scrap metal.

A long stretch of silence followed. Finally, Chang-wei lowered his pickaxe. With his chest heaving, he staggered towards the fallen engineer on the ground. Whoever it was, he hadn't moved since I'd come to the bailey.

I rushed forward to join Chang-wei, slowing down warily as I passed the metal corpse of the automaton. The elekiter in the automaton's torso remained cold and black.

When I came to stand beside Chang-wei, he had gone still. His face was void of any expression as he stared down at his fallen colleague. I only caught a glimpse of the body before I took Chang-wei by the shoulders and turned him away. He followed my lead like a carved puppet, his limbs heavy and lifeless.

I didn't want to inspect the body, but as yishi, I had to be certain he was dead. Steeling myself, I looked back to the ground. The man's skull was shattered, his face pulverized into a pool of flesh and blood. What remained was an empty cavity, much like the thing that had caused his death. I forced back the bile rising in my throat.

One couldn't look too long at something like that without losing one's mind. As brief as the glimpse had been, I couldn't erase the horrid image. It would never go away.

CHAPTER 4

"*C*hang-wei."

Chang-wei charged down the corridor as I called out to him. We had left the courtyard in disarray. Kai had regained consciousness quickly, which was a good sign. I suspected his ribs were broken and that he would suffer lingering effects of a blow to the head. He was able to walk well enough for the others to take him back to the infirmary. Another of Chang-wei's engineers who had been trapped in the cage had suffered a broken arm.

Then there was the faceless man who lay dead.

"Engineer Chen! Chang-wei, stop for a moment."

He didn't stop. He shoved his way into a workroom and I stubbornly followed.

The room contained several workbenches covered in tools and mechanical parts along with a scattering of books and schematics.

"This is all garbage," Chang-wei spat, shoving at the disarray. A pile of coiled wire fell to the floor.

I'd never seen him like this before. Chang-wei was typically so methodical and controlled. He grabbed at the papers now, stacking them into a pile until it toppled over. Unsure of how to react, I bent to retrieve the pages.

"Leave them," Chang-wei snapped, his voice shaking. "It all needs to be burned."

He fell back, brow furrowed and expression hooded. There was an uncommon wildness about him. A crack in the stone foundation.

"Was this sabotage?" I asked tentatively.

"No. It was all me. This is my failure."

I tried to reach for him, but he sank down onto a stool and laid his head into his hands. It was frightening to see Chang-wei this way.

The skin on the back of one hand was discolored. "Let me see," I said gently.

He tried to pull away, but I moved slowly and remained firm. I took hold of his wrist as if he were made of glass.

"It's a burn," I said.

It must have happened when he destroyed the elekiter device. Chang-wei turned his face away from me as I inspected the wound. He breathed hard, struggling to regain what little composure he could.

I glanced up. "Does it hurt?"

"We've been pushing hard day and night," he choked out, refusing to look at me.

"I know."

"There's nothing to show for it."

"It will be alright—"

"*Liu is dead.*"

I couldn't find anything to say to that. Chang-wei took a shaky breath and, for the next long moments, there was nothing but awful silence between us.

"How long has it been since you slept?" I asked finally.

He turned to look at me. His eyes still had the dark and haunted look I'd seen before, but there was a wild light inside now. His fingers curled over mine. Without a word, Chang-wei pulled me close. Suddenly he was kissing me, his mouth closing hungrily over mine with a lost and desperate energy he'd carried with him from the bailey.

He circled his arms around me, but I was too startled to respond. Chang-wei was always in control of his emotions, but after everything that had just transpired, all of his control had been torn away.

Nothing about this felt right. I broke away from the kiss. "We can't."

He still held onto me, his embrace gentle now. "I know."

It had been a long time since we'd last kissed and this wasn't the way I'd hoped for it to happen.

Chang-wei's eyes were clear as they looked upon me, though his expression remained troubled. Even when a knocking came at the door, he refused to look away.

"I can't talk to them right now," he said, his throat tight.

His hands fell away as I stood and went to the door. It was one of Chang-wei's assistants. I spoke to him briefly before closing the door again.

I seated myself on a wooden stool beside him. "I told him you were assessing the problem."

"The Directorate will demand a full account. I'll have to go before them." He rubbed a hand over his eyes. "Just not right now."

"You should rest," I said again, hurting for him.

His thoughts were fragmented. Every line in his face, his very posture revealed how exhausted he was. Down to the bone. I didn't have any answers for him, but if Chang-wei didn't rest he was going to break — if he wasn't broken already.

"An endeavor like this should take years," he muttered. "I pushed too hard. I lost control of it."

"You need to rest," I repeated firmly.

There was a sleeping pallet stashed in the corner. The engineers must have been working night and day. I unrolled it and set Chang-wei upon the bedding.

"The official review is just days away," he protested, as I lowered his head down on the pallet.

I didn't know what that meant. "Just a few hours," I urged. "To clear your mind."

He reached out to grab my hand as I rose. "Stay with me." A hint of desperation crept into his voice. "I'll sleep if you stay with me."

It was inappropriate. Everyone outside knew I had followed Chang-wei into the room and there would be talk, but I was afraid of what would happen if I left. I lowered myself down beside him. His eyes remained open, watching me.

"I've failed, Soling." His voice caught. "This entire mess is my fault."

He took everything too personally.

"Sleep," I implored. "You promised."

He finally obeyed me and closed his eyes. Sleep didn't come until a little while later, but it did come. I watched as the tension drained from him. His breathing deepened and fell into a heavy rhythm, even if his body never relaxed completely.

The Directorate was asking too much of him. The Emperor was asking too much.

His queue had fallen over his face, catching on the edge of his collar. I smoothed the braid away from his face. His brow remained creased as if he were still awake and searching for a solution.

I'd come to feel so much for Chang-wei. Even though we were no longer betrothed, I still cared deeply for him.

When I was certain Chang-wei was soundly asleep, I rose and went to the door. Po was hovering in the passageway to give me a report of what was happening. I sent him for bandages and ointment.

Chang-wei's hand still needed tending to. Though a burn

was the least of anyone's worries, my thoughts were fractured as well. It would help me to keep busy. A minor wound was something I could actually treat and make better.

As I crossed the workroom to return to Chang-wei, I almost stepped on the papers he had shoved to the floor. I bent to pick them up, but the one at the top of the pile made me pause. The writing on it was unintelligible to me, but I recognized the language. It was the left-to-right snake script of the Yingguoren.

The paper was in Yingyu—in English, as they called it. The ink was still fresh.

I HID the paper with the foreign writing into the middle of the pile. It was dangerous having a letter like that around for the wrong people to find. Fear and distrust of Western ways had only gotten worse since the war. Foreign holdings within the treaty ports had grown in size and wealth, while civil war tore our land apart.

I was only able to keep Chang-wei away from the vultures for a few hours. He slept the entire time, as promised, even if it was a fitful sleep.

During that time, I applied ointment to the burn and bandaged his hand loosely. The skin had turned an angry red color. It would blister and crack but would eventually heal over several weeks. The worst of it would be the pain.

I was more concerned for Chang-wei's mental state. I didn't know if Liu, the engineer who was killed, had been a close friend, but that didn't matter. Chang-wei was Head Engineer. He would claim full responsibility for all of the men in his charge, for better or worse.

From the sketches and models in the workroom, I could see all of the work that had gone into building the automaton. Unlike the rest of the staff, I had an idea what the various parts that were being molded and forged would eventually become. I knew of the hitokiri assassins and karakuri machines that had inspired Chang-wei's design. I had been present when he had revealed his vision in grand fashion before the Emperor.

Chang-wei had proposed an army built of machines. Rather than sacrifice the lives of our countrymen, we would dispatch automatons, like puppets without strings, to fight in our stead. But the Emperor was so eager to have his mechanical army that the Factories were being pushed to the breaking point. The engineers in the citadel had taken unnecessary risks and they had paid for it.

Our people were still sacrificing their lives without ever setting foot on a battlefield.

Several hours passed before another knock came at the door. Inspector Hala came himself this time and I lacked the authority to send him away. Regardless, I braced an arm against the doorway and stood firm when he started to enter.

Chang-wei came up behind me. "Inspector Hala."

His voice was rough from having just awoken. Hala's gaze darted to Chang-wei then back to me. I stepped aside so Chang-wei could address him properly.

"The Directorate awaits your incident report," Hala said.

"I'll have the report prepared by first light tomorrow."

"The Directorate would prefer you deliver a report in person. Immediately."

A chill went down my spine. Chang-wei would be held responsible for everything that had gone wrong. Knowing him, he would insist on taking responsibility, but it wasn't entirely his fault. No one person could claim sole responsibility for everything that had happened here, except for the Emperor and his Grand Council. Their unreasonable demands had ground everyone to the bone.

But that sort of talk against the throne was forbidden. I bit my tongue and prepared my retreat, ducking into the passageway and sweeping past Hala.

"Yishi Jin."

It was Chang-wei who called after me. It was the first time I could remember when he'd referred to me in such a stiff and formal manner. Hala was still watching.

"Engineer Chen," I replied in kind.

"Thank you," he said, lifting his bandaged hand. He held my gaze for a long time after, even though the inspector was waiting.

As I turned to go, something unexpected happened. Inspector Hala caught my eye as well. Instead of the steely glare that I expected, he gave the smallest of nods. As if we were collaborators in a scheme.

CHAPTER 5

Two days later, I learned exactly what was meant when they spoke of an official review. Representatives from the imperial court were scheduled to visit Hubei. There would be someone from the Ministry of Science as well as members of the Emperor's council, all anxious to check on the progress of their war machines.

Outside of the citadel, the work crews were pushed to get all the assembly lines fully operational. They removed broken equipment and scrubbed down or replaced anything with signs of fire damage. It was so much theater and all for nothing. What the imperial court wanted to see wasn't in the factories, but at the citadel where the engineers had been working to assemble the machines behind raised walls.

On the eve of the official visit, I took my acupuncture case and made for the citadel. I told the guards at the gate that I was Zhuzhi yishi and needed to see Engineer Chen. After a brief delay to check on this and that, they let me in without much hassle. Why hadn't I attempted this earlier?

Chang-wei was in the same workroom, though it had been tidied up, swept and organized. To prepare for the imperial visitors, like the rest of the compound, I was sure. I cared more about how Chang-wei was doing.

"I came to check on your hand," I said.

He lifted it with a questioning look, as if he'd forgotten it was still bandaged.

"If it heals improperly, you might lose feeling or mobility. That would be disastrous for our illustrious head engineer."

The corners of his mouth lifted the slightest bit at my exaggeration. He appeared much calmer than the last time I'd seen him, though there was an odd stiffness about him.

He surrendered his arm to me then, stretching it across the worktable. I unraveled the bandage and held his hand gingerly in mine to examine how the burn was healing. The patch of ruined skin ran over most of the back of his hand and his fourth and fifth fingers.

Chang-wei's fingers were long and dexterous. I stared at them, the memories of the last time I'd been alone with him in this room flooding back. When he'd kissed me as if he couldn't help himself.

He was subdued now. So restrained that it made me wonder if my memories were even real.

"Is it bad?" he asked quietly.

"I have a salve to aid the healing. You should also apply oil as it heals," I told him, avoiding his eyes. "It will help the new skin and keep it from tightening and scarring."

"I have scars from another electrical burn," he recalled.

I did look up then. His eyes were fixed onto me, searching and intense. He was referring to the marks on his chest. I'd used an elekiter device to restart his heart when it had stopped beating.

"I'm fortunate you're always around to heal me."

My heartbeat quickened. "This one isn't so bad." I focused on covering his hand with a new bandage, hoping he couldn't see the flush rising to my cheeks. "You were the one that saved us."

He'd run up to the automaton to disable it, even after seeing how easily it could kill a man.

His expression clouded over. "I didn't save everyone."

I started to insist that he couldn't blame himself, but I stopped myself. Chang-wei wouldn't be who he was without the twin weights of duty and responsibility on each shoulder.

"The imperial Chief Engineer will be here tomorrow," Chang-wei said. "I won't be able to hide anything from Kuo Lishen."

Chief Engineer Kuo had taken over as head of the Ministry of Science after my father was removed. At one time, he had been a close acquaintance of my father's. They had come up through the same class and were promoted in parallel up the ranks. I remember hearing Kuo Lishen's name frequently in our house when I was young, but I knew little of what was spoken back then. I had been a child with a child's lack of cares.

After the empire's defenses had failed in the Opium War, my father and his closest associates had fallen into disgrace. Before the war, he'd warned the Grand Council that the Qing empire's defenses were no match for western steamships and that the Ministry of Science would need to learn and adapt.

At first, he'd been ignored, then later condemned as a traitor for advocating what was denounced as western thinking. The rumors had gone so far as to insinuate that he was a collaborator and that was why our defenses had been defeated so soundly. There was no evidence of such treachery, but it didn't matter. It was what Father's enemies chose to believe.

While many of Father's colleagues had fled or were expelled, Kuo Lishen had thrived. He'd taken on the highest post in the Ministry and became a trusted adviser to the new Emperor, young Yizhu, when the crown prince took the throne.

I didn't trust Kuo. And not only because of his superior attitude toward Chang-wei. He and my family had some unfavorable history, I was certain of it.

"Chief Engineer Kuo will have to understand that you can only do so much," I insisted.

Chang-wei exhaled long and slow, as if the effort of breathing pained him. "I'm going to be relieved of my duties."

"You don't know that."

"Maybe I should be removed."

The thought left me cold. I'd come to Hubei with him. We were in this together.

"This entire endeavor was your vision," I reminded him.

"Sometimes I wish it hadn't been."

He met my eyes with grave seriousness while I stared at him in shock.

"Come with me for a moment," he said finally.

I followed him out of the workroom. We walked through the corridors until we reached a flight of stairs. Chang-wei lit a lantern before we climbed up to the battlements.

The evening was just upon us and there was still a faint light from the parting sun on the horizon. Wisps of smoke puffed up from the factory chimneys from the last production runs. Little points of light had started to appear in the makeshift village just beyond. I'd never been up on the battlements before and had never been able to see the full expanse of the factory grounds from on high.

At either end of the wall, two watchtowers rose high over the compound. Guardsmen were rotated through watch duty day and night. Indeed, I could see the glow of lanterns up in the towers right now.

"I want to show you something," Chang-wei said.

We walked side by side along the battlements to the far side of the Citadel. From there, I could see beyond the wall that enclosed the Factories. There was another enclosure, a flat area that might have been used as a training yard when the compound had been a military encampment. My breath caught in my throat as I realized what I was looking at. There, spaced out like pieces on a chess board, were rows upon rows of automatons. A full regiment of machine warriors.

"Are they operational?" I asked, my throat dry.

"Not yet."

I didn't know what I felt upon hearing that. Relief?

"The gearworks are in place," Chang-wei went on. "The joints and levers to facilitate motion. But the control pathways—"

The intricate patterns the women were weaving in the Song Shan workroom.

"The controls are still faulty—as we saw." His voice dropped away.

"You'll find a way to fix it. You know it can be done."

Chang-wei nodded. "Because it's been done before."

In Japan, they had been called karakuri — mechanical puppets. Most had been created to perform a single task, but we had seen one machine with a more sophisticated design. This particular automaton had behaved as if it were a samurai warrior, going so far as to sacrifice itself for its mistress.

Chang-wei shook his head. "We don't have enough time to find a solution."

The delegation from Peking would be here tomorrow. "It would be short-sighted of them to punish you for what's happened. The Yingguoren have been occupying our ports for years now. If it takes a little longer to build a proper defense—"

"These aren't meant for the foreign invaders." He let out a breath. "The machines will march on the Taiping rebels."

A shiver went down my spine as I looked out over the rows of armor-plated warriors. The machines were being built to cut down our own countrymen.

~

ON THE DAY of the official visit, my directive was to go about my duties as usual. The delegation had little interest in the day-to-day operations of the Factories and no interest in the injuries suffered by the crews. If anything, the Directorate wanted the physicians and other caretakers out of sight.

I assumed the official review would come and go without any need of my services, but I assumed wrong.

Inspector Hala came personally to summon me to the citadel in his impassive and commanding tone.

I hurried to keep up with his long stride. "May I ask for what purpose?"

"You were present at the recent incident," the inspector replied. "Your perspective is of value to the delegation."

What did the Directorate expect me to say? It might help Chang-wei to have a supporting voice, but I shared his reservations about the automatons.

"I also just learned of your role," the inspector continued.

"My role?"

"Your particular history with Engineer Chen. You have insight into his mental state." The inspector turned to look at me. With his narrow face and protruding eyes, he gave me the impression of a mantis on the prowl.

I stopped cold. It was well-known that Chang-wei was my father's protege and it was no secret we were once betrothed. The thought that the imperial court had any interest in personal matters between us made my skin crawl.

I was certain now that anything I revealed to Hala would be used as ammunition.

The inspector continued his march to the citadel. Once we arrived, I immediately sensed the atmosphere had become more restrictive. We passed by several series of guards as well as officials in imperial regalia as we went through the corridors.

We continued to a new area of the stronghold I hadn't been to before, eventually winding around into an interior training field. I found myself facing row upon row of ominous and face-less automatons.

Even though they were just empty shells without the elekiter devices required to power them, the sight of them still sent a cold wave of dread through me. Especially after seeing what just one of them could do when activated.

The entourage from Peking was moving among the automa-tons to inspect them. The machines towered head and shoulders over even the tallest person, who happened to be the Chief Engineer himself.

Chang-wei was at the head of the procession dressed in a formal court robe with his queue neatly braided to trail down his back. His cap was set with a peacock feather to denote his rank. I barely recognized him in the regalia.

I looked down at the gray tunic I wore accompanied by slip-pers that were scuffed from daily use. They were covered with a layer of dust.

"The automatons are designed to be fitted with weapons," Chang-wei was saying. "But the protocols for weapons-use have not been fully tested."

He was speaking to a tall, bearded official. Chief Engineer Kuo Lishen.

"Your work is incomplete then," Kuo replied sharply.

"Unfortunately, that is correct."

"How much more time do you need?"

I didn't hear Chang-wei's answer. The small, slight figure that followed behind the Chief Engineer caught my eye. The functionary was dressed in a mandarin jacket and trousers, a plain uniform denoting a lower rank. A pair of dark-rimmed spectacles were set over the bridge of his slender nose. He balanced a book over one arm and appeared to be transcribing notes.

The entire delegation moved down the row of silent warriors and the functionary disappeared momentarily behind one of the automatons. I hurried to catch up to them. When the group came back into view, I saw who I thought was a man was actually a woman. And not just any woman.

She glanced over at me and her eyes grew wide behind the round lenses of her spectacles. It was my mother.

∽

Mother broke away from the group of officials to come to me. Chief Engineer Kuo was left staring after her but said nothing. Perhaps audacity came with age or, more likely, this was another sign of my mother's selective ability to disregard the world around her.

"Soling, I was hoping to see you," she said, her face bright.

Aware that everyone was watching, I pulled her aside into the corner of the yard. It was far from private, but at least we were away from the center of things.

"What are you doing here, Mother?"

She adjusted her spectacles, which I'd never seen her wear before. "I'm assisting Kuo. You haven't been home in over a year, Daughter. Not even for the Spring Festival."

"I sent letters," I said guiltily.

The last one was months ago. Hala and his agents pored through anything that was sent from the Factories to ensure that production of the automatons was being kept a secret. Each facility built the component parts without ever seeing the whole of what was being assembled in the citadel. As a result, my letters had always been bland and perfunctory, inquiring about my mother's health and my brother's studies. Little had I known—

"How long has this been going on?" I asked, looking her over.

"Kuo had work for me to do. You remember."

Kuo Lishen had given my mother some calculations to perform when our family had first returned to Peking.

When I looked at her notes, I could see details about the conversation along with other scribblings - figures, geometric diagrams, equations. As if the linear conversation between Chang-wei and the Chief Engineer weren't nearly enough to keep her occupied.

I had known that she and Kuo Lishen had some longtime association. It was common knowledge that Kuo and my father had attended the Academy together, but I'd since learned that my mother was there as well for at least one term. She'd sat for the imperial science examinations before it was discovered she was a woman.

"Are you here in disguise?" I asked in a lowered tone.

Mother glanced down at her clothing, touching a hand to the mandarin jacket. "Oh, this. No, it's not necessary anymore. The Ministry will accept a woman's work in its hallowed offices as long as she doesn't take on any position of power. I still find it's easier to move through Peking dressed like this. People ask fewer questions and somehow I feel more like myself."

I was astonished at the change in her. I was used to watching my mother with such care. Most of my memories from my childhood were of her shut away, her eyes glazed and vacant from opium smoke. The memory of that image left me cold.

"You seem...well," I said uncertainly.

I didn't know how to be around this other version of my mother. One that was vibrant and clear-headed and clever. This woman was a stranger.

She grew quiet as well, also aware of the rift between us. It was more than a difference of being apart for a year.

"I am much better," she said finally. "I don't need that poison anymore."

I hadn't asked about the opium directly because I was afraid to know. Her addiction had taken up so much of the space between us for all of my life.

"That's good to hear, Mother."

I certainly hoped it was the truth, but why couldn't I completely believe her?

It was easier to speak of work. "So, you're the Chief Engineer's assistant?"

She looked over to Kuo Lishen whose gaze fixed onto us even as he continued walking with Chang-wei. "The circumstances are...complicated," she said beneath her breath.

I followed behind her as she rejoined the committee.

"Yishi Jin is the acting Head Physician of the Factories," Chang-wei introduced me when I came to his side.

I performed the necessary greetings and obeisances and was met with a circle of dour faces. There were three other officials in attendance in addition to Kuo Lishen. I understood them to be representatives from the imperial Grand Council sent by the Emperor. They didn't give me the courtesy of who was who before beginning their questions.

"You were present at the incident that occurred here last week," one of the officials began. "When one of the engineers was killed."

"This servant did not witness those events, Honorable Sir."

"But you were present when the machine was eventually deactivated?"

"Yes, sir."

A barrage of questions followed. How many men were present? What was the nature and seriousness of the injuries? I was certain all of the details had been given in a stack of reports. I'd had to write several myself describing the fractures that Kai had suffered as well as describing what had happened to the engineer who had been killed. I still had nightmares about him and his face, the face that I would never see.

Despite all the paperwork, the officials were still intent on questioning me directly. I consciously avoided looking over to Chang-wei as I answered, though I couldn't help but wonder if they had asked him the same questions and were looking for someone to either confirm or dispute his version of events.

"What weapons were employed against the machine?" Kuo asked. "Were they effective?"

The answer was that we had employed every weapon we could find. And no, they weren't effective until Chang-wei had disabled the automaton himself.

The most senior of the officials spoke last. He had gray threaded through his hair and beard. He'd remained silent for the entire interrogation until that moment.

"What did you feel upon seeing the machine for the first time?" he asked me.

I could remember the grind of the metal gears, the lone figure lying still in the dirt with a pool of blood beneath him. And the hulking, inhuman frame of the killing machine as it attacked the cage where the engineers were trapped.

"Fear," I replied, unable to lie. "It was like looking upon a demon."

CHAPTER 6

"Kuo Lishen came to me about calculations for a massive airship," my mother recounted. "It was a dragon in the sky with impressive red sails."

Mother and I sat in her room for our evening meal. All of the officials and councilmen and functionaries were meeting elsewhere, and we hadn't been summoned to join them. I much preferred it this way anyway. A simple tray of rice and pickled vegetables sat between us along with a plate of fried bean curd and sweet wine. The wine was an indulgence.

"It was *enormous*. The size of a mountain." My mother became animated as she spoke, with her eyes bright and dancing. "I worked out the calculations and the thing would never fly. No engine could lift it. It would have been disastrous to even try to build it."

"What was its purpose then?" I asked, scooping up a mouthful of rice with bamboo chopsticks.

"To look fearsome and impressive?" she wagered with a shrug. "Then I unrolled the second plan and what could it be? An ocean junk, one that looked like any other ship except—"

"The size of a mountain," I finished for her.

She nodded, stifling a laugh.

"And it would never have floated?" I asked.

"Oh, it would have. But nothing could ever propel it. It would have been more useful in pieces."

"Zheng He's treasure ships were supposed to measure forty-five *zhang* in length." It was the sort of detail my parents would have once been intent on telling me.

"This design was larger than a treasure ship," Mother said. "Obscenely so."

I was getting a glimpse of what my mother might have been like had things been different. Flowing with conversation. Excited about minute numerical details.

"I've known Kuo Lishen for a long time," she continued. "He was never particularly clever. No sense of ingenuity. Just a big talker."

Mother paused to pick up a slice of bean curd. It was habit for me to watch over her, looking for signs that she wasn't well. Was she eating enough? Sleeping enough? Was she anxious?

From what I could see, she really did look better.

"Kuo has other talents. Sometimes I think if Kuo had been promoted to Imperial Chief Engineer and had to deal with politics while your father had remained in the background—" She fell silent.

For a moment, we both sat quietly, picking at the food.

"But your father was also good at convincing people," Mother resumed. "He wasn't just an engineer. Everyone respected him. They admired him."

There was no scenario where the cannons didn't fail. Where the Westerners didn't take over our ports and my father wasn't blamed for the empire's inability to defend itself. It hurt to think of the dark and inevitable fate of things.

This was why my mother didn't like to dwell on the past.

The past was a problem that couldn't be solved, no matter how hard one tried. Mother was a solver of equations. A finder of logical inconsistencies.

At least my mother wasn't avoiding the past anymore, but the brief memory of my father was all she was able to endure. When she spoke again, it was about an entirely different subject.

"You and Engineer Chen seem close."

Heat rushed to my cheeks. I took a sip of the rice wine to stall.

"That's good to see," Mother assured.

I took another sip. Swallowed deliberately.

"Your father and I have known Chang-wei since he was very young. About the same age as Tian is now. He was almost like a son."

I'd heard all of this in some way or another, but that had been before I'd known who Chang-wei was as a person. We weren't allowed to see one another after our marriage was formally set up. Probably so he wouldn't think of me as only a child when we finally did meet. He'd passed the imperial examination and Father had arranged for us to be wed when I came of age.

Hearing my mother repeat the story now warmed me. In some ways, Chang-wei had known my family, my father and mother, better than I had. He'd known them before the war. Before my father's execution. Before my mother's addiction to opium.

"He reminds me a little of your father," Mother said.

I blushed even more furiously.

"Clever," she went on, not noticing. "And determined."

There was warmth in Mother's eyes. She reached out to tuck my hair behind my ear, something I couldn't remember her doing since I was very young.

"The last ten years have been difficult," she acknowledged.

"But everything is better now." It was a question as much as a response. Our family was back in Peking. Tian was going to attend the Academy.

Slowly, Mother nodded.

We finished our meal. Mother spoke of how Tian was doing. My younger brother was attending a school in Peking for lessons in astronomy and mathematics.

At the end of the evening, Mother invited me to stay in her chamber that night and we prepared for bed. I watched as she took the pins out of her hair. As she let it down, I could almost see a vision of the past. My mother, young and ambitious. Willfully chasing her own dreams.

Mother had left her family to go to Peking and enroll in the Academy. She'd been completely alone and fending for herself when she'd met my father. She'd turned away from her parents, never to see her family again. In contrast, thoughts of my family and my duty to them were never far away.

"It's fortunate that you were able to come, Mother," I told her. "I miss you and Tian."

She smiled faintly. "I asked to come. Kuo was convinced it was a good idea."

I arranged my sleeping pallet beside hers. "I didn't realize you and Chief Engineer Kuo had such a...a close association." Saying it aloud put a sick feeling in my stomach.

"I've been helping him and he's been helping me as well. Can you fetch my comb, Soling?"

As I reached into her pack for the wooden comb, I noticed a handful of small yellow packets of paper, folded in little squares at the bottom of the pack. I stared at them, my heart pounding out a dangerous rhythm. I picked up one of the packets and ran it between my fingers, feeling for the contents inside.

"Can you find it?"

I jumped, startled. "Here it is."

I grabbed the comb and handed it to her, trying to calm myself, but it was no use. Mother pulled the comb through her long hair while I laid down on my pallet, staring up at the ceiling and unsure of what to do next. What to say.

Inside the packets were two hard, round tabs. Pills.

"At first, I was worried you were going so far away," Mother said, setting her comb down and turning down the lamp. The room went dark. I could hear her shifting on the mat as she lay down. "But then, I thought of how I was your age when I left my family to go to the Academy. I was only nineteen years old."

"Mother, I'm twenty-one years old now," I replied absently.

"Oh really? So old?"

"Yes."

"Where has the time gone?"

THE NEXT MORNING, the officials were to make their tour of the factory facilities. I left Mother after our morning tea to hurry back to my office. Inside my pocket was a yellow packet I'd managed to slip out of my mother's belongings.

Only when I was shut away inside the office did I dare to unfold the paper. Inside were two white pills. The inscription on the packet indicated they were opium cessation pills. Pills like this were distributed in opium refuges and dispensaries in larger cities.

I didn't know what to think of my mother trading one substance for another. She seemed better, but all of my old doubts and fears came back and I started to panic. I needed to return to Peking. I needed to be there to take care of her and my brother — but then I stopped myself.

I wasn't a child anymore. I could talk to my mother about this. Still, the thought of confronting her made me so nervous. I folded the packet back into a square and tucked it into my pocket.

Outside, the morning gong was sounding for the workers to make their way to the factories. I could see the groups moving from the village toward the facilities. It was time for me to make my rounds.

Inside the infirmary, Little Guo was propped up in bed. His wound was on the mend and he was back for the follow-up procedure. An engineer from the citadel had come to take measurements for the mechanical leg. I waited for him to finish and take his leave before approaching.

The youth was able to push himself into a sitting position using his elbows. He was in much better spirits than the last I'd seen him.

"Yishi Jin," he greeted. "Thank you for this. Jiang told me all you had done. If not for you, they would be sending me home as a cripple."

"Where is your home?" I asked, sitting down on the stool beside him.

"Sichuan province. I've been away for a long time."

"You've been at the Factories for less than a year," I pointed out.

"Yes, seven months now." His face may have held the rounded innocence of youth, but his eyes were shrewd and intelligent.

I continued with the acupuncture session while he watched me with a look of intense concentration. It was good to see the incision from the amputation was healing. There was no further loss of feeling or mobility in his leg.

"The engineers will be able to start fitting you with your leg soon."

"*My* leg," he echoed. "It sounds strange to say that."

"It will feel strange at first, but you'll adapt quickly."

He nodded, his hand straying to the token that he wore around his neck. The same wooden carving I'd seen right after the accident.

"Is that from your family?" I asked.

Guo tucked it back into his tunic. "A souvenir," he said, then turned the conversation back to me. "Yishi, you've been gone for the last few days."

"A lot of official business to see to."

He nodded, his dark eyes remaining fixed on me. "I heard there was another accident."

I kept my expression neutral. The only accident he could have been talking about was the incident with the automaton, but the happenings at the citadel were kept secret.

"What have you heard?"

"That there was a machine malfunction. The engineers at the citadel lost control of one of their...inventions."

I leveled my gaze at him. "Even engineers make mistakes. Fortunately, everything was brought under control quickly."

"Good thing that no one was hurt."

Except for the man who was killed. And Kai had been thrown across the yard. I felt a pang in my chest but said nothing. I had the distinct impression the boy was testing me.

"You're interested in machines," I ventured.

He shrugged. "Sometimes."

Poor farm boy from Sichuan, indeed. "You remind me of my brother. He was always fascinated by mechanical things. I wonder with such an interest in machinery, why weren't you assigned as an operator? Seems to be a waste to have you in maintenance."

"Who cares what a young fool like me wants?" His mouth curled cynically, making him suddenly appear much older. "I'm small and can slip into places. One goes where he fits. In any case, an operator's job doesn't require so much knowledge, does it?"

"Oh?"

"Pull a lever. Check a valve. The same repetitive job over and over."

"You can learn how everything works," I suggested lightly.

"What's really interesting isn't what's built in the factories," Guo insisted. "It's what happens afterward."

"What happens afterward?"

Guo smiled a little. "With all those little parts. I suppose it's a mystery."

I left Guo a little while later and searched out Kai who was attempting to move a crate of supplies into the storage room despite having his ribs wrapped tight.

"What are you doing?" I chided, rushing over to support the weight of the crate in my much smaller arms.

"It's not so heavy," Kai insisted.

"You're a bone-setter. You know how you need to rest to heal."

He graced me with a crooked smile. I ordered him to go and get some rest, but stopped him as he started to leave.

"Kai, did you tell anyone about what happened at the citadel?"

His grin faded to be replaced with a serious look. He came back to me, lowering his voice before speaking. "I said nothing. I know how secretive the factory authority is about what we're building here. But the others—"

We had rushed to the citadel with a small crew. Surely, it wasn't a serious problem. There were always rumors and whisperings of what we were doing. But still, rumors were different from confirmed knowledge.

"Is there a problem, Yishi?"

I shook my head. "It's nothing. Get some rest and heal up."

"Happy to get the day off." He grinned and granted me a bow before leaving.

IT WAS mid-day when I saw my mother again. She was speaking to Chang-wei outside of the offices and they appeared deep in conversation. Chang-wei had his head bowed solicitously. Mother presented a much smaller figure beside him, wearing her official robe and headdress that marked her as part of the imperial entourage.

He was always courteous when addressing Mother. I'd heard it from more than one person, including from my own mother, that my father had treated Chang-wei like a son, but I knew nothing about Chang-wei's actual family.

He never spoke of family. When he spoke of his past, it was always about Peking and his time at the Academy and the Ministry. Occasionally, he would mention being abducted and taken to the West.

Our pasts had intertwined long before we met. They involved the same people. The same events had torn our lives apart in different ways, but there was still so much I didn't know about him.

They both looked over at the same time to see me watching them. Chang-wei took a step back as I approached and I thought I saw a spot of color on his cheeks. I had to have been mistaken. I looked over to Mother whose smooth features revealed nothing.

"Soling," she said, taking my arm. "Engineer Chen and I were speaking of the developments over the past year," Mother began. "And how much progress has been made."

"Perhaps less progress than the Directorate would like," I replied. "Some call Engineer Chen overly cautious, but he always has everyone's best interests in mind."

Chang-wei was giving me a strange look and I shot him a small frown, trying to decipher what he was trying to say.

Mother gave my arm a squeeze. Now something most

certainly was amiss. Mother rarely showed such open affection and definitely not in public.

"Daughter," she continued warmly. "I am glad I was able to come and see you."

I inquired about the factory inspection briefly, but the entire time I was thinking of the packet of pills I'd found in her things.

"So, what were you two discussing?" I asked.

Oddly, Chang-wei stiffened.

"Jin *Furen*," he intoned, using the traditional honorific to address my mother. "Soling."

He lingered over my name and I felt a little lurch in the pit of my stomach.

"If I may take my leave now." He bowed toward Mother, gave a small nod to me, and then headed off quickly in the direction of the citadel.

"He's been worried about his work in the citadel," I explained, trying to account for Chang-wei's anxious behavior.

Mother followed his retreat with her eyes. "He really does remind me of your father."

"Is that good or bad?"

Mother didn't answer directly. "Be careful of losing yourself in another's ambitions," was all she said.

We continued, still arm in arm, to the offices.

"Chang-wei doesn't have to worry so much about proving himself," Mother continued as I led her inside. "Kuo Lishen recognizes his talent."

"How involved are you with the war council's review, Mother?"

She seemed to know so much about what was happening inside the council.

"I know nothing of those politics," my mother insisted. "I just know Kuo Lishen. He is one who has always recognized the talents of others, as compensation for lacking any talent of his own."

Kuo again. What was my mother's connection with the Chief Engineer?

"You said you were helping him, and he was helping you. What does that mean?"

She sighed, wandering over to the bookshelf. I'd forgotten how much Mother loved books. Too bad there were nothing but ledgers and records there. We hadn't kept many books after leaving Peking, but now that we had returned, perhaps she could gradually build up her collection.

"Your mother needs something to occupy herself, Soling. If there's nothing ahead but the emptiness of the hours, my mind wanders."

Mother touched a hand to the ledgers, but her mind was far away. In her voice, I sensed that same vulnerability that always filled me with dread. She was thinking of the past. Thinking of the things that she'd lost. My hand trembled as I reached for the pills in my pocket.

"Have you been taking these?" I asked, pulling out the folded yellow paper.

She turned to stare at the packet in my hand.

"I found these in your belongings, Mother."

"Your mother only has those in case she needs them," she replied, retreating into formal tones.

I realized what had me so shaken about the cessation pills. It was the reminder that no matter how vibrant she appeared, my mother was still fragile. She was still fighting her addiction.

"I know it's not easy," I said.

My instinct was to caution her against trading one vice for another, but the effect of the cessation pills was supposed to be milder than that of opium smoke. At least, that was the opinion of those who trusted in them. I started to hand the pills back to her.

"I haven't needed them," Mother assured me, looking directly in my eyes. "And I won't need them."

Her confidence had me more worried than the pills. It echoed the glimmer of hope I would feel whenever Mother would try to stop smoking opium in the past. The moments of clarity would never last. I had stopped believing long ago, but I had to leave those doubts behind us now.

"It was Kuo Lishen who insisted I procure the pills," she said, coming back over. "I told him the same thing — I don't need them."

She became focused again, calling for a clerk to fetch some records. It was quite unsettling to see my mother in command.

"These production numbers are fundamental to understanding how the factory has been operating," she told me. "And Chief Engineer Kuo wants to review the engineering designs."

"You'll be assisting him with that as well?"

"Along with someone from the Ministry. Kuo Lishen was never one for details," Mother said with a rueful smile. "He was always better at communicating with the imperial court."

A sinking feeling formed in the pit of my stomach. Kuo had been part of the Ministry of Science under my father. If his role was to communicate with the imperial court back then, how was it that my father took the blame for our defenses failing? And then Kuo was elevated to Chief Engineer in the aftermath.

Was he doing the same thing now? Using Chang-wei to get the work done and then collecting the rewards? Avoiding the blame should the project fail?

"Are they going to replace Chang-wei?" I asked directly.

Mother looked surprised. "I don't imagine they could. Engineer Chen is more than capable. No one knows the production details better than he does."

I told her about the accident, not just about the accident at the citadel, but all the other accidents as well.

"Chang-wei feels responsible for what happened here," I told her. "He doesn't have control over the machines."

I could see her processing the information.

"I'll see what the Chief Engineer's perspective is on this," she said finally. "In any case, we'll know by tomorrow."

"What happens tomorrow?"

"The imperial delegation will go to the Directorate with its decision."

CHAPTER 7

I was summoned to the citadel again the next morning. I couldn't imagine why the delegation would still need me, but an order was an order. Fortunately, my duties were light that morning and I was able to re-assign most of my tasks.

The guard detail at the citadel was still on alert but allowed me in once I showed my summons. Once inside, I was surprised to be met immediately by Chang-wei. He intercepted me in the main passageway to pull me into a what looked like a book room.

"Soling," he greeted, seemingly out of breath.

"Engineer Chen."

I was immediately aware of the difference in how we addressed one another. Me, formal, as was customary for us in public. Him, much too familiar.

"Someone sent for me," I began.

"That was me." Chang-wei was standing close and there was an odd light in his eyes as he regarded me. "I sent for you," he repeated unnecessarily.

"What's happened?"

Chang-wei lifted his hand, but whatever he meant to do, he

must have decided against it because he let it drop. He ran his teeth over his lip nervously.

"Chang-wei?"

"I should have asked you this yesterday. I spoke with Jin *Furen*. I spoke with your mother."

I frowned at him. Yes, I was well aware of my mother was also Jin *Furen*.

"After all that has happened," he went on. "I didn't think it was possible. I didn't think I was worthy. But over the last year. And these last few months—"

My frown deepened. I didn't want to say anything for fear he'd lose focus—what little focus he possessed at the moment.

"Soling." He spoke my name tenderly. He did touch me now, though just the edge of my sleeve. Still, it made my heart flutter. "I asked your mother for permission to marry you." Finally, he allowed himself to take a breath.

I couldn't do anything but stare up at him. Dark circles hung beneath his eyes. Chang-wei looked exhausted, the same way he'd looked for the last months, but for once there was something else behind the tiredness. A spark of light.

"What did" —I swallowed, surprised to find my throat so dry — "she say?"

I had so many questions. So many, but that was the only question I could form. My heart was pounding hard. I couldn't be certain I'd heard him correctly. I remembered seeing him with Mother yesterday. Mother's oddly affectionate manner toward me afterward suddenly made sense.

"She told me I should probably ask you." He paused, looking boyish in his uncertainly. "So, I'm asking."

Chang-wei had done so much for my family. And there were times in the last year when I felt close to him followed by times when I didn't — it was hot and cold with Chang-wei. I couldn't deny that he was dear to me, but I was surprised he would be thinking about such personal things now. He was typically focused and absorbed in his work.

Then I remembered how he'd kissed me just days ago not far from here. Someone as brilliant as Chang-wei could certainly focus on more than one thing at once, couldn't he?

I was blushing. I could feel the heat high on my cheeks and burning at the back of my neck. I opened my mouth to speak.

"Don't answer right now," Chang-wei implored suddenly.

I clamped my lips closed, more than a little perturbed.

"Kuo Lishen and his delegation are to present their verdict. You should know what it is before deciding whether—" He hesitated, his eyes fixed onto mine. "Whether I'm even worth considering. I just wanted you to know that, despite what their decision may be, this was always my intention."

The words were spoken gently. His voice played along my spine. I wanted to tell him of course he was worth considering. I'd never considered anyone else.

"When did you know?" I asked, instead of all the more sincere, more feeling and grandiose things I should have said.

He licked his lips. "When did I know what?"

"That this was your intention?"

"Oh." His gaze wandered upward, searching. My heart thudded, once, twice.

"That first time I saw you again in Canton," he replied. "All grown up."

My chest felt like it would burst. I wanted to throw my arms around him and tell him that I didn't need to wait. I didn't care if he was to be stripped of his rank and removed from the Factories. What mattered was what he and I meant to each other.

It was a messenger who stopped me from pouring out all the thoughts swimming inside me.

"Engineer Chen, you're required in the Director's office."

Chang-wei acknowledged the messenger with a curt nod before looking back to me.

"I'll be right here," I assured him.

He reached out to touch his fingertips to the back of my hand before following the messenger out into the passageway.

I remained just inside the book room, thoughts of all that had just happened swirling around me like the images of a dream. Chang-wei, asking to marry me. Wanting me to be his wife. He'd known since that first moment we'd met in Canton.

A guard patrol passed through the corridor outside and I glanced up just in time to catch a glimpse of them. One of them glanced over at me before quickly jerking away. The patrol didn't pause to ask about my presence as they marched on.

The guardsman who had turned to face me had looked disturbingly familiar. The jagged features, the chin scraggly with stubble. Jiang Wen. From the Tai Shan facility.

Jiang who was supposed to be in Tai Shan Facility right now, working the line.

I ran out into the passageway. The patrol had disappeared down the corridor and I started in their direction for a few steps before I stopped. Then I spun around and ran back in the opposite direction, toward where I'd seen Chang-wei disappear.

The messenger had said they would be in the main hall. I didn't know where that was, but I ran through the corridor, glancing into the rooms. There was the workroom where I'd been with Chang-wei the other day.

Finally, I found a pair of guards standing before a door.

"Please, I must speak to the Directorate," I implored as the guards blocked my way. "There's going to be another attack."

I didn't know for certain, but it made sense. With the representatives from the Emperor's war council and the entire Directorate all in one room. I pleaded with the guards, my throat constricting with a rising panic.

The two men regarded me warily. One held me back with a

raised hand as the other reached for the door. As it opened, I was given a glimpse of the inner chamber. The three members of the Directorate sat behind a raised platform like magistrates hearing a case. The entire imperial delegation was assembled there with Kuo Lishen at the front, dressed in regalia.

"We commend the Directorate and your engineers on this great success," Chief Engineer Kuo was saying.

Chang-wei's voice rang out in response. *Chang-wei.*

"The automatons aren't ready. They don't work." His voice came from somewhere on the far side of the room.

Mother was standing just behind Kuo Lishen. She turned when the door opened and saw me. Her eyes widened with concern. The next events unfolded all at once as I tried to push past the guard with a warning hanging on my lips.

Mother started toward me. Kuo Lishen turned to see what had distracted her.

"Sabotage—"

That was all I could get out before the explosion shattered the air and I was thrown to the ground.

I was on my hands and knees in the hallway. I'd barely lifted my head to see the gray smoke that had flooded the room before there was another explosion. I ducked my head, hearing the splintering of wood. Then shouting. The ground trembled beneath my knees.

The next moment stretched on forever. When I finally dared to look up, I couldn't see a thing. There was movement inside the fog before me. The guard beside me had also been thrown to the ground. I saw him struggle to stand, his hand braced against the doorway.

My first attempt to get up failed as I staggered. There was a ringing in my ears.

JEANNIE LIN

"Mother!" My voice sounded muted, as if coming from far away. I coughed as smoke billowed out from the chamber.

My mother was in there and so was Chang-wei. A tight knot of fear formed in my stomach. I crawled forward, then once again struggled to my feet while using the doorway for support.

The smoke hung thick and I could hear voices crying out from inside, hurt. Needing help.

I couldn't wait to see if there were any more explosions, I needed to get inside. Pressing an arm over my nose and mouth, I pushed forward. My eyes teared up and I blinked furiously to try to clear them. Through the smoke, I could see people struggling to regain their feet. Several dark figures remained on the ground unmoving.

"Mother," I cried out again, squinting through the haze. She should be close. I had seen her right before the explosion.

A hand settled on my shoulder. "Soling?"

It was Chang-wei.

"Are you hurt?" I demanded.

"Are *you* hurt?" he echoed.

I could barely make out his face, but he seemed unharmed. He hooked an arm around me, and we held onto each other as I searched for my mother. The smoke had dissipated enough that I could make out more shapes. I stumbled over something and saw that it was an imperial headdress with a peacock feather attached.

Looking up, I saw someone huddled on the floor before me. Kuo Lishen.

"Are you hurt, sir?"

He groaned, grabbing onto my arm as he struggled to stand. Beneath him was my mother, sheltered from the blast by Kuo's body. She was dazed, but I was able to help her to her feet. A feeling of relief flooded me as I held onto her.

"I'm going to take Mother outside," I shouted to Chang-wei.

My ears were still ringing, but his must have been as well.

84

He'd been closer to the blast. He waved at me, go, then turned to help Kuo Lishen.

By the time Mother and I made our way out to the corridor, more help had arrived. Guardsmen ran into the chamber to pull out the others.

I kept moving in the opposite direction, away from the disaster until the air was clear enough that it didn't hurt to breathe. Mother sank to the ground with me beside her.

"Are you alright?" I asked her.

She stared up at me but didn't answer. Her face was covered with a layer of soot, and I was reminded of pulling survivors from the accident at Tai Shan. This would be much, much worse.

Gradually, her breathing calmed. Mother reached up and touched her hand to my cheek. I pressed my forehead to hers.

"Daughter." She put her arms around me, pulling me close.

There was so much to do. I needed to get to my feet and start right away, but for a moment I was grateful to be held by my mother and comforted. I knew the worst was yet to come.

CHAPTER 8

T he hours after the explosion were a blur.
      There were injuries. There was death — just as I
feared.

A temporary infirmary was set up at the citadel. An additional crew came from the factories led by Kai, who, against my original orders, did quite a bit of lifting and carrying.

Nine people had been inside the room. There were three members of the Directorate along with Chang-wei and then the five members in the delegation. The Directorate appeared to have been the target of the attack. An explosive device had been planted in the bench; two of the presiding members had been killed instantly. The third was injured. Chang-wei had been close to the blast but had avoided harm by ducking behind a desk.

The delegation had also suffered severe injuries. Two members were burned so badly that I didn't know if they would recover. Mother had been the most fortunate. She'd been turned away to come toward me. Kuo Lishen's larger form had shielded her against the full force of the blast.

As I set about caring for the injured, the Inspector General commenced his investigation. It was routine by now, the process eerily reminiscent of the earlier accident at Tai Shan. I reported my sighting of Jiang at the citadel to the inspector. Within the hour, the inspector reported back to me that Jiang Wen had disappeared along with a number of other workers. It wasn't until I was able to return to the infirmary several days later that I discovered Guo had gone as well. I had to assume Jiang had come for him.

With Guo's amputated leg, he'd slow down the escape. Yet they'd risked taking him. He had to be important to them — or maybe there was more of a sense of loyalty and brotherhood among the rebels than we realized.

Inspector Hala and his men were unable to find any trace of the rebels in the factory village or beyond. They'd managed to plan a clean escape route along with the attack.

Chief Engineer Kuo suffered burns and contusions from debris. He'd likely been saved from more serious injury by turning toward the door as well. He was confined to bed for a few days afterward, with my mother tending to him. I still wasn't clear of the ties between them. The Kuo Lishen I knew of was a selfish, power-hungry bureaucrat with little talent, as my mother herself described. Yet he'd thrown himself over her without a thought.

The part about being power-hungry still seemed correct. With the only remaining Director unable to resume his seat due to injuries, Kuo was the one to take over leadership of the Five Factories. He issued a directive for production to increase, even while the citadel was recovering from the tragedy. Chang-wei, who'd escaped with hardly any injury at all, was removed from the engineering corps and taken off of construction. Instead, he was assigned to investigate the explosive and incendiary device involved in the blast. Chang-wei bit his tongue about his objections and threw himself into his work.

"It's a good thing the production lines weren't affected by

the accident," Kuo said when I visited him along with my mother.

I decided that I still didn't like him. It was a week after the explosion. By then, we knew three people in that room, including one from Kuo's own delegation, had been killed by the explosion.

By the time two weeks had passed, the factories were busier than ever. Kuo Lishen was off of bedrest and it was clear that imperial authorities would be taking a more direct role in how the Five Factories were run going forward.

Eventually, Kuo Lishen summoned me directly to him. I came to his private studio, an office that he had commandeered from one of the directors who'd perished in the blast.

When I entered, he greeted me cordially and invited me to sit, calling for a servant to bring tea. I sat across from the Chief Engineer with my hands folded in my lap, as I waited for the tea to be served.

Given Kuo Lishen's much higher status, I kept my eyes lowered which meant I was only able to take him in with sideways glances. His dark beard was neatly trimmed and added an imposing look to his face. His features were sharp, his nose hawkish. A nick across one cheek was still visible, but healing.

"I knew your father, Miss Jin."

This might be the first he'd ever addressed me directly.

"So my mother has told me," I replied.

"We attended the Academy together."

I knew this as well, but it was strange to hear such pleasantries from the Chief Engineer. Since I'd known him, he'd antagonized Chang-wei, casting doubt on his loyalty, and clashing with him over status in the imperial court.

The servant returned with a tray carrying two teacups. A pungent herbal smell rose from Kuo's cup once he lifted the lid, reminding me that he was still taking a medicinal tea to dull his pain. Though his injuries were less serious than the others', he'd still been badly burned and bruised.

I drank my tea silently while he drank his, wondering why he'd called me and what were his hidden reasons for doing so.

"Engineer Chen was Jin Zhi-fu's brightest pupil," Kuo continued. "He honors your father's name with his accomplishments."

Yet my father's name was a source of disgrace in Peking, by imperial decree. I didn't say it aloud, but Kuo must have seen something in my expression. He set his tea down and folded his hands in front of him, regarding me with a dark look.

"It was a tragedy, what happened to your father."

I couldn't keep quiet any longer. "Fortunately, the same fate didn't befall you, Chief Engineer."

"No. Fortunately, it did not."

Mother had told me Kuo Lishen was an opportunist. He was more a flatterer and interloper than an engineer. I had to believe it given how he'd now taken over as Head Engineer in the factories, holding authority over Chang-wei even though Kuo had not been involved in any of the accomplishments of the past year.

"Chen Chang-wei has had to prove himself against unfortunate circumstances for the last ten years. His mentor's loss of face and his own capture by the Yangguizi." Kuo's lip curled around the less than polite term used to refer to Westerners. "It was hard for the Emperor to trust someone who'd spent so much time among foreign devils, but Chang-wei managed to convince him."

"Chang-wei is one of the most loyal people I know," I declared, bristling at the Chief Engineer's disparaging tone.

He raised his eyebrows at that. "He must be. And very clever."

I wanted to ask why he'd asked me to come. The sooner he

told me, the sooner I could leave, but etiquette demand that I wait patiently.

"It seems Chen Chang-wei will have yet another chance to prove himself," Kuo Lishen said, his tone indicating that it was undeserved. "Due to his foreign connections, the imperial delegation decided Engineer Chen would be the best person to send to Shanghai."

Shanghai? Chang-wei was leaving?

Kuo saw my look of shock. "Shanghai has been occupied by rebel factions for over a year now. Arms and supplies come into them from what should be our ports. The city is key to beating back the rebellion, but the imperial army has been stretched thin, divided between controlling the growth of the rebel army in Nanking." His lip curled. "As well as other uprisings emboldened by these traitors."

"But what of his work here?" I protested. "The automatons haven't been perfected. There's still so much to be done—"

"Engineer Chen will be stepping down from his duties at the Factories. It's clear that tighter control is needed."

It was exactly as Chang-wei had predicted. "Chen Chang-wei knows the design and what's needed better than anyone."

"We have what we need from him here," Kuo replied dismissively. "I'll remain as acting Head Engineer while Engineer Chen can better serve the Emperor's interests in Shanghai."

Of course, Kuo would now take over. All he could see was the triumph of presenting a fearsome mechanical army to the Emperor, but Chang-wei knew the machines were ready for battle. He had told me it might be years before the controls could be properly developed. I doubted Kuo Lishen would take the care to do it properly.

"The delegation has already sent their recommendations to the Emperor," he went on. "Chen Chang-wei will make contact with the former intendant of Shanghai who has escaped to the foreign concession. Loyalist forces are preparing to retake the Old City."

Chang-wei was once again being set up for failure.

"Sir, if I may ask, what does this have to do with me?"

"Though it may surprise you to hear it, I did consider your father a friend," the Chief Engineer confessed. "Which means, I do feel some responsibility to see to the well-being of his family."

I didn't believe him. He'd done nothing while my mother fled with my brother and I, hiding away in poverty and exile. But then again, for whatever reason, he had put himself in harm's way to protect my mother just weeks ago.

"I know that you and Engineer Chen are close and I feel there is something you should know." He leaned closer, offering a level of confidence that I didn't welcome. "I have reviewed the accounts of what happened in that chamber several times, and there's a question that I can't answer. Aside from the Directorate, Chen Chang-wei was the closest one to the location of the explosive device. Yet he escaped any harm." He paused, his black eyes boring into me. "Tell me, Miss Jin. How did he know to duck behind that desk so quickly?"

I NEARLY COLLIDED with Chang-wei outside in the corridor.

"Soling." He looked me over. "What's wrong?"

I stared at the container he had balanced in his arms. "What is that?"

"It's a model. A re-creation," he replied impatiently. "What's happened? You look upset."

"A recreation of what?" I insisted.

He let out a sigh. We were at odds, but I was still flustered from the conversation with Kuo Lishen. I wasn't yet ready to accept that Chang-wei was being sent away.

"This is an acid timer mechanism," he explained, tilting the box so I could see the glass vial attached inside. "This was how the perpetrators were able to build a delay into the explosive device. A strong acid is kept at the neck of this glass compartment. Once the acid dissolves this metal strip, the chemicals inside these two compartments will mix together—"

"You're leaving," I blurted out.

He looked startled. "For Shanghai," he conceded, shifting the large container to keep it from slipping from his hands.

"Why didn't you tell me?"

"There hasn't been any time," Chang-wei began, then stopped, his jaw hardening. "There never is any time for us, is there?"

He spoke quietly. His expression was the same thoughtful, serious one I'd come to associate with Chang-wei. His mind was always grinding away at something. I'd come to hope that, at least once in a while, his thoughts would come back around to us. The last time we'd spoken, he'd asked me to be his wife—and then nothing.

"Everything is happening very quickly. The delegation sent its recommendation to the war council and planning is already underway."

Those weren't the words I was hoping for from him. I bit my tongue, trying to listen as patiently as I could.

"Chang-wei," I interjected. "Last time we spoke. You said…"

His skin flushed. "I know."

For a moment, I had the wild thought that he no longer meant it. He'd reconsidered. He didn't want me after all.

Chang-wei looked down helplessly at the unwieldy container before bending to set it off to the side on the ground. When he straightened at least we were able to face each other without any obstacles in between us.

"I know," Chang-wei repeated, softer this time. His eyes darkened as he regarded me.

I didn't realize I'd been holding my breath. "With you going so far away—"

He blinked at me, looking confused. Would he really leave with his question, *the question,* unresolved and hanging between us?

Suddenly the corners of his mouth lifted. "I won't be too far. You're going as well."

"To Shanghai?" Now I was confused.

"Did you think you would be rid of me so easily?" he asked with a rueful smile.

He still hadn't answered my question. Or rather, his question...the one he told me not to answer. But that was before. Did he actually want me to give him an answer now?

Chang-wei could be so frustrating. Maybe I didn't want to marry him. I could figure it out if my heart wasn't pounding so hard just being near him.

"Why would I need to go to Shanghai?" I asked. It was the simplest of the questions I had for him.

"Well, not quite to Shanghai. The city has been overrun by rebels and we'll need help getting to the foreign concession through the treaty port." Chang-wei looked very serious now. "And Yang Hanzhu has always regarded you more favorably than he regards me."

PART II

THE HIGH SEAS

CHAPTER 9

Ningpo was a bustling port city, a mix of languages and faces. Like Shanghai, it was one of the treaty ports that had been opened up to trade after the Opium War. I elbowed and shouldered my way through the crowd on the busy street, moving toward the teahouse on the corner. The unpleasant smell of sea and sewage hung in the air, and I was eager to find refuge. A passerby with sun-dark skin barked something at me as I brushed past. I couldn't understand him and kept moving. He also didn't pause. Politeness didn't serve well on streets like these. One would get nowhere.

I'd studied up on Ningpo before arriving in the city. Ships from all manner of origins docked there. Goods, legal and illegal, were shipped or smuggled through the ports. Chang-wei told me it would be like Shanghai. I had been to Shanghai and, I could say this much at least, Ningpo was not Shanghai.

In Shanghai, there had been boundaries. Places that were Chinese and non-Chinese. In Ningpo, those lines had eroded. Its rules were its own. Ningpo might be on Qing soil, but a foreign landscape had been carved out of its streets. I was the interloper here.

The teahouse was crowded in the morning hour. I entered alone, ascending the wooden steps and weaving past patrons on my way to the upper floor. I was grateful to find a seat, newly vacated, next to an open window. No sooner did I sit down did a server arrive to pour tea. Now that I was at a safe and more calming distance, I took the opportunity to survey the street down below.

It looked just as bustling from above. In Peking and in Hubei, all countrymen were required to wear their long hair braided into a single queue. It was a sign of loyalty to the Qing. Here, there was no such rule. Men wore their hair in varying lengths and styles, some with hair shorn close to their heads and others in what looked like long tangled knots. Here and there, I spied the lighter coloring of the Western sailors, still such a strange sight to me.

From the high vantage point, I could at least breathe a little easier. The air was filled with a grit of salt and steam. I sipped my tea and looked to the stairs just as a graceful figure ascended to the upper floor. There weren't many women in this area, which was perhaps why she particularly drew my attention.

The woman met my eyes. Without waiting for an invitation, she came and seated herself across from me.

"Soling-san," she greeted.

"Satomi-san. You look well."

It had been a year since I'd last seen Sagara Satomi. She was dressed in a mismatch of clothing, leather and silk with no sense of origin or conformance to fashion. Which was to say she appeared at home in Ningpo. The polished handle of a firearm protruded from her belt. Her skin had darkened, taking on a warm tone from days in the sun.

"I had to be sure it was you who sent the message," she told me.

"I was expecting Hanzhu to come."

"He still thinks this is a trap. Though he does send his greetings. His fond greetings, I was to say."

The server came around again to set down another cup. Satomi left the tea untouched as she continued.

"I saw that you didn't come alone. I spotted Chen Chang-wei situated just inside the front door wearing a rather...interesting hat." Her eyes danced with amusement.

Apparently, Chang-wei and I made miserable spies. "He bought it from a trader from Macau," I explained sheepishly.

"Your engineer is not one for disguise. He looks like an imperial agent trying not to look like an imperial agent."

I blushed at the mention of Chang-wei as *my engineer*. "I assure you this is not a trap, Satomi-san. You and I have history together. Certainly, we can trust one another?"

She shrugged. In the past year she seemed to have picked up some of Yang Hanzhu's mannerisms.

Satomi and I had fled through the Nagasaki countryside together, fighting armored assassins sent by the shogunate. But, more importantly, Satomi had lost her father the same as I had. He'd been a trusted engineer to the Emperor of Japan, until he wasn't. In many ways, we were mirror images of one another. Satomi had found her freedom, escaping to the seas. I, however, had spent the last year doing the bidding of the very powers that had executed my father. I was doing their bidding now.

I shook away the thought. "If I could just speak to Hanzhu."

"He wouldn't have sent me if he meant to refuse you, so tell me what it is you need."

"We need passage to Shanghai."

Satomi made a face at that. "Shanghai was captured by insurgents last year. What do they call themselves—the Small Swords."

"The rebels only control the old Chinese city. We need to dock in the foreign concession."

Her frown deepened. "An even more difficult feat."

"Not for Yang Hanzhu."

Hanzhu was considered a privateer in polite circles, a smuggler in less polite circles. He came from a wealthy family who had disowned him, from what I'd heard. After the war, Hanzhu had cut off his queue in defiance of the Emperor, but that wasn't always who he'd been. Like Chang-wei, he'd served in the Ministry of Science under my father. He was a gifted alchemist and had a hand in refining the gunpowder fuels used to power the empire's ships.

"Yang-san hates foreigners," Satomi reminded me.

"You're a foreigner," I countered.

She didn't flinch. "He hates the Yangguizi," she corrected. "Though lately, he seems to hate everyone."

I watched her expression. "How is he?"

Satomi let out a slow sigh. Taking hold of the teacup, she turned the porcelain cup in a slow circle without lifting it to drink. "A lot has happened in the course of a year."

It must be lonely floating adrift at sea all the time. Yang Hanzhu was marked as a traitor by the Qing empire and Satomi could never return to Japan. They were both in exile.

"I wouldn't ask this of Hanzhu if there was any other way. He may not care about the empire, but he was always close to my family. I'm doing this for them."

"Family honor," she murmured solemnly. "I remember what that was like. The sacrifices required to uphold it."

"Will he see me?" I pressed.

"Is it just you and the engineer?"

I nodded and Satomi stood. "Yang-san will always see you."

I tossed a coin on to the table and followed her to the stairs. Satomi moved with a long, confident stride which led me to believe she regularly frequented places like Ningpo.

Every table below was filled. The teahouse had become even more crowded since I came, but it was two spots near the door that drew my attention. Chang-wei was positioned at one table with his face hidden beneath a dark, wide-brimmed hat. Across the aisle, however, was another familiar face.

"You didn't come alone either," I remarked.

Makoto was one of Satomi's countrymen who had also left the island empire of Japan when Chang-wei and I had made our escape. A year on the seas had given him a lean, careworn look.

I'd first encountered the swordsman in Nagasaki when Chang-wei hired him as a guide to smuggle us outside of the foreign section. His expression was one of quiet watchfulness as he surveyed the room. He and Chang-wei sat with two tables between them, quietly facing off against one another. Makoto acknowledged my presence with the tiniest of nods and stood to join us. His katana hung prominently at his belt.

"Chen-san," Satomi greeted at the same time as she passed by Chang-wei before exiting.

Chang-wei and I had dressed as plainly as possible to try to disappear into the crowds of Ningpo. His jacket and robe were brown in color. Mine, a drab, chalky blue. But I could see what Sagara was talking about when it came to Chang-wei's disguise. It wasn't so much his manner of dress as it was his demeanor. Straight-spined with a sense of rigid formality. He certainly needed more than a large wool hat to look like he belonged in the squalid streets of the port city. I found it endearing.

"What is it?" he asked, seeing my smile.

"It's nothing."

He scrambled to his feet. "Is it done then?"

Outside the press of the crowd was once again upon us. I had to lean close to his ear to be heard.

"You know it's never that easy with Yang Hanzhu."

Makoto fell in behind us. For a moment it felt like old times, like it had been with the four of us in Nagasaki. Bonds formed quickly when you had to fight for your lives together.

Satomi made a path toward the docks. As we neared the customs house, we passed by a series of yellow decrees pasted onto the public wall. Rewards offered for known rebels and pirates, from what I could see. I caught the three characters of Yang Hanzhu's name inked in red among them.

The waterfront provided a wider avenue, but was just as busy. A group of sailors passed by and Satomi slowed to catch the conversation before the sailors melted into the crowd.

"For a long time, Ningpo was the only port where the Shinajin would allow delegations from Nippon," Satomi said over her shoulder. "There are still many trade ships that dock here from our empire. Makoto and I try to search for news, but sometimes it's just a comfort to hear our mother tongue."

"What news is there?" I had to practically shout to be heard.

"The gaijin were granted trading access in Nippon, but without the devastation of a war."

Chang-wei had gone to Nagasaki a year ago hoping to forge an alliance, but our two nations were separated by more than a stretch of sea. Japan had been closed off to the outside for hundreds of years and both the Qing emperor and the shogunate were set in their ways.

The dock was filled with all manner of travelers. Unlike Shanghai, which had separated the foreign concessions into specific areas outside the walls of the old city, Ningpo was a stewpot mixture of seafarers. There were the lighter-skinned Yangguizi amidst darker-skinned traders from Macau. Regardless of clothing and origin, they all had the sun-baked and wind-swept look of those who sailed the seas. A mix of languages flowed into the ports where they all merged together to form a common language. The Canton dialect of the south seemed prevalent. Out of every five words, I recognized one.

"Passengers," Satomi announced to a representative from the port authority, slipping a silver coin to him in the same breath. She kept on moving.

We navigated through the wooden docks to a sleek vessel with furled sails.

"Has Yang traded ships?" I asked. Yang Hanzhu had always sailed on a massive war junk.

"Yang-san won't set foot in Ningpo," Satomi replied. "Or any other port controlled by the imperial authority and especially not the treaty ports. He's become more suspicious."

"*More* suspicious?" I asked.

"He's instructed me to bring you to him." She regarded Chang-wei. "And you as well, Chen-san. But the only way to see him is to sail out with us."

Chang-wei looked to me.

"It's where he has the advantage," I said quietly. "He won't speak with us otherwise."

He calculated the risks and came to a decision. "Out to sea then."

CHANG-WEI STOOD beside me on deck as we watched the shore recede.

"I hope he can be reasoned with," he said. "There are many lives counting on us getting to Shanghai."

I couldn't see how the plan was in any way reasonable. If we managed to get Hanzhu, a noted outlaw, to smuggle us into Shanghai, we would then have to collaborate with foreigners. All of this to re-capture the city from insurgents.

"I trust Hanzhu," I told him.

Chang-wei took in a breath. "I don't."

Yang Hanzhu had saved our lives more than once. I didn't understand the nature of the rift between them. They'd once been colleagues and had referred to each other as brothers — though that may have just been a courtesy. Whenever Yang Hanzhu and Chen Chang-wei came face-to-face, there was an undercurrent of discord between them. Like two poles of a magnet refusing to come together. When asked, all they would tell me is that they disagreed on everything and always had.

Given that Yang Hanzhu had cut off his queue and declared himself an outlaw while Chang-wei still served the imperial court — these things were obvious signs of the greater rift between them.

Chang-wei continued, "My contact in Shanghai tells me the Small Swords have fortified the old city. The rebels made an agreement with the foreign powers to leave their territory in the concession alone as long as the Westerners don't interfere. The ports in the foreign concession are still open for trade. In fact, they're even busier now that the customs house is unable to levy any tax on their shipments. Our best chance of getting into Shanghai is through the foreign concession."

"Your contact is that Yingguoren — Burton?"

I pronounced the foreign name as well as I could. Burton was a foreigner, nearly as tall as Kai, with square shoulders and a square face. He was pale-skinned with shockingly yellow hair. When I'd met him, it was the first time I'd seen anyone who looked like that. Whether Chang-wei considered him a friend or just a useful ally, I wasn't quite sure.

"He's not from Yingguo. He's Meiguoren," Chang-wei corrected. "*American.*"

I didn't know if that was better or worse or all the same. We had never gone to war with Meiguo, but they brought in opium all the same, caring nothing for our laws.

"When we see Hanzhu, I think it's better if you speak to them," Chang-wei suggested.

"I'm not so sure about that—"

"It's possible he's sympathetic to the Small Swords in Shanghai, which would mean stop all negotiation immediately. And then, possibly, try to escape with our lives."

"Chang-wei," I began in a warning tone. "Hanzhu has never

aligned himself with the Taiping movement or any other rebellion."

He had just rejected Qing rule and taken to sea. He operated outside the laws, which is exactly why he was useful now.

"We need to negotiate passage to Shanghai for me and my crew and our cargo."

I tensed at the mention of Chang-wei's involvement. He was the one with the foreign contacts and better able to move about the concession, but I still didn't like it. Chang-wei wasn't a soldier. He was an engineer.

"What if Hanzhu wants to know why?" I asked.

"Then tell him."

"That you're bringing weapons to Qing loyalists?"

He sighed. "I don't see how we can avoid it. As long as the rebels occupy the city, foreign influence continues to grow stronger. Perhaps Yang will see it that way. He may have objections to the Qing government, but surely he doesn't want to be ruled by foreigners."

The insurgents had occupied Old Shanghai for over a year. All of the officials and citizens loyal to the Qing had fled into the concession areas of Shanghai occupied by Western powers.

"If he insists on knowing any more, tell him our aim is to establish contact with the circuit intendant, Taotai Wu."

Chang-wei had been tasked with bringing word from the Emperor to the intendant. Taotai Wu had been appointed administrative control over Shanghai by the Qing government. The uprising had momentarily stripped him of power, but he remained connected to the loyalist forces who had gathered in the region. There had been skirmishes between the loyalists and the Small Swords, but the Old City was shielded by a defensive wall the loyalists couldn't breach. To prevail, they needed support from Peking that had been slow in coming.

Over the last year, the Taiping rebel army had grown into the hundreds of thousands, swallowing city after city. The

Emperor's forces were struggling to hold onto territory and couldn't spare any troops to re-capture Shanghai.

The Emperor's Grand Council couldn't spare any more soldiers. The loyalists would have to make do with the gunpowder and weapons Chang-wei managed to smuggle in.

"Will the Westerners allow munitions into the foreign concession?" I asked.

"They've been doing so. How do you think the rebels are being supplied?"

I squeezed my eyes shut, trying to make sense of it. "Maybe you need to be the one to make your case to Hanzhu."

I wasn't any good at keeping the alliances straight. Everything was becoming entangled and there was no telling who was friend or foe.

"Yang will refuse simply because it's me proposing it. But you. He holds you—" Chang-wei struggled to find the words. "With some regard."

Regard? I frowned at him. Yang Hanzhu had been a family acquaintance. I'd known him before ever meeting Chang-wei. Hanzhu was older than him by five or six years. As a child, I'd referred to Yang Hanzhu as "uncle". He would show me his experiments when I visited his laboratory. Perhaps that was why Hanzhu remained sentimental towards me, but he was also shrewd. He'd know I was just parroting Chang-wei's demands.

"Hanzhu resents both the Qing government and the Ying-guoren," I reminded him.

"Then tell him we can pay him."

"Insult him like that and he'll surely throw us into the sea." I paused, considering carefully what Chang-wei was proposing. "If I can convince him—"

He straightened, listening.

"If I can convince him, then you'll take me with you to Shanghai."

Chang-wei tensed, a protest already forming on his lips. We were interrupted by Satomi returning from the main deck.

He held my gaze for a second longer, frustrated at not being able to respond, before turning to her. "Sagara-san. Thank you for your assistance bringing this meeting together."

"So formal," she mused. "I'm not so formal in your language. We'll reach Yang-san by first light tomorrow morning. He's not so far if we sailed directly, but there are matters of caution."

"There's no one following," Chang-wei assured.

"So you say. But the imperial navy aren't the only ships we're evading nowadays."

I recalled the yellow notices calling for Yang Hanzhu's capture. "Who else?" I asked curiously.

"Imperial ships. Foreign ships. Pirates from Macau. Pirates from Canton."

"It's thieves stealing from thieves out on the water." Makoto came to join in. "There's not a stretch of coastline that someone hasn't laid claim to, demanding a water tax for safe passage. This is why our fleet was formed. A lone ship couldn't survive."

"How many ships are under Yang's command?" Chang-wei asked.

"You see, Shinajin. Questions like that make people suspicious of you," Satomi said with a sideways glance.

"I apologize. I'm always curious," Chang-wei replied.

"A scientist's curiosity or an imperial agent's?"

He bowed, conceding both his innocence and complicity at once and Satomi smiled back at him. I was given a glimpse of how charming Chang-wei could be.

"It's not command so much as...*sōgo ni yūekina*," Satomi explained. "A mutual arrangement. This is the fastest of the smaller ships."

The engine started with a rumble beneath our feet and the vessel picked up speed through the water. The battened sails were rotated and adjusted to reduce the drag from the wind.

"Between Yang Hanzhu and his engineer, he's able to outfit these ships with the fastest engines in the water," Chang-wei observed.

"The engines themselves have been a problem," Satomi concurred. "We've been chased by pirates wanting to steal our ships to salvage the engines. Then there's the matter of the bounty on Yang-san himself."

"The engineer is more valuable," Chang-wei said bluntly. "It's still Old Liu Yentai, isn't it?"

I looked to Chang-wei. He'd been captured by the Ying-guoren during the war and forced to labor in the engine room aboard their steamships. It was how he'd learned about the inner workings of the foreigners' war machines.

"This is why Hanzhu wouldn't go to Ningpo," I said.

The notices for Yang Hanzhu's capture suddenly made more sense. The battle for control of the empire was becoming one of engineering.

Despite its small size, the ship we were on was outfitted for battle. Chang-wei lifted a tarp to reveal a portable cannon underneath before Makoto tugged the cover back in place. There was also a supply of clay jars stashed on deck. I assumed they were fire bombs which were a favored weapon of Hanzhu's. The chemical compound within them ignited on contact and would even burn on the surface of water.

Below deck there was a compartment where we could rest at night and stay away from the sun. There was no privacy there, just space for us to sleep along with the crew as they rotated in and out.

That night I was pressed close to Chang-wei. His arm draped around me in the dark.

"Yes," he said softly.

"Yes, to what?"

"Shanghai." He was formless in the darkness.

"I thought you would say that it was too dangerous."

There was silence. I wished I could see his expression, not that I could always read it. But I'd become better over the last year together.

"I considered all the possible alternatives," he admitted finally. "Shanghai is, unfortunately, the best scenario."

CHAPTER 10

Chang-wei sighted land on the horizon just after dawn. He lowered the set of field glasses and held them out to me. They were crafted from solid brass and weighed heavily in my hands. I lifted them to my eyes, taking a moment to steady myself against the slow roll of the deck.

"There." He helped me direct the glasses to the correct area.

"I see it."

"An island," he said. "There are many small islands off the coast of Ningpo. Some were used as enclaves by outlaws before they were raided by the imperial navy."

Apparently, they were still in use.

"We've done everything Yang Hanzhu wanted," Chang-wei went on. "We've put ourselves completely at his mercy. I hope it's enough."

Just the thought of seeing his old colleague did something to him. His spine went rigid with tension and his jaw set into a hard, unyielding line.

I handed the field glasses back to him. "What happened between the two of you?"

"I don't know if anything ever happened. We were never friends."

They had both served in my father's Ministry but in different departments. Hanzhu in alchemy and Chang-wei in engineering.

"It might have something to do with how your mother favored Yang and your father, myself," he admitted after a pause.

"Why would it matter who my mother favored—?"

Chang-wei met my eyes but said nothing.

Realization finally struck me and my face flooded with heat. "Both of you wanted to—?"

"Marriage is an arrangement between families," Chang-wei said, redirecting his gaze to the horizon. "Yang Hanzhu really was the better suitor. He was a few years older than I and already established within the Ministry. Everyone knew that he came from a wealthy family."

"I was only nine years old at the time," I mused.

Chang-wei would have been eighteen years old, having just passed his exams.

"What about your family?" I asked because I was too curious not to.

"I came from the orphanage. I have no family."

I was struck speechless. He said it so simply, as if it were nothing. We had been through so much together and I had never known. Chang-wei never spoke of family so I'd never asked. It would have been impolite to do so.

"Your father took me in," Chang-wei explained. "Initially I fetched things for him, did small tasks in the various workshops and laboratories. I greased the gears, scrubbed the equipment clean. Whenever I could, I would try to read the books I found lying around. I'd scrub my hands for an hour, I was so afraid of leaving dirty prints on the pages."

I tried to imagine him, a skinny boy with dark and curious

eyes, gingerly opening a newly discovered book with careful hands.

All of the sudden, I understood the reason for Chang-wei's unshakable loyalty. His loyalty to the Emperor. To my family. Our arranged marriage would have been akin to my father taking Chang-wei into the family. Like a son.

Chang-wei needed to belong to something. It didn't matter that court insiders whispered that he was *hanjian*, disloyal. It didn't matter if they accused him of being a Western-sympathizer or dismissed his continued sacrifices.

"My father always spoke so highly of you," I told him, knowing my words wouldn't be enough for him.

"Your father was a very good man," Chang-wei said, his voice thick with emotion. "You should know all this, who and what I am. Before—"

His voice trailed away. Before I gave him my answer.

I parted my lips, ready to give him my answer now. It wasn't who he was or where he came from that made me hesitate.

Chang-wei was finally making a name for himself because of his earnestness and his intelligence. And his undying loyalty. Our family name could have once lifted him, but it had since become a source of disgrace. In the past, our arranged marriage would have benefited Chang-wei, but being associated with the Jin name now could only drag him down.

Chang-wei was looking at me intently, but I couldn't bring myself to say yes yet. There were things he should know about me as well. And duties we had yet to complete.

"Tell me about the orphanage," I said instead, shyly.

He tried not to look disappointed. "There were twenty boys there, young and old." He drew me closer until I could feel the front of his robe brushing against my shoulders. A small shiver ran down my spine. "I was always getting into trouble, they said, before I could even remember. I liked to take things apart…"

A SHORELINE EMERGED in the distance along with a set of sails like large red wings. I peered through the field glasses to see another vessel nearby in the water. And another closer to shore.

"We'll signal them," Satomi said, coming up behind us.

The crew assembled a launcher that consisted of a hollow iron tube erected on top of a stand. It looked like a small cannon. Satomi inserted a bamboo rocket before lighting a fuse. The rocket shot high before exploding in a puff of blue smoke that hung in the air. Several minutes later, there was a similar reply from the distant fleet.

"Soon now," Satomi said.

Our vessel sliced through the water to rejoin its sisters.

"Remember what we spoke of," Chang-wei told me in a low voice.

As we entered the bay, we could see a dock along the shore and a few wooden structures inland that appeared out of use. The fleet had taken temporary shelter in an abandoned enclave but wouldn't remain for long.

"We just float from island to island," Satomi said wistfully. "Some large, some small. Some more dangerous than others."

Even though much of the fleet had gone ashore, Hanzhu remained on his flagship anchored in the water. He was waiting on the main deck for us as we climbed aboard on the rope ladder. He peered down at us. A brown cigarette rested between his fingers, emitting a thin plume of smoke.

He was dressed in a Western-style trousers and boots with a leather waistcoat fitted over his shoulders and fastened with a row of silver buttons. He wore foreign clothing in defiance of the Qing government with its strict edicts regarding dress and appearance.

The most shocking part of Yang Hanzhu's appearance, however, was his hair, which he let hang loose to his shoulders.

No matter how many times I saw him, the rogue appearance was still a shock.

"Jin Soling." A slow grin spread across his face revealing even white teeth. Then he glanced behind me, and the smile disappeared. "And Chang Chen-wei."

"Elder brother," Chang-wei began respectfully.

Yang met my eyes, deliberately overlooking Chang-wei. He took a long drag of his cigarette, blowing out a stream of smoke. "So, what fool's errand have you been sent on this time?"

"Uncle," I began respectfully.

He made a face.

"Thank you for agreeing to see us."

"This must be a greatly unpleasant task hearing how stiff and formal you sound," he interjected with a snort before turning to address Chang-wei finally. "No ships following you? You didn't send a spy kite after us?"

"No, Elder Brother," Chang-wei replied. "Not this time," he couldn't help adding.

Hanzhu fixed his eyes on him. They were black and penetrating, set deep in his face and gleaming with intelligence.

"We need your help," I interrupted. There was no use in letting the two of them be reminded that they hated one another.

"*You* need my help?" Hanzhu asked, his tone suddenly gentle, but no less sharp. "Or is it that boy Emperor who likes to give orders while sheltered away in the Forbidden City."

I stiffened. It was difficult to hear the Emperor treated with such disrespect.

"I'm here to speak on the Emperor's behalf, for his sake as well as mine."

Hanzhu held my gaze a moment longer before rolling his eyes.

He turned to Satomi. "What's the news in Ningpo?"

"The reward for your capture has doubled. Five hundred taels of silver. Dead or alive—"

"I haven't done half the things they say I've done!" he ranted. "I didn't sink those river junks at the Pearl delta. I never sacked Xiamen."

"They say you raided a trading fleet and burned fifty crates of opium," Chang-wei chimed in.

"Well, I did do that," he admitted begrudgingly. "Those foreign devils keep bringing in more of that poison. You would think the Qing authorities would thank me for that transgression."

The opium trade was illegal in our country, but the treaty ports were enacted so the foreigners could continue to smuggle it in plain sight. And our people — I couldn't help but think of my mother — our people kept consuming it. Opium was a festering, open wound that would not heal.

Yang turned and started walking. Satomi indicated that we should follow and I quickly fell into step behind him.

"It's getting harder to roam about in exile these days," he complained.

He tossed the cigarette overboard into the sea before reaching the stairs and descending. Satomi glanced once over her shoulder. She gave me an encouraging nod before ducking below.

There was almost a sense of homecoming, being back in the hold of Hanzhu's ship, though it wasn't necessarily a joyous occasion. While we were here, we were under Hanzhu's protection, but we were also at his mercy.

Chang-wei and I followed Satomi and Hanzhu to his workroom which he'd specially built on board in order to continue with his alchemical experiments. He was obsessed with the study of opium and the varying compositions of the drug. Hanzhu was convinced that the opium shipped through our ports had been tampered with to make the drug more addictive, more destructive. As if opium wasn't destructive enough as it was.

The wooden counters were currently bare and the equipment stowed away, but there were times when Hanzhu would disappear down here for days. A massive herbal cabinet with an array of drawers spanned the far wall. A series of cabinets lined another wall, filled with bottles and glass containers that had to be secured against rough seas.

Yang rounded the worktable and turned to face us, hands braced against the surface of the counter as he waited for our proposal.

"We need passage to Shanghai," I began. "But the Small Swords rebels control the main port right now."

"That is why you want me to dock in the foreign concession," Hanzhu completed for me.

I could see an immediate sneer of refusal on his lips, but he held himself back. At least for the moment. "What is the purpose of this foolish mission?"

"To provide support to allies sheltered in the concession," Chang-wei replied stiffly, despite his earlier plan that I do most of the talking.

"While the Qing army mounts an attack from outside the city."

"Yes."

Hanzhu narrowed his eyes. "And how do the Yangguizi figure into this?"

The temperature in the room seemed to drop. I glanced between Yang Hanzhu and Chang-wei. Even Satomi, who had remained off to the side, straightened.

"The Westerners have remained neutral," Chang-wei said evenly.

"So they say."

Listening to the two of them speak, I was aware, more than

ever, of how the Ministry of Science was an extension of the Ministry of War.

"If this plan doesn't work, the imperial forces will need to find another way," I pleaded. "A direct attack on the city will risk a drawn-out battle. There will be more suffering and death."

"Soling." I could see the tiniest cracks forming in Hanzhu's hard exterior. "How did you become so involved in all this?"

His gaze flicked accusingly over to Chang-wei.

"The entire country is involved," I deflected.

There were uprisings in the north and south on the mainland. The Taiping rebel army had taken Nanking as well as a string of major cities. Hanzhu had once declared that the empire deserved to fall, but I couldn't believe he truly meant that. Not when the collapse of the Qing would come with so much bloodshed.

"You picked the wrong person to ask for help," Hanzhu said bitterly. He and Satomi exchanged a look. "Is there anyone who isn't hunting us nowadays? We'd need to navigate past the rebel lookouts, the imperial navy, and all of these cursed pirates who want to scrap my ship for parts."

"I know you're not motivated by money," I began tentatively.

"What gives you that impression?" He patted the pockets of his waistcoat, searching until he found his cigarette case. "There's not a single vessel in this fleet that doesn't need repair."

I took a breath, praying that Hanzhu wouldn't be offended. "The imperial court will pay you handsomely with silver."

He sneered, "The imperial court wants me thrown in prison."

"Then perhaps there is something else you might consider. Something more valuable to you than money," Chang-wei said.

I glanced at him in surprise.

"What is that?" Hanzhu asked warily.

"Amnesty."

Outwardly, Hanzhu's expression revealed nothing. He opened the metal cigarette case, seemed to remember he was near all kinds of flammable substances, and snapped it shut before shoving it back into his pocket.

"The empire has offered amnesty before in times when it was deemed beneficial to form alliances out at sea," Chang-wei went on.

"I'm aware of the history," Hanzhu replied coldly. A beat passed between them. "The Emperor has offered this?"

"I can propose it to him."

"*You.*"

The one word said enough. How little Hanzhu trusted the empire. How little he trusted Chang-wei's place within it.

Chang-wei nodded, as earnest as I'd ever seen him. "We once worked together for the good of our country."

"I'd rather take the money," Hanzhu declared with a sharp laugh. "But no amount of money is worth what you're asking. I don't deal in opium and I don't work with foreigners."

"But—"

He held up a hand to cut off my reply. "It was good to see you, Little Soling, alive and well," he said while ushering us toward the door. "Please try to stay that way."

I STARED AT THE DOOR. Hanzhu had shut it without a word of farewell, leaving Chang-wei and I standing in the passageway.

"Perhaps with some time," Satomi suggested gently, having been herded out of the laboratory along with the two of us.

Chang-wei's expression remained unreadable. Had he expected any different?

Satomi gestured toward the stairs, but I reached for the door instead. I slipped back inside the laboratory, pulling the door closed behind me.

Hanzhu had gone to the cabinets at the front. He was searching through the drawers, opening and closing them in sharp, agitated movements.

"Do you want to watch it all burn?" I asked loudly.

He stilled, his back to me. The Western jacket give him an angular, box-like shape. It was another layer of armor, of distance.

"You're not doing this for profit, or even for revenge," I pressed. "Is it just for the sake of watching everything fall apart?"

"That would be a rather empty pleasure." Slowly, he turned to face me. "Why do you keep working so hard to defend the empire?"

"I'm not protecting the empire."

"It destroyed your family," he reminded quietly.

His mood had changed now that it was just the two of us.

"My family still lives in Peking," I told him honestly. "My mother and my brother. We can't all just go jump onto boats and drift about at sea."

Hanzhu grinned, challenging my assertion with his smile alone, but there was something flat behind his eyes. Tinder without a spark to ignite it.

"The Qing Emperor doesn't deserve your loyalty," he admonished lightly.

"This is the world we live in."

It was the world I knew, even if it was a flawed one. I wanted my family to not only survive but thrive within it. The rebellion brought its own kind of madness and its own injustices.

"What about your family? Aren't you concerned for them?" I asked.

The Yang family had been involved in the salt trade for generations and ran a large merchant fleet. Hanzhu been a fugitive for ten years now, separated from family and country. He might be more comfortable than most at sea, but everyone had their limits.

Hanzhu's smile disappeared. "My family will have no problem surviving regardless of who controls the empire. They were born of this kind of strife."

"My family won't be so fortunate."

His eyes darkened. The rebels were taking cities and slaughtering the Manchu. Perhaps he could dismiss the bloodshed and suffering as unavoidable, but I couldn't.

Hanzhu held my gaze for a long time before letting out a slow breath. "I don't want to watch it all burn," he said finally. And then, "How much silver are we talking about?"

CHAPTER 11

T he exchange happened in the dead of night. The imperial ship landed upon the agreed upon location and unloaded the cargo on to the dock. A small team stayed behind with the enormous crates while the imperial ship sailed away.

By the next morning, Yang Hanzhu came in with his head ship and fleet to retrieve the goods. I was relieved to see Kai among the crew as they worked to load the goods. I didn't recognize the others.

Chang-wei had disembarked to supervise the loading while I remained on board the war ship. From the size of the cargo, I imagined we'd be here for hours.

"Little Soling, off on another adventure," a gravelly voice said behind me.

I turned around to see Liu Yentai, stout and covered in soot. Heavy leather gloves covered his hands and forearms. His mask and goggles were pulled down to reveal a wide grin. "That scoundrel Yang didn't tell me you were on board."

"Old Liu. I should have come down to see you," I began guiltily.

Liu Yentai waved away my apology. "Everyone forgets the engine room when things are running smoothly, eh?"

In truth I was so occupied with negotiating our passage that I'd forgotten. Liu Yentai had been close to our family since before I was born. He took my side by the bow to view the activities below.

"Chen Chang-wei," he said thoughtfully.

Chang-wei and his crew had rigged a pulley to lift the crates into the hold.

"That boy's still in the Ministry," Liu remarked.

Chang-wei and Old Liu got along well from what I recalled. Much better than Chang-wei and Hanzhu did. I imagined Liu was like a grandfather who looked upon all of us as children who needed to scrape up our knees, fight amongst each other, and eventually find our way.

"How is your mother?" Liu asked fondly.

"She's much better," I said and meant it. "She's happy. Doing calculations again."

"That's what it would take," he said with a laugh. "Do you know she was part of the team that built the first imperial airships? Not that she would know a thing about how an engine fires or what needs to be done to lift the structure. But if you stripped everything down to the numbers, she would know what would work and what wouldn't."

"Maybe one day she and you will be able to see one another again," I suggested.

His cheerful mood immediately darkened. "I don't think that will ever be."

Liu had escaped Peking with Yang Hanzhu after the war and had stayed away from the mainland for a decade, preferring a life of exile. Even though he still wore his hair in the traditional queue, braided and wrapped around his neck like a scarf, he was as much of an outsider as Hanzhu.

"If only we'd been able to find her," Liu said with a sigh.

"Find her?"

He looked back at me. I could see the pale outline around his eyes where the goggles had been. "On the day of your father's execution, the Ministry was in disarray. I commandeered an airship and several of us planned to make our escape on it. Yang Hanzhu went to find your mother."

I remembered that night. All of those memories were cloaked in darkness like a dream. Tian was only a baby. Our housekeeper, Nan, was holding him as she told me to pack our things. Mother was in my father's study speaking with a man who had come to the house telling us we needed to go.

"Kuo Lishen," I murmured.

"What?"

"It was Chief Engineer Kuo who came to our house that night," I realized. "To warn Mother."

"That bastard. He wasn't Chief anything then. Just a do-nothing, know-nothing, rich and worthless egg of a turtle!"

I stared at Old Liu in shock. If my memories were correct, Kuo Lishen might have been a know-nothing climber, but he must have helped smuggle us out of Peking that night. Much later, we learned that imperial authorities had come that very same night and burned down our house. What would they have done to us if we had stayed?

A sudden thought came to me. "Old Liu, who else was with you in the airship?"

"There were five of us, all members of the Ministry. We needed enough people to operate the airship. For a while, we stayed together, but gradually went our separate ways. Those men were still young with their life ahead of them. They'd come from their hometowns to Peking. With the Ministry gone, they could still return to their families."

Liu was reluctant to tell me more. Chang-wei was still part of the Ministry and thus loyal to the Emperor. By association, I suppose I was as well.

"We'll have a chance to talk more soon enough as we sail for Shanghai. You can tell Old Liu all the news of Peking and what you've been doing," he said cheerfully.

I nodded though it had been more than a year since I'd been in the capital. And I didn't know what I could say about my life when we weren't supposed to speak of the Factories to outsiders.

Thinking about the Factories, however, reminded me of something I was still trying to figure out.

"Do you know anything about this symbol?" I pulled out a paper from my pocket and unfolded it to show to him. I'd drawn what I could remember of the spoked wheel pattern I'd seen on the amulet that Little Guo had worn.

Chang-wei had suspected that the sabotage had come from one of his engineers. I wondered if it was possible that the rebels had infiltrated the Factories with someone from outside who had that knowledge.

"It looks like a wheel or a gear," I explained. "I was wondering if it might be familiar to you."

Liu merely frowned at the drawing. "Never seen it before."

We were interrupted by Liu's apprentice, a boy who'd grown quite a bit taller since I'd last seen him, at that phase when his arms and legs looked just a little too long for his body. He must have been sixteen years by now. Like Liu, he wore a leather apron and gloves with a face mask pulled down below his chin. They were nearly copies of one another, though the apprentice was now taller than his master.

"Master Liu." He held a metal carrying case which I presumed contained Liu's tools.

"Are you called *Benzhuo* or *Congming* nowadays?" I asked him. Liu was in the habit of calling his apprentice Clumsy or Clever, depending on his mood. I didn't know if he had ever been given another name.

The boy, who was really a young man now, smiled at me shyly. "Still 'Clumsy,'" he revealed.

"He's always Benzhuo, this one," Liu said gruffly. "We should be worried now that he's taking on his own ship."

"Just the engine room," Benzhuo clarified for me.

"Just?" echoed Liu. "Running the engine is more important than being captain."

There was some maintenance on the other ships they needed to see to while the fleet was ashore. I watched the two of them disembark, young and old. Old Liu might call his apprentice clumsy, but I see the pride in his eyes. What he said was true about the value of running the engine. With piracy and smuggling on the rise along the coasts, ships run on gunpowder or steam were the fastest in the water. The advantage of a good engineer who could keep things running smoothly could mean life or death.

The smaller vessels that had sworn allegiance to Yang had been fitted with gunpowder engines, but each one also required resources. There were constant repairs, parts for replacement, a supply of gunpowder, food, water. What used to be a single war junk under Hanzhu's command had become a collective.

As to the imperial bounty on Yang Hanzhu's head, the Emperor understood how the knowledge men like Hanzhu and Chang-wei carried with them were potential weapons. There was a similar bounty on Liu Yentai and any of the former Ministry members who were still known to be alive. The former Emperor had turned his back on learning and science and any advancement that had been deemed foreign. The ignorance had forced the people who could have saved the empire into hiding.

Or even worse. Into rebellion.

~

AFTER SEVERAL HOURS, our cargo was finally loaded onto the flagship. Chang-wei was coming onboard with Kai and the rest of our team when they were met by Satomi and Makoto.

"We're here to escort you below deck to a holding area," Satomi explained.

I hurried over to them. "Is this necessary?"

"It's necessary."

Beside her, Makoto didn't move or speak, but I was more than aware that he was samurai, or former samurai, and was armed with two extremely sharp swords. Hanzhu was conspicuously off-deck.

"It will only be until we are underway to Shanghai," Satomi explained. "There are logistics that need to be attended to beforehand."

"I understand," Chang-wei replied. When he met my eyes, his expression remained neutral.

The others with him didn't appear to share the same sentiment, but Chang-wei was in command. Kai looked the most anxious of all. Makoto watched the larger man with an eagle eye.

We descended below deck and were ushered into a compartment. There were chains attached to the wall. At the sight of them, Kai turned to flee. Both Chang-wei and I had to reach out, a hand on each massive shoulder, to still him.

"The chains will not be used," Satomi said gravely. "I apologize that this is how Yang-san feels he must treat even his friends. There is more light up here than down in the cargo hold."

"How long?" I asked.

"Not long," was all she would tell me.

They left, locking the door behind them. For a holding cell it wasn't the worst. There was enough space for us to sit on the floor, even stretch out. There were six of us inside, with me, Chang-wei, Kai and the three others who were assigned to this mission. I learned that the men had been staffed at the citadel and were part of the engineering corps.

Kai retreated to the corner, looking miserable.

I went over to him. "Are you afraid of enclosed spaces?" I asked quietly.

He shook his head. Shortly after the ship moved out to open water, I realized why Kai was so nervous. He suffered from seasickness. His complexion took on a decidedly green look as he sank his head onto his arms.

"He was this way the entire way to the island," one of the engineers reported.

After knocking on the door, someone finally came and I was able to ask for preserved ginger from my medicine case. I didn't know if it would help, but Kai took it from me with a grateful look before sinking his head back down.

Everyone else had settled into their spots in the cell. I went to Chang-wei who sat with his back propped against the bulkhead. He had pulled out his journal from his jacket, prepared to pass the time patiently in contemplation.

He glanced up as I approached. "It's not so bad. I would have expected to be locked in the entire time rather than just for the time they need to replenish supplies. Yang likely has supplies stashed in an enclave somewhere and he doesn't want us or any of his many enemies to discover it."

"Is this what this is?"

"I'm almost certain of it. We're going to make a run on Shanghai. We'll need gunpowder."

Hopefully it wouldn't be long before we were released. I had spent a good deal of time at sea, usually on Hanzhu's flagship. Though I didn't suffer from seasickness, I did prefer the fresh air above deck whenever possible.

One benefit of the current arrangement was we that had a moment of privacy away from Yang Hanzhu and his crew.

"Would you really have petitioned for amnesty for Hanzhu?" I asked.

Chang-wei directed his gaze back to his journal. "He doesn't want it."

"But would you have pleaded with the Emperor on his behalf?"

"I would have tried."

Chang-wei's position within the imperial power structure was uncertain, but he had managed to convince the Emperor more than once. He was the one who had proposed an alliance to Japan. He was also the one who had submitted plans for the manufacture of the automatons.

I thought of everything Hanzhu had revealed to me when we were alone.

"Hanzhu is not a criminal," I asserted. "He's not really a traitor."

Chang-wei let out a breath. "He is a criminal. And it's the Emperor and his inner council that decides who is or isn't a traitor."

WE WERE RELEASED AFTER HALF a day as promised. Kai staggered above deck, found that looking at the rolling ocean all around him didn't help, and promptly staggered back down.

Chang-wei and I were brought to Hanzhu's laboratory. He stood, jacket removed and shirtsleeves rolled up, over a map.

"Two days to Shanghai," Hanzhu declared, showing the course on the map. "If we don't encounter any obstacles."

"Seems a roundabout way," Chang-wei remarked.

Hanzhu refused to spare him a glance. "Water taxes and my refusal to pay them."

I remembered how Satomi had spoken of parties claiming territorial rights all along the coast.

"Waterways are like roads," Hanzhu explained conversationally. "Except no one can see them. You can't know them unless you travel them often enough and they continually change. Those of us who listen for news at every port and navigate carefully have a chance of avoiding danger. Everyone else just falls prey to whoever is the first shark to come along."

Chang-wei didn't argue. "Two days then."

"We'll enter the Huangpu inlet and dock in the foreign devil's settlement."

"In the Meiguo section." Chang-wei opened his journal to show us a picture of the flag with white stars on a blue background alongside red stripes.

"I know Meiguo," Hanzhu replied, exasperated.

The two of them were going to be at each other's throats for the entire time. At least for now they were snapping softly.

In appearance, they couldn't be further apart. Chang-wei in proper Manchu attire, his queue neatly braided. He appeared the cultured gentleman, while Hanzhu wore his Western buttons and sleeves with careless disdain, his hair unkempt and a growth of stubble roughing up his jawline. It was the scholar and the rogue to any who would look upon them.

Yet it was Hanzhu who had come from wealth and Chang-wei who had come from nothing. Even so, they were not so far apart as they would like to believe.

"Once you reach Shanghai, I'll abandon you to sail away with your silver."

Chang-wei nodded. "I wouldn't think to ask for anything more."

"Shanghai isn't the same as you remember," Hanzhu warned. "On land or at sea. The waters surrounding it have become so treacherous that the Qing authorities have even hired pirates from Canton to fend off pirates from Macau. Pirates fighting pirates." He gave a bitter laugh.

"That's why I thought of you, Brother."

Hanzhu's grin faded and he took on a serious expression. "Any ship that looks to be carrying anything valuable is a target. Any ship that looks to be vulnerable is a target. We'll be traveling with two smaller, more maneuverable vessels. Each outfitted with cannons and a crew prepared for battle. Hopefully any pirates we encounter will see that we're armed and ready and decide whatever we're carrying isn't worth the fight."

"Your formidable reputation may be of use here," Chang-wei observed.

"There are two edges to that sword," Hanzhu snorted. "Light and dark. Dead or alive."

CHAPTER 12

We emerged above deck to a cloudless sky. The vessel cut a line through the otherwise calm water, propelled by the gunpowder engine. The sails were simultaneously unfurled and angled to catch even the slightest breeze, taking advantage of wind and fuel.

I had spent time on board this junk before and returning to it was much like coming back to visit the home of an old friend. The layout and locations of the ship were familiar, as were the routines the crew would engage in. I recognized most of the faces on board. Yang Hanzhu had assembled a close-knit crew that had remained together for several years now. Satomi and Makoto were the newest additions.

Little Jie was no longer little. Nor did he look like the street rat I'd met who had first brought me to Yang. He must have been twelve years of age by now. I found the boy hanging up on the battens of the main sail as I came to the quarterdeck.

"Miss Jin," he called down to me from on high with his skinny legs hooked over the bamboo frame. He freed one hand to wave at me in a gesture that made my stomach lurch.

"Be careful up there," I scolded, which set him laughing. He looked more sure-footed climbing the sails than I was moving on dry land.

There was a barge master who everyone referred to as Master Yim. His skin had the leathery look of a lifelong seafarer, making it difficult to tell his age. I placed him ten years older than Hanzhu based on his steady and even-tempered nature. He was one of the few crewmen who had kept his queue, which, at least to me, gave him an air of propriety.

Satomi made it known to us that Master Yim was the stand-in authority who kept an eye on the day-to-day running of the ship as well as conditions in the fleet. Though Hanzhu was the ship's owner and captain, he was prone to disappearing into his laboratory for days at a time.

As for the rest of the crew, it was comprised in part from the merchant shipmen who had once been employed by the Yang family and then a band of characters Hanzhu had taken on in his travels through various ports. Like in Ningpo, the language spoken was a base use of Canton dialect with a mix of words and phrases adopted from other tongues. Common shipboard terms served as an underlying backbone. It was a language of strangers from different lands attempting to make meaning between them.

Chang-wei stayed above deck just long enough to see that his team were settled before disappearing below to catch up with Liu Yentai in the engine room. Satomi came to me then.

"Will you have tea?" she asked.

I followed Satomi to the galley. There was a stove there in the small cooking area. She poured tea into two chipped porcelain cups and offered one to me which I took gratefully. We returned above to the quarterdeck to drink by the last of the day's light. My hands curved over both sides of the cup, letting the warmth seep through. Hot tea signaled normalcy. I took a calming sip while watching the waves.

It had been a long time since I'd last been out at sea, with nothing to see but water from all sides. One easily lost a sense of time and space. Perhaps an experienced sailor might have some compass or map in his head to track where he was, but for me, I was nowhere. I was in-between until setting foot on land again.

Satomi drank her tea beside me. The falling sun cast a warm glow over her face. We were the only women on board. On a typical day, this meant she was here alone among this rough-and-ready lot. Yet she appeared more at ease, less wary and reserved than I remembered her.

"Does this life suit you?" I asked.

"It has to," she replied, non-committal. A light scattering of freckles lay across her cheeks.

"Do you ever think of going home?"

"It's not possible," she replied curtly. Then softer, "Maybe one day, one of these many islands we flit to and from will capture my interest."

It sounded like a far-off fantasy. "It must be hard to be constantly at sea."

"I was always surrounded by the sea in Nippon." She sounded far away.

We drank our tea in silence for a while before Satomi spoke again. "Yang-san thinks there will be war again."

I thought of the rebels. Of the battles at Changsha and Nanking and Shanghai. "There's war now."

Still, Satomi's words caused some alarm.

For the last year, Satomi had lived just beyond the shoreline, in places where boundaries and nations blurred. As part of Yang Hanzhu's retinue, she would have witnessed growing tension between the foreigners and the Qing empire. Between Japan and the other neighbors. If Hanzhu was becoming more fearful, I needed to be as well.

"Hanzhu trusts you," I remarked.

"He allows me passage for as long as I require."

"I think it's more than that."

Hanzhu and Satomi had formed a connection upon their first meeting. They were fellow exiles by choice.

"Yang-san is an eccentric. A madman," Satomi said as a matter of fact. "There is something about that that feels very familiar. Even oddly...comforting." She caught herself and straightened with a frown. "What about you and Chen Chang-wei?" Satomi asked, changing the subject. "One would have thought the two of you would be married by now."

My heart thudded. "No one thinks that. There are...too many other things going on. With the empire. With the uprisings." I made a motion to drink even though my tea was nearly gone.

Satomi shot me a skeptical look. "Yet here you are, the two of you, still together. And you saved his life."

Chang-wei's heart had stopped on the journey back from Japan to Shanghai. I'd managed to revive him.

I stared at the leaves at the bottom of my cup, trying to hide the skip of my pulse. Every mention of Chang-wei did this to me lately. Satomi and I were friends, but not the sort of friends who shared such personal details. Even if we had faced life and death together.

Still, I hadn't had the chance to talk to anyone about Chang-wei's proposal. There had been my mother — but then death and disaster had struck. Perhaps it was a bad omen.

I shouldn't be thinking that.

"He wouldn't marry me just because I saved him," I protested, my face growing hot. Was that why he'd proposed? Duty? A sense of debt?

Satomi held out her hand for my empty cup. "Better that he owes you than that you owe him," she assured, her lips curving upward in a knowing smile.

When night came, we retired to our respective berths. I passed Chang-wei as I moved toward the draped area at the forward end. Satomi's berth was located there, which I'd be sharing. The section was separated with a curtain to provide some privacy. The crew slept in close quarters on the ship, with bunks arranged into lower and upper levels. Satomi had more space to herself than the others as the topmost bunk was left empty.

"Will you be alright?" Chang-wei asked me.

There was a dark smudge over his left cheek. Everything in the engine room was covered in a layer of soot. I resisted the urge to wipe it away. The gesture would seem too intimate. Wifely.

Even unspoken, that word was strange, with a heaviness attached to it that sent a flutter to my stomach. Or perhaps that was just the roll of the ocean.

"I'll be fine."

"The others and I will be at the opposite end. If you need me."

I nodded.

"Sleep well," he added.

We weren't saying anything of importance, yet this somehow felt like the best conversation we'd had in a long time. The time away for a night's sleep suddenly felt like a parting, even though we were sure to see each other in the morning not long from now.

"Sleep well," I replied.

He even bowed at me as we awkwardly parted. I turned quickly to hide my smile.

I AWOKE ALONE in the berth and saw it was morning by the swaying light seeping from the deck hatch.

The sleeping arrangements were sparse. Satomi had taken the lower bunk while I slept on the upper level. When I opened my eyes, she was already gone.

The sea had been calm through the night and sleep surprisingly restful. It still took me a moment to stretch out the knots in my back and neck. I could hear the sounds of many footsteps overhead. Combing my fingers through my hair, I repinned it into its usual knot and straightened my appearance before passing through the curtain.

The bunk area was empty. I climbed up the stairs to the main deck and was greeted by the rush of wind and the rustle of the fan-like sails overhead. The crew were already at their morning tasks. Little Jie ran about with tea and stopped in front of me to pour a cup.

"Are you going to fight the Small Swords in Shanghai?" the youth asked brightly.

I was taken aback by such a direct question. "I am not much one for fighting—"

"I hear the rebels have superior kung-fu skills. There were roving bands of fighters all over the city that used to battle each other, but then they joined together and kicked out the crooked Taotai."

Jie grinned at me, fully excited as if he bore some grudge against the former official. Maybe it was a grudge against any authority.

"What else have you heard?" I asked.

"They're calling for everyone to join them. Fight the Qing, preserve the Ming!"

I wasn't sure he was aware that I was Manchu and Qing. Or even what was meant by preserving the Ming, a dynasty that had ended two hundred years earlier.

"That sort of talk would have you imprisoned on the mainland," I chided gently.

His grin only widened. "That's why I'm at sea. Though I might jump ship in Shanghai."

"To join the rebels?"

"And learn some fighting skills! I've been trying to get Makoto to teach me, but he won't let anyone touch his swords."

Makoto was currently scrubbing the deck with the other crewmen. Maintaining the ship, in a ritual of swabbing, sealing and repairing, was a constant battle against the elements.

"Perhaps keep pestering Makoto," I suggested, a bit unsettled at the casual way Jie talked of rebellion. "He was once samurai."

"I knew it!"

I handed the cup back to Jie and the boy scurried off to carry on with his duties. Searching about, I spotted Chang-wei and Satomi on the raised quarterdeck, deep in conversation. I climbed the stairs toward them and caught part of the conversation about the roar of the wind.

"How long did it take to perfect the sword fighting patterns?" Chang-wei asked.

"...my father studied the sword from a young age...simplify the concepts..."

I could only hear part of Satomi's reply. Interestingly enough, fighting skill seemed to be the topic of the morning. As I came closer, I heard Satomi mention the name "Yoshiro" and it all became clear.

Yoshiro had been an invention of her father's. A mechanical karakuri warrior created to act as Satomi's bodyguard. Though it was mute, it had been able to move, walk and even wield a sword. She spoke of Yoshiro with emotion, as if it were a companion and not just a machine. Even I had assumed Yoshiro was human before his secret was revealed.

"My father was removed from Edo and put on house arrest," Satomi was saying. "In isolation, he had a lot of time to develop his karakuri. I would see him creating wire patterns and then patiently testing them, making a small change, testing again. As a child, I didn't understand what he was doing. Yoshiro started as a toy for me, like any other karakuri, but he gradually learned how to do more and more.

"I was always careful when working on Yoshiro after my father passed away. I lacked my father's knowledge of engineering and I knew if I broke anything inside, I'd be unable to fix him. Inside his frame there was a complicated mesh of copper wires and panels."

Like what the women in the wire room had constructed. I came up behind Chang-wei, but remained silent.

"Sagara Shintaro was assassinated shortly after the Opium War," Chang-wei surmised. "Which meant your karakuri servant remained operational for eight years with hardly any maintenance."

Chang-wei had managed to re-create something similar to the karakuri. His automatons walked about and appeared to react to movement and sound, but their behavior was crude in comparison to what Yoshiro had been able to do. Unfortunately, Yoshiro and all of the intricate wiring inside the automaton was lost. The machine had been beheaded by the shogunate's assassins and its secrets left to rust among the weeds.

"I still have my father's journal, if you would want to see it," Satomi offered.

"My knowledge of *Nihongo* is unfortunately limited."

"If you ever have a month to spend at sea, I can translate," she suggested.

He bowed graciously. "I would be honored."

Chang-wei's reaction to Satomi's offer was a little too warm. I stepped forward to position myself conspicuously beside him.

"Soling-san," Satomi acknowledged.

"Satomi-san."

That came out colder than I'd intended. What had come over me? Satomi was a friend. A tall, clever and confident friend, who was able to discuss mechanical things with Chang-wei in a way I never could.

Whoever said that envy was like a grain of sand in one's eye was wrong. It was an entire beach.

My face heated at my display of jealousy, though Satomi was polite enough not to mention it. She bowed and returned to her duties, leaving Chang-wei and I staring at one another. My stare was decidedly pointed.

"What?" he asked, all innocence.

"Translation?" I questioned evenly.

"My interest is purely academic."

There was the barest hint of a smile on his lips. I turned sharply to present him with a stark view of my profile. Let him study that for a while.

Eventually, Chang-wei rounded up his team and went down to the engine room to see if they could be of use. Even though we had paid Hanzhu in silver for the excursion, it still seemed necessary to make ourselves useful while on board. If nothing else, it passed the time.

I went to inspect the medicine cabinet, which was stored in the cook's galley and consisted of jars and bottles and an assortment of herbs. For the rest of the morning, I set about replenishing any medicines that were low. I searched out the required components from the laboratory and mixed a batch of Jinchuang ointment used to treat wounds. There were a few other common remedies that were always of use — a powder for upset stomach, a salve for burns — the same one I had used extensively at the Factories.

Several of the crew remembered me from the last time I was on board and came to inquire about various aches and ailments. Kai managed to acclimate himself a little to the rocking motion of the ship. He came above board to make some conversation, at one point engaging in a game of dice with the crewmen where he proved himself to be a poor gambler.

It was during the mid-day meal that Liu Yentai came to me with his mask and goggles removed. His face and hands were for once scrubbed clean. The engine wasn't running at the moment. We were sailing on the power of the wind and the current.

"I set Chang-wei and those boys to scrubbing the engine room," he said with glee. "And threatened to cut off Chang-wei's fingers if he tried to modify anything."

Lunch was a bowl of rice porridge and salted fish. Old Liu sat down with me above deck to enjoy the sun while we ate.

"I thought about that symbol you spoke of," he said. "It might be associated with a merchant or trade guild."

"I wondered if it could be a symbol of rebellion used by some faction."

He sighed. "To the Great Qing, any group banded together is considered a threat. This constant fear will be their undoing. The Middle Kingdom is a vast place. People must have their clans and sects and inner circles. It is human nature to seek kinship."

The Qing Empire had been broken by war and addiction. Sensing weakness, rebel factions quickly formed and splintered off. Old loyalties had resurfaced. It was very much like, as Satomi described, so many little islands.

"Our family is back in Peking now," I told him. "I wasn't sure it was the best place to go, but nowhere else seemed safe either. Tian is studying and preparing to enter the Academy."

This should have been a good report, my family was safe and cared for, but I felt guilty relaying all this to Old Liu.

"Peking is as good a place as any other," Liu replied gruffly. "What's important is who you surround yourself with. Don't be too trusting, Soling. Your father was a little too optimistic in that respect. Everyone respected and listened to him. Zhi-fu thought that would last forever."

"Mother is working with Kuo Lishen."

Liu started swearing again. "Mistaught, snake-tongued, unfit son of a dog," he spat.

"I think...I think Mother believes she can control him."

"Your mother is clever," he conceded. "Just like your father was talented. But not for games like those. Kuo has always been an opportunist. You need to tell your mother to stay as far away from him as she can."

Kuo Lishen had taken over the Directorate after the governing body had been all but destroyed by the explosion. Even this brash move on Shanghai had been his plan, not Chang-wei's.

Had Kuo sent us sent into danger to take on all of the risk while he alone would reap the rewards?

CHAPTER 13

There was more swearing later that afternoon when Yang Hanzhu emerged from below deck.

Hanzhu was conversing with Master Yim when Chang-wei approached. There was a parcel tucked beneath Chang-wei's arm which he'd retrieved from his bunk. I'd wondered what it was.

"I have something for you, Brother Yang," Chang-wei said.

Just the use of the honorific set Hanzhu on edge. Chang-wei ignored his skeptical look and held out the parcel. When Yang made no move to take it, Chang-wei carefully unfolded the white cloth to reveal a long triangular flag displaying diagonal red cross bands.

Hanzhu's expression turned to stone. "No."

"This is to signal to our connection in Shanghai and to indicate you're registered to trade at the treaty port."

"A foreigner's flag," Hanzhu said through his teeth.

"This doesn't represent any of the nations in the concession. You're not declaring any allegiance."

Hanzhu regarded him with eyes narrowed, unconvinced.

"Consider it not a matter of honor, but practicality."

Chang-wei folded the banner neatly back into its triangular parcel and offered it out once more. "At your discretion, Elder Brother. If you decide this suits your purposes."

Hanzhu directed one of his deck hands to take the flag as if he didn't wish to touch it himself.

Later, Chang-wei went out on the utility boat to taxi to the auxiliary ships at Old Liu's behest. According to Liu, the operators throughout the fleet were all hacks and the engines needed some maintenance.

By that time, the sun was dipping low over gentle waters. A cool evening breeze had begun to pick up, when I saw one of the crew working the rigging on the main mast. He attached a white and red banner and pulled the lines to raise it high until the signal flag flew from the top mast.

Hanzhu came up beside me as I stared up at the red stripes. The breeze caused his rogue hair to whip about his face.

"A matter of practicality," he said with a shrug.

Chang-wei noticed the flag overhead upon returning to the deck.

"You two are exactly like brothers," I remarked, seeing Chang-wei's smug look. "It's too bad you don't get along."

"We get along well enough." He searched for Hanzhu and found him at the helm. "It can't be easy for him, being constantly on the run."

We watched as Satomi came to Hanzhu to tell him something. They stood close as they spoke. Hanzhu's fingertips grazed Satomi's long sleeve lightly before she moved away. Chang-wei looked to me with eyebrows raised.

"Hanzhu...who would have thought?" he said under his breath, eyes bright with amusement.

"Like brothers," I repeated.

I thought of what Chang-wei had said the other day about amnesty as well as what Liu Yentai had observed about the Qing government. The lines between enemies and allies were quickly eroding. Even the shogunate in Japan had been forced to be pragmatic about trade with the West.

Would Hanzhu ever be able let go of his feuding to earn a pardon? Would he ever want one?

The newly raised flag rustled overhead in the wind. It was a fragile symbol marking a new Shanghai, a place in its infancy and home to constantly changing alliances.

As it turned out there was nothing, certainly not a strip of cloth, that would protect us from what was coming.

"A ship. To the east."

The call from a crewman was followed by coordinates I couldn't understand. Yang Hanzhu was immediately called up from below. He lifted a pair of field glasses to his eyes, aiming them to the horizon. I followed his gaze but could only discern the smallest of blots in the distance. Sailors must have been accustomed to searching out such anomalies.

Chang-wei surveyed the horizon as well before coming to my side. "It's too soon to tell what sort of ship it is."

The only thing confirmed was that there was more than one and they were indeed moving toward our position. Yang called for a change in direction. After an hour, it was determined that the fleet did not appear to be following.

Tension drained from the crew, but not nearly as quickly as it had come. Master Yim doubled the watch duty for the remaining daylight hours and through the night.

That night I retired with Satomi to our bunk.

"Well, a little drama does make the day go faster," she said as we prepared for bed. "When I first came on board, days would last forever, but it's gotten better. Having an assigned watch and a set of tasks to perform daily does help mark the time. Otherwise, there would be nothing to do but stare at the sun crawling across the sky."

She undid her gun belt and set it aside. "Having new faces on board is also a welcome distraction. New stories to listen to," she added, lying down.

"When is your watch?"

"The morning watch. Up before dawn."

As I climbed onto the upper bunk, I noticed Satomi had placed an old, weathered journal beside her headrest.

"Is that the journal you and Chang-wei were discussing?" I asked from above her.

"It contains my father's writings. The book was one of the few things I was able to take with me from Japan. All I have are the firearms, this book, and my memories."

"Does it help having someone from your homeland with you?"

"You mean Makoto-san? We sometimes speak of Nagasaki, but we try not to reminisce too much. Homesickness only makes this exile more painful."

We'd spoken throughout the day in small snatches over conversation. Satomi described how she had taken on the role of Yang Hanzhu's bodyguard whenever they were on land and also maintained the ship's arsenal of firearms. There was another crewman, as assigned gunner who managed the gunpowder supply in the magazine.

I glanced at the rifle she'd laid down beside her bunk. "Is it dangerous at sea?"

"We've engaged in battles before," she confided. "Yang-san tries to evade before there's any danger, but it's not always possible. With our engines, the best strategy is to outmaneuver any potential attackers."

We were finally alone, so I had to ask. "Are you pirates?"

There was silence down below.

"Yes," she said finally. Then, "No."

I crawled to the edge of the bunk to peer down at her. Satomi lay stretched out with her arms folded. The look she gave me was clear-eyed, at peace with everything she was telling me.

"Most of our transactions involve transporting salt and gunpowder. We've received requests to join one raid or another, but Yang-san always declines. He prefers to answer to no one. Sometimes we transport supplies to places we're not supposed to, which does pay more."

"But not opium."

"Never opium. And there's so much of it. Yang-san can't hold himself back when we encounter an opium runner."

She extinguished the lantern and darkness surrounded me. The boat swayed beneath us in a gentle, rolling motion.

"I must apologize for my behavior earlier," I said after a moment.

"There's nothing to apologize for."

"I saw the way you and Chang-wei were talking and I couldn't help wondering—some things I've been wondering about a lot lately."

"What things?"

The image came to me of the two of them, heads close. Chang-wei had looked completely absorbed in the conversation, his eyes bright with interest. I couldn't help but wonder if it wasn't for an old promise to my father, if it wasn't for duty, would Chang-wei have wanted me?

"I didn't think I'd be the jealous sort," I told her helplessly.

It was so difficult to sort out all of these feelings. Chang-wei was the only person I'd ever thought of in this way. Since I was a child, I'd assumed if I were ever to marry, it would be to him, as a matter of course. But things were different now.

I'd always found him disturbingly handsome. Mostly because I was supposed to be too practical to be distracted by something like that, and yet I was. He was intelligent and protective. Everything he did was with a sort of singular intensity that fascinated me.

Ever since his marriage proposal, I found myself thinking of him all the time. I kept wondering whether he really meant what he'd said when he'd asked to marry me. Whether he still meant it.

"It shouldn't matter this much. I shouldn't be so bothered," I fretted. "He should be able to talk to anyone he wants."

My face heated while Satomi laughed softly.

"Your engineer was really only interested in Yoshiro and whether my father had written any instructions or explanations in his journal."

"I know." Which is why it was embarrassing to so become emotional over it. And for Satomi to have witnessed it. I needed to change the subject. "Did your father write much about his inventions?"

"His mind would dart around like a hummingbird. There are notes and diagrams interspersed with observations and odd philosophical passages. I thought I could read his journal to understand him, but I know him no better than before."

In the darkness, her voice took on a sorrowful note.

Chang-wei had taken the secrets of the elekiter technology Satomi's father had developed to power the automatons. Was Satomi aware of it? What would she think if she knew her father's invention was being re-purposed for war?

"Your father created Yoshiro to protect you. It was an act of devotion."

"He did it just to see if he could," Satomi insisted. "He would become fixated on a problem sometimes and stay up days without sleeping to try to solve it. Yang Hanzhu is the same way. Sometimes I worry about it."

"Why?"

"He was fixated on the idea that your countrymen are being poisoned."

"We are being poisoned," I argued.

"I'm starting to believe it as well," she agreed, to my surprise. "In Nippon, we've long thought that the scourge of opium was a weakness of the Shinajin. That it had nothing to do with us if we kept to ourselves. Now I've seen evidence of something more frightening than opium."

She told me of an encounter they had had on an island at one time chartered by the Qing Empire as an opium refuge before falling into disuse.

"There was an island of people suffering from a strange sickness. They were mindless beasts, ready to attack anything in sight. What's worse, they had been abandoned there by the men who were in charge of the opium refuge."

"I know of this sickness." I had seen how it rendered a person mindless and ravenous.

"Whatever this new plague is, it might have been started from within. By your own empire," Satomi said. "Are these rebels the true enemy? Are they the ones you really should be fighting?"

I didn't have an answer. My world, our country was being torn apart bit by bit. Opium had been the start of it, but it wasn't the only thing killing us.

I took that last thought with me into sleep.

IT WAS STILL dark below deck when I heard the pound of footsteps followed by the urgent clang of a bell.

Satomi clasped my shoulder in a firm grip, jolting me awake. "We need to take our positions."

I dragged myself up. "Positions? What's happening?"

Satomi lit the lantern before pulling her boots on. "Someone's approaching. A possible attack—I'll find out more above."

She fastened her belt, taking a moment to check the pistols, then slung a rifle over her shoulder before grabbing the lantern. She disappeared through the curtain before I could climb down from the bunk.

I fumbled around in the dark for my slippers before leaving the berth. Crewmen rushed by as I moved through the passage-way. Finally, I reached the galley where some light from outside streamed through. It was there that I found Chang-wei when we collided into one another.

He steadied me in his arms and a rush of relief flooded through me. "Soling. Our people are assembled at the far end of the hold."

I held onto him as he led the way. Someone shoved past us in the opposite direction, heading above deck. The hold cleared out as the crew readied itself for confrontation.

"Do you know what's going on?"

"Not yet." His arm closed around me as he urged me forward. "I'll find out more after we get to the others."

Kai was assembled with three of Chang-wei's engineers. They were gathered near a porthole that looked out into the water. Chang-wei left me with the group to go topside.

"There are five or six boats gaining on us," Kai reported. I couldn't tell if his pale complexion was due to tense situation or his general seasickness. "They're small, like fishing boats. They can't do anything to a ship this large, can they?"

I looked out through the porthole. From there, I could see two of the vessels trailing behind our ship. The others must have been on the other side and not visible from our vantage point. Were they attempting to flank us?

I didn't know enough about ships or sailing to make any guesses, but the fact that these smaller vessels would attempt to surround a larger ship signaled ill-intent. It was like a pack of wolves closing in on prey.

Chang-wei came back to us with his report. "It might be pirates. Likely from Canton."

I tried to remain calm. "Are we in danger?"

"Small raiders like these shouldn't be underestimated. It's harder to target them with heavy cannon. They can launch fire-bombs as a distraction before boarding. Or they may be trying to lure the two convoy ships away, but Yang wouldn't fall for anything like that. He's just going to try to outrun them."

The engine roared to life below us, sending a low rumble throughout the hull, vibrating the deck beneath us. I glanced outside to see the boats gradually drifting farther away until they were dots in the distance.

"Nothing to worry about," Chang-wei said evenly, though his jaw remained tense. "Did you sleep well?"

I wasn't swayed. "Will it become less dangerous the closer we get to Shanghai?"

He didn't answer.

"*Chang-wei*," I prompted sharply.

"With the breakdown of imperial oversight in these waters, the abundance of valuable cargo, legal and illegal." He glanced out through the portal. "Fleets don't operate alone out here and small ships can easily serve as scouts for larger ones. We won't be out of danger until we safely reach land."

CHAPTER 14

I t was only hours later when the next alarm came.

"Devil ship!"

The entire crew went fully alert. With my naked eye, I could see the plume of smoke that billowed from the ship in the distance.

"It's a steamship," Chang-wei said, coming up beside me at the rail. He lifted the field glasses to inspect the ship.

I'd seen the foreign transports from afar while docked at port. This was the first time I'd encountered one at sea. It was bearing down at us at a fast pace, growing larger by the minute. A black menace on the water.

"Yingguo," Chang-wei reported. "From the flags."

Hanzhu stood on the quarterdeck with cigarette in hand. He'd been there since the morning when we'd evaded the raiders. "Those foreign devils get paid per head. They don't care who it belongs to."

I looked to Chang-wei, who didn't disagree.

Hanzhu allowed himself one more drag, exhaling slowly, before stubbing it out against the case.

"Engines!" he commanded.

The deck was already in motion. An alarm bell sounded to signal the engine room as Hanzhu took the helm. The barge master ordered for the crew to man the cannons and the gunners assembled quickly. Each of the cannons required a team of men to load and fire. Another team wheeled out a wooden frame affixed with a sling arm designed for launching fire bombs.

Chang-wei took hold of my arm. "Soling, I think you should get down below."

"No." Satomi appeared beside us with Makoto close behind. "We need everyone."

She thrust a pistol into my hands and tossed a rifle to Chang-wei. The next moments were a shuffle of gunpowder, bullets, and shouted instructions. All the while, the Western ship loomed closer.

Chang-wei moved us against the wall of the forecastle and checked his rifle before looking through the field glasses once more. "They're hailing us," he called out. "They want to board."

"Fuck their ancestors to the eighteenth generation!" came Hanzhu's reply from the wheel.

"He's always been like this," Chang-wei said apologetically, seeing my wide-eyed look. "He just usually holds back around you."

As if I cared about swearing at the moment. I was in a ship stocked full with black powder and guns about to face off against another ship with even larger guns.

"Isn't Yingguo aligned with us against the rebels?" I asked.

I jumped as the thundering boom of cannon fire shattered the air.

"Warning shot," Chang-wei explained, surprisingly calm. "None of that matters out here, I'm afraid."

We weren't supposed to be here as far as the Qing government was concerned. There was no one to hold to account if we were blasted out of the water.

My pulse raced. Kai clamored up beside us, pressing his large frame against the forecastle.

"I don't know how to use this," he said, indicating the pistol in his hands. I took it from him.

Chang-wei's men emerged from the hatch, surveying the gun deck and the flurry of activity around them.

"I'll send them to the engine room," Chang-wei said, darting away. I watched his back as he left, biting down the urge to call him back.

By now the engines below us were churning. One had to shout to be heard over the roar. The foreign steamship had gained on us. Yang Hanzhu's war junk was smaller and more maneuverable, but was it faster?

I turned back to Kai and quickly gave instructions on how to use his weapon before handing it back. If we were boarded, the firearms would only afford us one shot each. Neither of us had the skill to reload for a second shot.

"Do we tend to the injured?" Kai asked me.

In the Factories, that had been our duty. Here, I doubted we'd have that luxury. This could very well be a fight for our lives.

"Afterward," I told him.

If we survive.

ANOTHER SHOT from the devil ship split the air and my insides shook. I hated that sound.

The foreigners were still out of range, but not for long. I thought I heard the splash of a cannon ball plunk into the water, but it was followed by a hissing sound. Moments later, a cloudy mist rose to surround us.

I'd seen Yang use this trick before. He'd discharged barrels of a chemical substance which mixed with the sea water to bubbled up as a thick fog. It would keep the steamship from pinpointing our exact location as well as knowing how the convoy ships were positioning themselves.

Chang-wei came back to us. "All warning shots so far. It doesn't appear the naval vessel is aiming to shoot us out of the water," he said. "Which is perhaps our only advantage."

He handed me and Kai plugs of wax to put into our ears. Before I did so, Chang-wei stopped me with a hand on my wrist.

"Stay safe," he implored softly.

"You stay safe," I commanded, not as softly.

The surrounding sounds became muffled and distant once I inserted the knobs of wax into my ears. The next roar of cannon fire shook the deck and I was grateful for the plugs. The volley had come from our own guns. I looked up to see the steamship lined up along our port side, exposing its own array of weapons. The thing was massive, rising high above us like a fortress. The wooden hull was plated with iron armor and steam shot from its exhaust pipe like an angry breathing monster. No wonder our sailors called them devil ships.

Pale faces peered down on us from the bridge. Yingguoren. Gun crews assembled behind the cannons as they prepared to fire.

Our two convoy ships had maneuvered to either side of the steamship to sling fire bombs on to the deck. Hanzhu was bringing the fight to them before their larger cannons came within range. All the while, the engines below continued to rumble and grind. I could imagine Liu Yentai shouting at the engine crew below as they shoveled gunpowder into the combustion chamber.

The chase was on, with Hanzhu steering the ship to present

the rear aft as we tried to retreat. It was a smaller target for certain.

Black ceramic shells resembling wine jugs launched from the convoys to smash against the attacking ship. Fire fanned out over the armored plates as the bombs hit, the flames spreading briefly before dissipating. Some of the bombs managed to clear the gunwale to land on deck, catching onto the wood and rigging there and igniting.

As the foreign crew rushed to tend to the flames, a shot came from the steamship directly at us, tearing through our main sail. I threw my arms up as a shield and ducked down. Another cannon blast roared, followed by the sickening thud and crunch of wood. The impact tossed me onto all fours. Vaguely, I became aware of Chang-wei crouched beside me. I braced my hands against the deck, feeling splinters of shattered wood and bamboo stabbing against my palms.

The devil ship was tearing us to pieces.

Black smoke clogged the air, stinging my eyes. Squinting through it, I struggled to my feet. Strong hands reached out to help me up. It was Kai. He coughed, doubled over, then searched through the smoke just as I was doing, trying to take stock of the damage.

Part of the gun deck had been shot through and one of the cannons destroyed. The gunner crew lay sprawled beside it, some barely moving, others not moving at all. The steamship was again positioning alongside us, looming even larger than before.

Something was amiss. The crewmen, who had mounted a coordinated defense before, were flailing and unable to regroup. Cannons remained unmanned, the injured staggered as they searched for cover. Smaller shots rang out now from the opposing deck, forcing us to take cover. Without the gunners, there was nothing to hold them off.

I searched across the gun deck and found a body laying

crumpled out in the open. My stomach sank when I realized it was Master Yim. Chang-wei followed my gaze and came to the same realization.

He met my eyes for only a moment before springing forward. Running at a crouch, Chang-wei shouted instructions at the gunners as he moved down the line.

"Kai!" I tugged on the big man's arm and gestured toward the unmoving figure behind the line of cannons.

Satomi was organizing a round of return fire from the crew. I ran forward as the volley started, ducking and praying amidst the noise and smoke. When I reached the barge master, Yim turned his head weakly toward me. Kai scrambled up beside me to grab hold of Yim beneath his arms and tug him toward the rail. Scant cover, but it was what we had.

I knelt beside Master Yim, searching for his wound while Kai hunched over the both of us, using himself as a shield. It wasn't a feat of bravery or even loyalty for him to be there. It was just who Kai was at his core.

I'd found where Master Yim was hit. A bullet had stricken the barge master's lower leg, shattering bone. He howled as I pressed against the wound. Hot blood seeped through my fingers and I fought a wave of nausea. There could be another injury. We needed to check before moving him.

Gesturing for Kai to take over at the leg, I examined Master Yim for other wounds and found another shot on his left side, hidden by his dark tunic. I pulled at the tear in the cloth to rend the edges open. The bullet had hit him low on his chest. Not near his heart, but near a hundred other vital parts.

I couldn't think of how bad it might be. He was still alive right now.

I peeled off my jacket to use it over the chest wound, allowing myself a glance across the deck as I pressed down. Chang-wei had reformed the gun line and was returning fire. Satomi ran to me. Leveling the rifle against her shoulder, she took aim at someone and fired up at the opposing deck. The shadow of the ship engulfed us, heralding doom. Steam rose like a great black ghost from its exhaust port.

Just beyond the plume of smoke, I saw a shape that made my heartbeat stutter. Master Yim had fallen unconscious while we tended to him and I gestured for Kai to apply pressure to the second wound while I fumbled for the barge master's field glasses. They had fallen to the deck. I lifted them with blood-stained fingers and directed the eyepiece upward and into the distance. One of the lenses had cracked and my hand shook so badly that it took a long time to center on what I'd seen.

My body went cold. I shouted at Chang-wei, but he was focused on the battle. There was wax in his ears, wax in mine. He couldn't hear me.

Without time to explain, I left Master Yim and ran to the helm. Hanzhu was at the wheel, grim determination on his face. I had to tug hard on his sleeve for him to notice me.

Once again, I shouted out what I'd seen, pointing to the sky and handing him the field glasses.

"An airship!"

He found it much faster through the glass than I had. "Yang-guizi," he muttered.

Before long, the devil ship would have air support.

I didn't catch what signal Yang gave, but a moment later the ship's drum began to beat. From the helm, I could see the convoy ships as they circled and pointed their bows toward the steamship like the tips of twin daggers. Suddenly both of the ships ignited, becoming engulfed in orange flames. I gasped as the engines fired and both ships shot forward. Were they sacrificing themselves?

The convoys picked up speed as they neared the steamship. The fire at their bows spread, licking down half the length of the hull. Then, at the last moment, the vessels snapped in half. The foremost sections continued to shoot toward the looming steamship while the aft section veered away to turn back toward the war junk.

I held my breath as the fire ships crashed into the hull of the foreign vessel. One stab after another, doused in flame. The impact was enough to penetrate the armored shell to feed on the wood beneath. The convoys continued to burn while our flagship cut away to make its escape.

CHAPTER 15

For the rest of the day, the crew remained on the lookout on the water was well as out over the skies. The battle might have been over, but our escape was far from the end of it.

What remained of the convoys had enough power to return to the main ship, but didn't possess the engines to be seaworthy. The skiffs were tied down and their crew welcomed back onto the junk. Among them was the young engineer Benzhuo, sometimes Congming, who received a scolding from Liu Yentai for sacrificing two perfectly good vessels. But instead of cuffing his young apprentice on the head, Old Liu cupped his soot-stained hand gruffly over the back of Benzhuo's neck and kept it there for a long time before letting ago.

Yang Hanzhu set about inspecting his ship and determining what repairs were required. The port side had been badly damaged. The gun deck torn to shreds. Holes in the hull that needed to be patched immediately.

Three crewmen perished in the battle. Their bodies were solemnly relinquished to the sea. Many more were seriously injured, including Master Yim who went under the surgeon's knife. The surgeon, who also happened to be the cook, was able to dig out the bullets lodged inside Yim.

Dig was the appropriate word, as there was little in the way of skill and much in the way of determination to the endeavor. Kai held Yim down throughout the operation as there was no amount of opium that could completely dull the pain.

Kai and I helped where we could, cleaning and sewing wounds. Setting and wrapping bones. Like we'd done at the Five Factories.

We'd escaped. We'd survived.

The crew remained watchful of the sea as well as the air. It was possible we were being tracked from the skies now. We didn't know if there were other naval ships coming to exact revenge.

Night came as it did, but tonight the watch detail was doubled. All lanterns on deck were to remain dark.

Sick bay was set up in a section of the sleeping berths. I stayed there late into the evening until Kai urged me to get some rest. He would sleep nearby and come find me if I was needed.

I didn't fight it. My body was merely hanging from my bones by that point.

Hanzhu intercepted me as I was making my way back to my bunk.

"Walk with me," he said cryptically, his sharp features ragged with exhaustion.

As depleted as I was, Hanzhu looked even worse. I followed behind him, watching the bob of the lantern he held, while I waited for whatever Hanzhu had in mind to reveal itself.

Wordlessly, he moved to the hatch and climbed down to the lower part of the ship where the cargo hold and engine rooms were located. The engines were silent at the moment, though the air below remained stuffy with residual heat. The burnt sulfur smell clogged my throat and I had to wrap a silk scarf over my face to filter it out.

Our destination was the cargo hold. Yang stepped into the bulkhead and beckoned me in after him. He set the lantern down and I could see the large wooden crates arranged inside, most of them standing taller than me. There was an assortment of tools laid out on top of one of the crates, which led me to believe that someone had already been in here.

"When we were loading these containers onto the ship, I did a cursory inspection. Firearms, Chang-wei claimed. Indeed, that's what it looked like to me initially. In this trade one learns not to ask too many questions in any case. And since Chen Chang-wei and I are old *friends*—" His lip curled on the last word.

I wasn't certain I liked where this was going. "If Chang-wei knew we were down here—"

"He won't be disturbing us," Yang said, taking up a pair of goggles. "Satomi's distracting him. With her journal," he added, seeing my odd look. He tossed the goggles to me which I caught, agitated.

"I didn't know you were the jealous sort," he said with a chuckle.

"I'm not jealous. I just—" I had nothing. It had been a difficult day. I'd had to clean blood from my hands not too long ago and now Yang Hanzhu was taunting me. I didn't have any patience left.

"What are these for?" I asked, dangling the eyewear from my fingers.

"Put them on."

I did as he asked, using the leather strap in back to adjust the goggles so that the lenses fit over my eyes. He donned a pair himself before throwing a pair of work gloves my way. They were thick, molded from rubber, and over-sized by far.

"Do you know what's in these crates, Soling?"

"Firearms," I replied weakly, a knot forming in my stomach.

It was what Chang-wei had told me.

Yang Hanzhu looked at me as if I were a child. There had been a time when I was a child in his presence, but that was long ago.

"I'm sorry I brought you into this," I said, pained.

Hanzhu waved it away. "I accepted the silver," he said brusquely. "I understood the risks."

"Your ship was under fire today. You lost men."

His mouth formed a grim line. "They knew the risks as well. Come help me."

He pulled a set of gloves on over his hands and kicked two stepping stools over beside the nearest container. Then he handed the lantern to me before gathering his tools.

"That devil ship could have blown us out of the water today," Hanzhu began. "But they were reluctant to fire directly at us, almost as if they were afraid to damage my ship too badly. Of course, I'm quite grateful. I'm attached to this thing, it being my only home for the last ten years."

"But they did fire on us."

"At the gun deck. The masts. That's not how you disable a ship."

He climbed onto the first stool and I followed his lead, climbing up on the second one. All the while, a seed of doubt grew inside me.

"The airship was what really made me wonder. We may have just happened to encounter a naval ship patrolling these waters. The Yangguizi have been vigilant around the treaty ports lately. Even though we're currently outside of the established shipping lanes, it's still possible this steamship was sweeping a wide area. But to have an airship also circling nearby?"

Yang had my complete attention now.

"It was as if they were protecting something. Surely it wasn't my life that anyone cared to spare. I thought, for a moment, it was a double-cross and Chang-wei had come up with this elaborate scheme to have me apprehended."

"He wouldn't do that."

"You know, I believe that as well." Hanzhu gestured toward me with what looked like a long iron spike. "So, I wondered if the Yangguizi had received some information. You know there are just as many spies around as pirates, nowadays. If the foreign navy somehow believed there might be something valuable in the cargo hold that they wanted to confiscate."

"Weapons are valuable," I suggested, my throat dry.

"Yes, my dear Soling. We are at war and weapons are valuable. Some more than others."

There was a large metal hinge lock over the crate. Hanzhu tapped a spot beside the lock to indicate where he wanted the lantern. Then he inserted the spike into the lock and appeared to shift the length of iron this way and that.

"Chen Chang-wei was trying to be clever," Yang said quietly, a look of intense concentration on his face. "There's a special design on these locks. A glass vial on the inside holding a strong corrosive. If the lock is tampered with or not opened properly, the vial will break, spilling the acid over the contents and destroying whatever is inside. But, if you know how the acid trap is constructed, it's fairly easy to manage."

My mind was racing. Chang-wei had described something like this. Not for a lock, but for a timing mechanism. The one what was used to trigger the explosive at the citadel.

"Would you know how to make one?" I asked

"Of course. I designed this lock when I was in the Ministry of Science."

I swallowed. Hanzhu couldn't have been responsible for the explosion that had killed half of the Directorate. He was isolated at sea. He didn't even know where the Factories were or what they were producing.

More importantly, Yang Hanzhu wouldn't kill so indiscriminately. His crimes were for destroying property, particularly opium.

"Hold this for me." Hanzhu shifted aside so I could grab onto the spike. "Hold it in exactly this position and hold it steady." He picked up another iron bar from the array of tools before pausing. "You do want to know what's inside, don't you?"

I nodded, my stomach knotting. "The acid lock. Is this a common design?"

"It's pretty simple in principle, but I can't imagine the exact design is too common. Ah, there it is. Hold still."

Hanzhu withdrew the iron bar and then used the head to pry open a hidden panel beneath the lock. He reached a hand inside and felt around before straightening.

"It will take both of us to lift the lid," he said.

I repositioned the lantern. Then I wedged the iron spike beneath the lid while he did the same with his tool. Together, we carefully raised the wooden cover and pushed it aside. Inside, I could see the large glass receptacle filled with a clear compound, just as he had described. Packed into the crate beside it were various metal plates and joints. Hanzhu reached inside to retrieve the most recognizable piece.

He turned the metal object around in his hands. "I've seen something like this before."

Hanzhu held up what looked like a large samurai helmet. It was the head of a killing machine.

I CORNERED Chang-wei in the galley. He was seated on a stool with Satomi across from him. Her father's journal and an oil lamp flickering between them.

"You didn't tell me the truth," I accused.

He stood abruptly, blinking at me in confusion. Then he saw Yang Hanzhu standing just behind me and understood.

"I didn't lie," Chang-wei asserted.

"You said we were transporting weapons to allies in Shanghai."

"These are weapons," he replied, too composed.

Not firearms, but automatons that didn't require any hands to wield them. My throat clenched as I realized I must have always known this was what Chang-wei was planning. I just hadn't wanted to acknowledge the truth.

"You can't control those machines. You know you can't."

Satomi looked from me to Chang-wei. "What machines?"

"Much like your father's karakuri," Hanzhu chimed in casually. "Though I doubt these are meant to serve tea."

Chang-wei straightened. "I don't see how this changes anything," he remarked, jaw tense. "When does a smuggler care what he's transporting?"

"Changes nothing for me, but it must make some difference to you, *Brother*," Hanzhu said, his tone cutting. He came forward to stand beside me. "Why so secretive, Chen? Why the lie?"

Hanzhu looked to me as he spoke the last part.

It did make a difference to me. From the moment Chang-wei had first proposed these machine soldiers to the Emperor, I had assumed it was to build up our defenses against foreign invasion. Then, when I'd learned they were to be used against the rebels, it was supposed to be in order to face the rebel army. But to use such weapons inside Shanghai—to have killing machines rampaging through the city streets where families dwelled…

"Kuo Lishen didn't take you away from the automatons," I realized. "You were just tasked with taking them into battle."

"I have to see this through," Chang-wei said.

"There are innocent lives in Shanghai," I protested. "You yourself said the machines were not ready."

His face was a mask. "They're ready enough. We considered everything, Soling. This is the best we could do."

165

Hanzhu sighed, "The impossible dilemma of trying to remain honorable while doing dishonorable things."

Chang-wei kept his eyes on me. "The Qing army is stretched thin. Every day the rebels grow stronger and we grow weaker, unless we can stop them now. The Factories couldn't produce fast enough to make a difference on the front line, but we can succeed in a targeted attack on the base of the Small Swords in Shanghai."

All I could think of were the lives lost at the factories. The lives lost on the ship. And more lives yet to be sacrificed in Shanghai. Each one a separate equation.

"This is the best solution," Chang-wei insisted, as if it would make it true.

"It's not," I replied with a heavy heart. "It's just the easiest one."

CHAPTER 16

Over the next days, we sailed into the shipping lanes that would lead us to the port of Shanghai. I grew apprehensive as we neared the international settlement. We gathered topside on the quarterdeck as the first promise of land appeared on the horizon.

"Will we be detained by the Yingguoren?" I asked Hanzhu.

He shrugged. "Hard to tell. No one entity controls the foreign concession. Shanghai has been carved up and sectioned out like a slaughtered pig. There's also a lot of looking the other way."

"Our agreement is with the Meiguoren," Chang-wei said. "We'll bypass the Yingguoren section to dock farther down the river."

The Americans. The British. More nations had laid claim to the treaty port in the time since I'd last been to Shanghai.

Conversation between all of us had been limited since the attack and the subsequent discovery of the automatons. I'd spent the last few days looking after the injured crewmen. From what I'd heard, Chang-wei was involved in repairs on the gun-deck and for the main mast. Despite being on the same ship, we'd seen little of one another until now. Chang-wei made an effort to catch my eye, but I didn't know what to say to him, so I made the excuse of needing to check on the others down below.

When I went to see Hanzhu to report on the health of his crew, he made a proposal.

He was in the laboratory, coat removed and sleeves rolled up. A series of glass vials and tubes had been set up with a flame burning beneath one beaker. The contents inside bubbled steadily away while Hanzhu bent over a notebook, scribbling something into the margins. He looked up as I entered, a set of steel-rimmed goggles hiding his eyes.

"Master Yim is doing better," I reported, hating to interrupt. Of all the injuries, the barge master's were the most serious. "He's awake and alert and able to drink water."

"You've changed, Soling."

I was taken aback by his directness. Hanzhu moved away from the apparatus and came toward me, removing his goggles. "You disappeared somewhere over the last year."

I bit my lower lip nervously. I'd forgotten that Hanzhu had some secret connection in Peking, maybe even in the imperial palace, but whoever it was hadn't known about Hubei.

"Now you've changed. You're different," he continued, not entirely disapproving.

I smiled faintly. "I'm older?"

"It's like you've seen things."

I had seen things.

"This is not the first time you've witnessed death," he pressed.

But it still gutted me every time. Even when I didn't know their names or their stories. I still mourned the crewmen we'd lost in the battle just days ago. "Why does this matter to you?"

"Don't go to Shanghai," he replied bluntly. "You don't want to."

"What else would I do? Stay here on your ship?"

He shrugged. Grinned. "It's becoming a haven for lost souls."

"It's not exactly safe." Hanzhu was constantly under attack by anyone and everyone.

"Neither is Shanghai. It's all becoming battlefield, Soling. You should realize that before going to Shanghai to save Chen Chang-wei from whatever fate he's chasing."

"It's my fate too."

"It doesn't have to be," he said gently.

"Chang-wei asked for permission to marry me."

Yang Hanzhu fell silent at that. It was hard to imagine there had been a time when both Chang-wei and Hanzhu were discussing marriage with my parents. It wasn't particularly to be wed to me as much as to my family.

"I'm surprised it took Chen so long to get around to it," Yang said after a pause. "As proper as he...claims to be."

As far as insults went there was no bite to it. Yang regarded me, his eyes searching. "I don't hate Chen Chang-wei. I don't even dislike him. I actually want very much for him to be able to take care of you and...all the other things. Chang-wei is only dishonest with you, Soling, because he's dishonest with himself."

It was the first time he wasn't taunting or testing. For once, Yang Hanzhu looked serious and even concerned. He didn't have the answers any more than Chang-wei or I did. His approach was to take to the seas, lash out, burn things. It wasn't productive, but I didn't know if assembling killing machines to march against our own countrymen was any solution either. It only had the appearance of purpose.

There was a hissing sound behind us. The beaker above the flame was bubbling over.

"On my father's head—" Yang swore and rushed to turn off the heating element.

I moved to help him but held back.

"Don't worry," he said, attending to the spilled chemicals

with a rag. "Nothing that would melt through steel here. Just a distillation process."

"I didn't mean to distract—"

"I'll just start it again. I have enough of these samples."

As he tidied the workbench, I could see several yellow paper packets lying next to a mortar and pestle on the back counter, triggering some inner instinct. My pulse skipped.

"What are those?" I asked.

He followed my line of sight to the packets and picked one up to present to me. "Cessation pills. They're supposed to reduce cravings for opium."

I turned the packet over in my hands, barely able to breathe. "Why are you studying these?"

"They've been distributed in opium refuges and missions all over the empire," he replied as a matter of fact. "The formula can be quite varied. Sometimes it's nothing but a mix of bicarbonate and ginseng. Some have a low dose of morphine which is, interestingly enough—"

"Derived from opium. You and your opium studies," I mused absently. The label was different from the ones that Mother had in her possession. The characters on this one were stamped in red.

When I looked up, Hanzhu was leaning back against the counter to watch me intently. "What is it, Soling?"

"I was just wondering if these work."

He shrugged. "Yes. No."

"You were studying a peculiar affliction caused by opium before," I prompted.

He nodded. "Now I wonder if it wasn't the opium that caused the sickness, but rather the intended cure."

I stared down at the packet in my hand. Yang and I had encountered what we'd thought of as a disastrous side-effect of opium-smoking. The condition made the afflicted out-of-control and violent, practically rabid.

Since that first encounter, I'd seen the phenomenon emerging throughout the empire. First in Changsha and then occasionally in the alleyways of Peking. I warned anyone who would listen about the strange affliction.

"My mother—" I choked out in alarm.

"What of your mother?" Hanzhu asked, eyebrow raised.

Hanzhu didn't know my mother had been addicted to opium. It seemed too private of a matter to bring up — even if Yang Hanzhu had been close to our family in the past.

Fortunately, my mother had stopped using opium, but I was constantly worried that Peking would bring back the dark memories and pressures that had caused her to seek out opium in the first place. Mother promised me opium was no longer a temptation for her, but she'd been tempted enough to visit a dispensary.

"How is Jin Furen?" Hanzhu asked.

I recalled how my mother had supposedly favored Yang Hanzhu over Chang-wei as a suitor.

"She's...she's well." As well as I'd ever seen her. I'd get a message to her to be rid of the cessation pills once I landed in Shanghai. "My mother is working for the Ministry again."

A sudden realization came to me. As close as she was to Chief Engineer Kuo's inner circle — did she have a part in this current strategy? Mother had a talent for separating options into numbers. This life for that life. The equations.

"Back under the loving care of the empire," Hanzhu remarked cynically.

"Mother needs to feel useful."

As did I. We were trying to reclaim our lives, our home. I couldn't pretend that the war hadn't happened or that the imperial council hadn't targeted my father, but I could hold that pain inside if it meant my brother would have a future.

Hanzhu refused to let go of his wounds. He'd stand his ground and fight against the tide.

"If the Qing empire falls, there are worse monsters waiting to take its place," I told him.

"Are they really any worse?" he countered.

Between foreign invaders and murderous rebel factions? The Taiping rebels hated the Manchu. Yang and Chen Chang-wei were both Han, but I was Manchu from my father's bloodline.

The Emperor was far from a capable and just benefactor, but he was young and he was trying to hold up the country. If the Qing government were to collapse, it would be like floodwaters breaking through a dam. There would be no stopping our many enemies, or the bloodbath that would follow.

"On the night your father was executed, I went to gather your family," Hanzhu reminded me. "There was room in the airship, but we had to go quickly. When I came to your house, your mother had already fled."

I remembered saying farewell to my father in the courtyard. When Kuo Lishen came to our gate later, I had hoped it was my father returning, but it wasn't.

Suddenly we were packing. Then we were leaving. I'd wanted to hold Mother's hand, but she had Tian clutched to her. Nan, our housekeeper, was the one who had pulled me along. If we had left in daylight, I might have clearer memories of what our life had been like in Peking. The memories that persisted were of that night and fleeing into the darkness with what few belongings we could carry.

"Things would have been very different if we had gone with you," I murmured.

"You would have been among friends," he said gravely. "We would have found a way to survive together."

Instead, we had been alone and shunned in the tiny village where we'd settled. Mother had fallen into dark times. There was the opium. The rice basket that was always empty. I'd sold our possessions to stay alive.

"You should be among friends now," Hanzhu went on. "No one knows what the future will bring, but you do know that there will be untold danger in Shanghai. Stay here, with me, with Satomi, until the danger is past. We can protect each other."

It might be a ship of lost souls, but Yang Hanzhu's war junk had come to my rescue before. He might be hunted by the authorities and wanted by the law, but he was in control of his own destiny. I couldn't say the same for Chang-wei. Or for myself.

"And then you can still marry that do-gooder Chen Chang-wei when all is done," Hanzhu added charitably. "You know he'll find a way to survive this madness to fulfill his promise. We all thought he was dead after being captured by the Yangguizi only to have him turn up alive. It's obvious there's fate between the two of you."

The word sounded strange coming from Hanzhu. He wasn't one to speak of fate. His proposal hovered over me like a storm cloud, as did his earlier warning.

It was all becoming a battlefield.

I FOUND Chang-wei at the bow of the ship as we navigated the river. He leaned forward on the rail, watching the movement of the water and the shifting view of the shore. From here, we could see the first glimpse of Shanghai in the distance. The waterway would take us through to the Bund, to the docks that served the foreign settlement.

The river was clogged with traffic. Ships flew flags from a web of nationalities and authorities. Overhead, airships could be seen heading to and from the landing ports. Here, Yang's ship would disappear into anonymity.

I rested my arms on the rail, my pose mirroring Chang-wei's. He looked lost in thought, a hundred things going through his mind. Yet I could tell he was acutely aware of my presence by the slight stiffening of his spine and the minute raising of shoulders. He was waiting for something. Almost bracing for it.

It was late in the afternoon, the sunlight flashed bright into my eyes in a last dance before fading beneath the horizon.

"This war will continue with or without you in it," I told him.

His knuckles tightened over the rail. "I can't wash my hands of this, Soling. I proposed the machines to the Emperor. I brought us to this moment."

When he spoke of us, he didn't mean he and I. He meant the empire.

"You had an idea," I protested. "It was just a beginning. You still have a choice."

"To stop?" Chang-wei shook his head. "That's not my choice. This can work, Soling, but only if I'm there to make sure that it does."

"You can't control those things—"

"I can now," he insisted.

I stared at him, searching his face for answers. He looked away. "I found a way to do it. This last month."

The last month when he'd worked night and day with hardly any sleep.

"We can save lives," he said quietly. "Prevent all-out war."

I didn't know if I believed it, but I was certain that Chang-wei did. When Chang-wei made a promise, he committed himself to it fully.

"Then I'm going with you to Shanghai," I told him.

He turned to me, his expression unreadable. "Alright."

I looked ahead to the city, trying to imagine what it was that he was seeing. The responsibility he must have felt on his shoulders to see this to the end.

When we had returned from Japan, we'd made a vow that we would take this journey together. This was before his marriage proposal. The vow was made before a lot of things, but it still held true.

"I know you asked Hanzhu to persuade me to stay," I told him.

He didn't deny it. The two of them really did have an interesting relationship.

Hanzhu's proposal had been tempting. Stay among friends. Don't think about Shanghai and leave what would happen next to fate, but I didn't believe in fate anymore.

The last time I'd seen my father, he'd held my hand and told me he had to go, accepting his fate calmly. Then I stayed while he left. My father had never come back.

I couldn't leave Chang-wei alone now, surrounded by enemies and questionable allies in territory that the foreigners had seized from us. He had to be able to trust someone. We had no one else but each other.

PART III

SHANGHAI

CHAPTER 17

The flagship approached the wharf on the north shore of the Huangpu River. We docked ahead of the river bend that led to the main part of the foreign settlement, allowing us to avoid the busiest section of the port. Even so, the Shanghai waterfront was a teaming, bustling place. We arrived in the late afternoon, just hours before sundown. Laborers were still hard at work loading and unloading.

The Yingguoren said that trade was the reason they had fought the war. The foreigners had demanded access to our ports. They wanted a favorable arrangement. But the crucial point was they wanted freedom to sell their opium. Their only cause was profit.

Even after the war, the opium trade remained illegal by imperial decree, but the Qing authorities could do little to enforce it at the treaty ports. The Westerners even enlisted companies run by our own countrymen to distribute the opium. That was the cruelest part of the enterprise — we were made party to our own destruction.

The rebellion in the Old City had further eroded Qing authority. The port in the concession remained functional, albeit under foreign control. With a combination of confusion and the right connections, a vessel could slip into the settlement by water, landing ridiculously close to the walls of Old Shanghai.

Fortunately, Chang-wei had a long-time associate in the treaty port. A westerner named Dean Burton who Chang-wei had met during his time among the foreigners. I'd encountered Burton the first time I'd come to the foreign concession in Shanghai. I'd never met one of the so-called "foreign devils" before.

As soon as we docked, a foreign official came to account for our arrival. Chang-wei produced papers, paid the customs fee and whatever bribes or gifts had been agreed to. As Yang had said, there was a lot of looking the other way.

The ground seemed to shift as I set foot on the shore, but it was only an illusion. My body had become accustomed to adjusting to the sway of the ocean, my senses compensating without thought. Now, on a steady surface, I continued to bob and wave expecting the rolling motion of the waves. Soon the feeling would pass and the journey by sea would be another memory.

I looked up toward the bow in a final farewell, but it stood empty. Yang Hanzhu had disappeared deep into the hold. He and his crew were itching to return to open water. There would be no coming ashore for drink and merriment here.

After the cursory customs inspection, we were met by a work crew led by Chang-wei's associate. Dean Burton was what one would expect from a foreigner. Yellow-haired and tall, with squared features. His shoulders were wide and draped in heavy fabric, elaborately sewn to accentuate those sharp angles. He removed a boxy-looking hat as he approached and flashed a grin that exposed a row of even white teeth.

"John," he said, in his peculiar Western way of mispronouncing Chang-wei's name. They reached out to clasp hands. I didn't understand his next statement, but it was accompanied by a glance upward to the mast which had only been partially repaired. The long tear ran down the red sail like a jagged scar.

It was a shock to see Chang-wei conversing in the foreigners' language. From what I gathered, most of the foreign traders in Shanghai spoke Yingyu along with a mix of other tongues.

"Miss Jin." Burton greeted me with a tilt of his head that wasn't quite a bow. I was surprised he remembered me after our one brief meeting.

"So honored to see you again, Miss Jin. You're tired from your journey. I've prepared lodging for your people."

Burton spoke a mix of Canton dialect and mainland Mandarin. His speech was oddly accented, but I could understand him well enough.

"Your Chinese has improved," I remarked.

He laughed at that, the sound thunderous in my ears. Burton was certainly a person who was comfortable taking up space in all dimensions.

"I have more opportunity to practice now so many people have come here."

A team of dock workers gathered to unload the cargo. Kai and Chang-wei's engineers moved to assist the men as they loaded the crates onto the back of a mechanical wagon. Burton had arranged for two transports to carry the shipment. From what I understood, Burton's business shipped and moved a variety of goods. Meiguo, or America as the Westerners called it, also had less visibility than the other major powers in the settlement. It made for the perfect cover.

As Burton and Chang-wei discussed logistics, I noticed the Chinese woman standing behind Burton. She looked familiar to me though I couldn't place when or where we would have met. She stood with spine straight, eyes watchful. Her hair was pulled back and pinned elegantly. She was dressed in a long-sleeved tunic with a series of silk frogs fastened in the front. A wide sash wrapped around her waist and her top was fitted over loose trousers. Burton called her forward to ask something, referring to her as 'Miss Wei.' From the ease of her movements, I could tell her feet weren't bound.

Miss Wei took care of directing the laborers as they unloaded the cargo and packed the wagons. Unlike Burton, she was able to communicate fluently with the workmen. Once the crates were secured, Kai and the engineers remained with the precious shipment while Chang-wei and I joined Burton in his steam carriage.

I seated myself in back and Miss Wei took the seat beside mine. She looked me over in one efficiently dispensed glance, nodded once, and then faced forward. I stared at her striking profile, with her long face and shapely nose, and was once again caught by the feeling we'd met before.

"A lot of changes since you were here before," Burton told Chang-wei as he wound a crank to prime the boiler.

I could hear the whir of a belt starting up. As the motor roared to life, Burton hopped into the driver's seat. Chang-wei arranged himself up front beside him.

The carriage was of Western design. It was steam-powered with a bass cylinder and pump assembly in the back of the transport. Once sufficient pressure built-up, the vehicle started forward.

"Mister Burton," I called, raising my voice to be heard above the motor. "If it's not too much trouble, can I send a message to Peking from here?"

Burton regarded me over his shoulder. "Our airships and transports aren't allowed beyond the treaty port, but Miss Wei can assist you in finding a courier."

Chang-wei shot me a curious look. I didn't want to trouble him with a letter that was meant for my mother. Hanzhu's theories about the cessation pills were just one part of his ongoing obsession with opium. At least that's what I told myself. Theory or not, it wouldn't cause any harm to warn Mother of potential danger.

I looked out the window as we rolled through the streets. The biggest difference was immediately apparent. The foreign concession had become crowded with Zhongguoren, with Chinese. Two years ago, it wasn't completely rare to see native Chinese in the foreign settlement, but we were there as servants and laborers. Now the streets were crowded with Chinese living among foreigners. Native people with braided queues and loose jackets and trousers walked among Westerners with pale-skin dressed in stiff, buttoned-up layers.

"Since the Small Swords took over Old Shanghai, we've had a flood of people from the city as well as the surrounding areas," Burton explained. "It feels like we're taking refugees into the concession every day."

"Refugees — in our very own country," Miss Wei remarked pointedly.

"Well, the municipal council takes care of putting them somewhere," Burton replied, either ignoring Miss Wei's remark or dismissing it completely. "The council is also responsible for policing, watching over things. Keeping the settlement safe."

The young woman's eyes narrowed at that.

"Building construction had been going at a tornado pace," Burton continued.

"That phrase might not translate well to our language," Chang-wei mused.

Burton laughed. "Right. Typhoon? Hurricane?" He cycled through words, finally hitting upon the correct one. "Whirl-wind. Very fast. Dwellings are being set up in a matter of days. The settlement is quickly becoming overcrowded."

"And Mister Burton has gotten wealthier by the hour because of it." Miss Wei played with her manicured nails as if sharpening knives.

"Some would say that American outspokenness has made an

183

impression on Miss Wei, but she's actually been this way the entire time I've known her," Burton replied cheerfully.

He turned to Miss Wei and made an expression by closing then opening one eye. Miss Wei did not return his smile even the slightest. All-in-all, a confusing exchange.

We continued on to a large brick building that Burton explained was one of his warehouses. The cargo was unloaded and secured inside and the movers were paid for their work before being sent off. Burton then dispatched his own people along with Kai and the engineers to an early supper.

"They must be famished after such hard work," he suggested amiably. Only when it was the four of us inside the warehouse did Burton start in on our purpose for being there. "There are some nuances you should be aware of before you do whatever it is you mean to do."

Miss Wei made a point of wandering some distance away, perhaps out of politeness. I stayed where I was beside Chang-wei.

"The French have declared support for the Qing government. The British consulate has tried to remain neutral."

He used a different word to refer to the Yingguoren. I was able to follow the conversation after some initial confusion.

"For right now, the Americans are of the same mind as the British. Staying out of any direct involvement, though there have been individuals joining up with the insurrectionists."

"What of the firearms sold to the rebels?" Chang-wei brought up.

Burton paused. "I haven't heard anything of that."

Out of the corner of my eye, Miss Wei's spine stiffened. She appeared to be inspecting a stack of smaller crates that had been pushed against one wall.

"From British traders," Chang-wei pressed. "And American as well. The Small Swords wouldn't be able to hold out in the walled city without outside support."

Burton let out a breath. "You need to remember that regardless of where the municipal council stand in regards to this uprising, the council is wary of giving imperial forces too much leeway. There was an altercation several months back when the Qing army attempted to set up camp too close to the border of the foreign settlement."

"It's a battle for territory," Chang-wei acknowledged soberly.

Burton nodded. "A dilemma for sure, but the Shanghai council is starting to sour on this rebellion. The overcrowding and this messy business of Western forces on both sides, fighting amongst each other. Rebel skirmishes are starting to interfere with trade. It's especially a problem if their armies intend to attack more treaty ports. I think your timing is good, just be careful of how you position yourself. Oh, and I can't have anything to do with this."

"Of course," Chang-wei assured.

Burton grasped his shoulder in a brotherly manner. "It's good to see you again, John. Don't get yourself killed, alright?"

I LATER BROKE AWAY from the group accompanied by Miss Wei. We were off to seek out a courier service that would deliver to Peking. Miss Wei moved confidently through the lanes in long, powerful strides while I made an effort to keep up.

In Peking, we would be called big-footed. It was a common custom among the Han for women to have their feet bound when they were very young. Bound feet served as a social signal in polite company. Miss Wei not having her feet wrapped tight could mean a number of things.

She could be Manchu like I was. The rebels were notably hostile toward people of Manchu ethnicity and she might have fled to the foreign settlement to escape persecution.

Another possibility was that she was Han, but her family

didn't follow the practice. My mother's family was Han, but they'd never bound her feet. As an only child, she was needed to work in the family paper mill. Binding Mother's feet would have been impractical, especially as she was never expected to marry. Perfect lotus feet were meant to attract a husband from a good family.

The final consideration was Western influence. Miss Wei had a firm grasp of Western customs and language. Perhaps she'd grown up among them. It was my understanding that Westerners found foot-binding very disturbing.

Whatever her story was, Miss Wei carried herself with authority among the workmen and even seemed to assert control over Burton himself. Burton had assured me it was perfectly safe for Miss Wei and I to go unaccompanied to the courier's office.

"Everyone in all the alleyways knows not to give Miss Wei any trouble. I'm a bit afraid of her myself," he'd told me, grinning.

As we wove through the streets, I became more and more curious about that statement. We passed by a group of not-entirely-upstanding looking men. They eyed us darkly as we passed, but Miss Wei breezed by without a moment's pause while I hurried along after her like a duckling trailing after its mother.

"There are several courier companies with land routes to Peking every couple days," she explained. "Going by airship will cost you more."

"Airship," I replied before remembering what Burton had said. "Are airships allowed to leave out of the foreign concession?"

"Only approved vessels. They're all captained by our coun-trymen. Of course, everything will be scrutinized by imperial agents at some point. It will cost extra to bypass that."

"That won't be necessary. It's just a letter to my mother." I wanted to let Mother know we were safe, as well as warn her about the cessation pills. I'd written the letter before we'd docked, using generalities as Chang-wei had warned.

"You're from Peking," Miss Wei said curiously.

"Many people are from Peking." In turn, I was curious to know more about her methods for circumventing the authorities. "Forgive me, but I keep having the feeling that we've met before."

"Ah, so you do remember," she replied with a sly smile. "I used to work as a hostess at a drinking house called the Dragon's Den. It was a gathering place for foreigners. When we first me, I warned you to be careful about trusting Dean Burton and Chen Chang-wei. I see you didn't heed my warning."

"I see you didn't either," I countered.

"Yes, well." She made a face. "I didn't expect the Old City to fall to a bunch of street gangs. Or for me to get stuck on the other side in the foreign settlement. I'm Wei Ming-fen."

"Jin Soling."

Ming-fen was much friendlier now that she was alone with me. Perhaps her snappish demeanor was merely a reaction to being out of place in the foreign settlement.

We moved down the alleyway, passing door after door on either side, very close together. A few were propped open, revealing tiny, one-room dwellings. At the far end, the alley opened up to a corner with shops and businesses. Once more, it was as if I had been transported to some faraway land.

The signboards were in Yingyu. The Westerners favored an orderly, stacked appearance to their buildings. There was a sense of pattern and sameness — one window after another in rows. Once we moved past that block, we were thrown into yet a different world. Here were the cluttered shops and hanging signboards of a Chinese city, an opportunistic space where every empty spot was filled. Vendors poured onto the streets with baskets. There were paper notices plastered on the walls.

The courier service operated inside a small door tucked in behind a printing house. I left my letter with the clerk at the counter and paid with a few cash coins.

"Burton, he isn't so bad," she admitted as we started back. "Or he's no worse than any other foreigner. He's been trying to help me. I don't have anyone else in this part of Shanghai."

"That must be difficult."

The rebellion had cut her off from her old life to throw her into this world between worlds.

"Were you working at the drinking house when the uprising started?"

Gradually, I pieced together the last time I'd seen Ming-fen. She had worn a scandalously form-fitting silk dress. Her lips had been painted a vibrant festival red.

I had considered, at the time, that she might be a prostitute.

"It was actually Burton who was caught on the other side in the Old City," Ming-fen explained. "I was trying to help him to safety. He had no idea about anything—" She stopped, letting out a sigh. "It started with the major street gangs banding together. Then the Taiping rebels got involved. I keep waiting for things to go back to how they were, but it's been over a year now."

"Do you have family in the Old City?" I asked, seeing the look of loss on her face.

She didn't answer and I immediately regretted asking something so personal. "It must have been frightening to witness the fall of Old Shanghai," I said to fill the silence.

"The Shanghai authorities surrendered rather easily. The Small Swords only killed the city magistrate that day and the intendant was eventually smuggled out of the Old City. Since then, it's been a standoff with the Small Swords inside the walls and Qing loyalists outside. It's like a heated kettle waiting to boil."

~

Burton and Miss Wei eventually left our group alone in the warehouse. Chang-wei's work could finally begin.

The first task was to move the crates into the basement beneath the main floor. The warehouse was previously used by opium runners and the entrance to the hidden lower level was through a removable section of the floor that could be easily concealed. The assembly work would be completed below, hidden from view.

Once the supplies were transported below, we gathered around Chang-wei for further instructions.

"The mission here must remain secret," Chang-wei said gravely. "Talk to no one. Our story is that I'm an inventor looking to make money off the foreigners and the businesses sprouting up in Shanghai."

"What do you invent?" Kai asked.

Chang-wei's lips quirked. "Mechanical puppets. That sing and dance — quite the novelty."

"Not so far from the truth," one of the engineers remarked.

The team would be working, eating, and sleeping here at the warehouse. I was to stay in the area near the front doors that was used for an office.

"This warehouse will remain locked. The windows will need to be covered and we'll stay on guard every night. Mister Burton tells me thieves are always a concern in the commercial wharves."

There were other logistical questions from the team. Like when assembly would begin.

The crates remained unopened. I couldn't imagine how long it would take Chang-wei and his small crew to assemble the automatons.

"We need to make contact with Taotai Wu first," Chang-wei explained. "Wu is the circuit intendant who escaped from the

Old City to the foreign concession during the uprising. He's still considered the administrative head of Shanghai and our liaison. There is a function tomorrow evening where the taotai is expected to be present."

I was as surprised as the rest of them when he told us the next part.

"I am to attend along with Miss Jin. Who will be posing as my wife."

CHAPTER 18

We spent the rest of the day securing the warehouse as Chang-wei had instructed. He opened the crates up himself for inspection. For each one, I noted how he reached inside to disarm the acid traps. He paused on one of the crates to stare curiously at the locking mechanism. That must have been the one Hanzhu had opened.

I said nothing.

The warehouse was located in the Meiguo section of settlement.

"*Ame-ri-can*," Kai pronounced slowly, testing the sounds. "They're like the Yingguoren?"

"It's another country across the ocean. They speak a dialect of Yingyu."

That was all I knew. The Americans had taken longer than the Yingguoren, the British, to establish footing in the treaty ports, but not by much. Dean Burton was from there and apparently became very offended if he was mistaken for Yingguoren.

Our meals were procured from nearby street vendors. Our countrymen had settled in the area surrounding the warehouse district. Tea and food sellers set up shop up and down the

JEANNIE LIN

streets just like in Old Shanghai. Kai and I had taken up that task of hunting down dinner.

"It's because we're clever enough to blend in," Kai asserted with an armful of wrapped rice cakes. As usual, he was the largest person around and it was impossible for him to blend in. "Truly, I never thought I'd see Shanghai."

For a bone-setter from a small village in Anhui province, the last few weeks must have been quite the adventure.

"You did well on the ship," I told him.

"I spent most of it seasick," he said with chagrin.

"You remained calm when there was danger."

He fidgeted nervously the compliment. "Just doing my duty, Yishi."

It still felt odd to have anyone deferring to me, especially someone as imposing as Kai. But for all his size and strength, Kai had a gentle soul. I remember how he'd shielded me as I'd tended to the injured barge master. Kai had also been the first to run into danger when the automaton had gone out of control at the citadel. He had been a good choice for this mission.

"Will you return to Anhui after this?"

"I would hope to return to the Factories. The money helps my family."

"I can help you petition for whatever position you'd like."

"Better than being conscripted as a soldier, Yishi," he said gratefully. "As big as I am, that's all people usually think I'm good for."

When night came, Chang-wei and the rest of our crew retired to the storage rooms in the back of the warehouse. Temporary lodging had been set up there with bamboo mats and cots. I retreated to the office near the front which could be closed off for privacy.

There was a mat and bedroll set up in the corner. Unlike the rest of the warehouse, there were windows in the office fitted with wooden shutters.

I lay back, blinking into the darkness. It was strange sleeping in this large old building, inside a fractured city split between rebel insurgents and foreigners. Yet, amidst it all, there was an air of the mundane. Like the metal components packed away in the crates — we were pieces waiting to be put together. Moments waiting to come together.

I wished that Chang-wei wasn't so far away that night so that we could at least talk. Whatever needed to happen, it would be soon and Chang-wei was at the center of it.

I also wondered what exactly it would mean to pose as Chang-wei's wife. It was a role I wasn't sure I was entirely suited for. It was also a subject Chang-wei seemed to be avoiding. He hadn't mentioned betrothals or weddings or anything even remotely personal since we'd left the Factories.

WHEN I WOKE up the next morning, it was to grunting and the sounds of heavy moving and lifting. I peered through the floorboards to see Chang-wei and his engineers setting up and constructing the assembly line. Kai was helping where he could, the strongest among them, and taking direction well.

I washed up before peeking outside the window into the street. The surrounding lanes had been quiet at night, but were waking up now to fill with carts and workmen. We would easily be able to hide our activities in the churn of commerce. Especially now when faces like ours were commonplace in the foreign concession. Ironically, it had taken the capture of Old Shanghai for us to reclaim foreign-controlled sections of the city.

Chang-wei came up to the main floor around mid-morning to hand me a folded slip of paper.

"Will you be able to manage?" he asked.

A deep line cut through his brow. Whether it was from

concern for me or his intense focus on the mission, I couldn't tell.

"I can manage," I assured him.

"And about tonight—"

"I can manage that also."

He met my eyes and held onto them. "Be careful."

I stepped outside and closed the warehouse door firmly behind me. From the street, there was nothing to set the building apart from the others around it.

I navigated back to the main road and hailed a rickshaw. The puller started off at a steady jog, his feet attached to pedals which cranked the small motor. We disappeared into the mill of traffic along the avenue, just another transport among hundreds.

Feeling a bit more secure now, I reached into my jacket to retrieve the paper Chang-wei had given me and opened it. The list was written in horizontal Yingyu script which I couldn't read. Just as I returned it to my pocket, I caught a glimpse of a radial pattern painted on the wall as we passed an alleyway. There were spokes spiraling out from a central hub, making it look like a wheel. I sat up straight.

"Uncle!" I called to the rickshaw puller. "Can we stop here?"

He couldn't hear me over the chug and creak of the rickshaw. I tried to call out again to get his attention.

"Almost there, miss," he assured me while the rickshaw's rusty gears whined away.

Was he was deliberately ignoring my request? The old puller likely wanted to earn his fare in the most expedient way possible.

I twisted around to look behind us but could no longer see the graffiti. That moment was gone.

I couldn't be angry. It wasn't easy to turn around in the street, and every step was extra distance and weight the rickshaw man had to bear. Despite feeling more than a little irritated, I sank back down in the seat. It probably wasn't anything important.

We neared a stone bridge and traffic slowed considerably as the rickshaw rolled onto it. The address Chang-wei had given me was on the other side of the creek. Brackish water flowed in the tributary beneath us. From the raised vantage point, I could see where the narrow lanes started to widen. The buildings became more Western in style and the street life sparser. Signs with hanzi characters gradually faded to be replaced with Western lettering.

The area I was in now was a crossroads of waterways and streets. The faces that stared out from carriages and doorways were light-skinned and sharp-featured. It was impolite to stare, so I looked beyond them to the street and the surrounding shops.

The rickshaw man wasn't familiar with the Western section so we circled about at least once before I told him to stop in front of a large storefront facing the water. Miss Wei Ming-fen came out to the front to wave me in.

I paid the rickshaw puller for his trouble and added an extra coin since he wasn't likely to pick up a fare on this side of the river.

"Miss Wei," I greeted, grateful for a familiar face. Today she was dressed in a long gray dress with loose sleeves.

"Miss Jin, you look well."

I looked uncertainly at the signboard with foreign writing. The name was painted in large gold lettering meant to impress.

"I was sent here for some things," I told Ming-fen.

"Let me see..." she began, glancing at the list that I held out. She made things easy, taking hold of my arm warmly as she led me through the doors.

A young man stood inside behind the counter wearing an apron. His hair was light brown and cut close to his scalp. I took him to be the shopkeeper. There were rows upon rows of shelves behind him, stocked full of various items. Dean Burton was a goods merchant and I assumed he owned this store. *A man who can get things* was how Chang-wei had described him.

Ming-fen said something to the shopkeeper in his language and he said something back in question.

"This is Mister Percival Lawrence," she said by way of explanation rather than introduction. The young man came to attention at the sound of his name. "Burton calls him 'Percy,' but he will not tolerate such familiarity from me. Mister Lawrence doesn't like me very much."

He did look very agitated when Ming-fen slipped behind the counter and started searching the shelves while armed with my list. Unlike me, she had no problems reading the foreign writing.

"He's Burton's clerk," she called out as she disappeared down one row. "We both work in this shop, though he does most of the speaking to customers as they're usually foreigners. No Chinese would pay these prices."

I looked at Mister Lawrence apologetically and gave him a small bow out of politeness. *"Good morning,"* I said, displaying the entirety of my knowledge of Yingyu.

In response, Mister Lawrence said something sharply to Ming-fen. She emerged from the depths of the shelves and set several small tins onto the counter before responding in an equally sharp tone. It was like watching a stage play.

"I'm telling him that if I have to read out the items, then I might as well get them," she told me. "Now he's insisting that I hand the list over to him." She did so, holding up the paper for him to snatch as she said it. "Business must be slow today."

Ming-fen continued our conversation while the shopkeeper gathered the rest of the items. "Mister Burton did say you, or rather the engineer, would be coming by today. He wanted me to tell you he's engaged with some business matters this morning, but he will be there to accompany you tonight. Do you dance?"

It was the oddest question I'd ever been asked. Dancing required years of training from a very young age.

"No," I replied cautiously.

"It's a different practice in the western way of things," she explained, seeing my confused look. "And about now, Mister Lawrence has realized there are items on the list that he would prefer I sort out after all."

With a smile, she held out her hand, not sparing the young man a glance. He came to the counter blushing and handed her back the paper.

"Come back here with me," she said with a conspiratorial look.

I followed her behind the counter, indulged myself with a quick scan of the novelties on the shelves, then ducked behind a curtain into a back room.

"Shanghai is like any port city," she said. "The men come and settle first. Merchants, businessmen, sailors. Not many women. Certainly not wives, at least not for a while. A young lady can make enough to eat doing nothing but smiling and pouring drinks. That's how I first came to this part of Shanghai," she explained. "For work. But so many of us have flooded into the concession over the last year, both men and women. In some cases, entire families. With the rebels ravaging the countryside, everyone is looking for a way to survive."

"And the coastlines are being ravaged by pirates," I added. If we couldn't end this war with ourselves, it was going to be bandits fighting bandits over the scraps of what was left of our land.

"Everything has changed very quickly. In Shanghai, the foreigners are the ones with the money." She let out a sigh, her expression darkening for a moment before she shook it off. "We all must adapt. Look at these."

She lifted a yellow dress from the counter and held it up to me. She paused, gauged my reaction with a tilt of her head, then picked up another garment. Blue this time, embroidered with a peacock feather design.

"Madame Yu is a seamstress on Hongkew Road. She recreates western styles from pictures she finds in the merchant's catalogs. Which one do you like?"

I had the sense of being swept beneath a crashing wave. "What are these outfits for?"

"The party tonight. I know what you need." Ming-fen lifted a third option, a dress in pale pink and trimmed with peonies. "A mix of styles," she said brightly. "Western and Chinese."

After that, there was a barrage of undergarments, which was what Mister Lawrence must have been blushing about. Ming-fen took time explaining and demonstrating all the ties and hooks before wrapping everything into a parcel that she tied with string. There was another parcel, already packed.

"For Engineer Chen. Oh, and one other thing," she added once we were done with the list. "That letter that you wanted to send to Peking? I had it diverted through Tianjin first."

I struggled to balance all of the packages in my arms. "Why?"

"The Qing authorities aren't the only ones watching closely. A letter to Peking might draw the attention of the Shanghai municipal council. Better to remain inconspicuous, right?"

CHAPTER 19

Later that day, as the evening neared, I was in the corner office with the shutters drawn and door closed, twisting around and around until my arms ached as I tried to tie the corset. Finally, I blew out a sharp breath and opened the door the tiniest crack. Defeated, I called for Chang-wei.

When Chang-wei came to the door, his eyebrows raised at the sight of me before he schooled his expression back to a neutral one. I had put on the under garments, but there was a whole other set of clothes to be worn over them.

"I need help tying the corset," I said, my face heating.

There was a pause before he spoke. "Turn around."

I did as Chang-wei asked, hoping I'd feel less embarrassed now that I was no longer looking at him. It didn't help. Chang-wei took hold of the laces in back and began to tighten them one after another, his hands working down my back. I could feel his every movement.

Chang-wei worked in silence while I stood as still as I could. There was nothing to break the silence aside from the soft tug of the laces and the deep and steady rhythm of Chang-wei's breathing behind me.

"I didn't realize Western women's clothing would take such effort," he said when the silence became too much.

"Men's clothing isn't as complicated?"

Chang-wei laughed a little. Hollowly. "Not nearly."

There was silence again as Chang-wei focused on looping the strings into a knot. He tightened it with a firm tug and then touched his fingers against the small of my back. His touch remained longer than it needed to before he withdrew abruptly. I turned around and realized that my shoulders were bare. I crossed my hands over them as a shield, then felt awkward for doing so.

"Do you need anything else?" he asked, swallowing.

"No. Thank you."

Was I imagining the flush to his cheeks? We'd become familiar with one another over the last year. Scandalously so, and I knew it. But this was...different.

It wasn't until he left that I let out a breath. I was determined to finish dressing by myself, even if I had to twist myself into knots to do so.

CHANG-WEI and I stood outside of the warehouse hours later waiting for Burton to arrive. I had managed the rest of the outfit myself. The Western-style dress was collar-less, with a neckline that slanted down, leaving my neck and collarbones exposed. For the scant coverage on top, there was an excess of material from the waist down where it billowed out like a bell. It had taken a while to struggle into once Chang-wei had left me and I still wasn't sure I wore it properly.

Chang-wei wore a heavy black coat with brass buttons over a linen shirt and trousers. His hair was still in its braided queue so at least he looked like himself. The suit itself looked so confining. I wondered if this was how Chang-wei had dressed when he'd been in the West. The strangest addition was a length of blue silk tied around his neck.

"It's called a cravat," he explained, smoothing a hand over the cloth.

When I asked, he didn't know what purpose it served other than fashion. It seemed like an ill-omen, to wrap a strip of cloth around one's neck.

The warehouse area was still and dormant at night. Aside from the two of us, the street was empty. Nevertheless, Chang-wei stood close with his hand resting lightly over my elbow.

"Are we attending a celebration?"

"It's just a social gathering. The foreign consuls will be there and Taotai Wu is in their custody."

"Is he a prisoner?" I asked, shocked.

"No." But then, "It's complicated. Wu is still the head of the circuit, but his contact with Peking has been limited. I've been told Wu attempted a counter-attack early during the insurgency. It failed and since then the foreign authorities have kept a closer watch on him."

The foreign powers were adamant about asserting neutrality. There were still ways to communicate with the Qing forces outside the city. Ways to send messages to Peking, but only after navigating a few obstacles like with my message for my mother.

"You don't really need a wife to speak to the intendant, do you?" I asked.

The corner of Chang-wei's mouth lifted. "You provide the appearance of respectability."

The steam-carriage arrived with Mister Lawrence in the driver's seat. He got out and greeted us with a slight bow before opening the door. I didn't know why Miss Wei found him so objectionable. He gave the impression of being a gentleman.

Inside I found myself seated across from Miss Wei Ming-fen

who wore a green dress with a phoenix pattern embroidered at the borders. Her hair was pulled back in an elegant coil that highlighted the clean line of her neck. Twin jeweled combs sparkled against the silky darkness. Upon closer inspection, I saw that the spine of the comb was shaped like a dragon with green gems set into the eyes.

Ming-fen looked like a privileged heiress while I was done up like an old housekeeper by comparison. My hair was pinned up in a simple bun as if to keep it out of my eyes while I scrubbed the floors.

Dean Burton sat beside her dressed in similar attire to Chang-wei in a dark-colored suit with a row of buttons down the front. His boots were leather and polished to a shine.

"You look very lovely tonight, Miss Jin," Burton said, which I took to mean I hadn't made any appalling errors. Then it was on to business. "I hear that Taotai Wu is meeting with the British consul under the cover of this social function. An official meeting would be too conspicuous given that the major powers of the foreign settlement have all agreed to stay out of the conflict."

Wei Ming-fen made another face, but Burton went on regardless. "Wu is usually surrounded by bodyguards, but Miss Wei and I have a prior connection to him."

"You're British. Wu has no reason to be afraid of you," Miss Wei remarked.

"Actually, I'm American," he reminded her, with a half-grin.

It looked to be some joke between them.

"What connection?" I asked.

The pair exchanged another look. "Miss Wei and I smuggled Taotai Wu out of Old Shanghai the day of the Small Swords uprising," Burton replied casually. "Since then, Wu has remained mostly in the American section for the last year. He was granted refuge at Russell and Company's."

"It's a trading house," Chang-wei explained.

Burton gave us a quick summary of the concession. Each of the foreign countries had their own allotted section controlled by the appointed consul. The Yingguo, or British concession was the oldest and most established. The entire foreign settlement numbered just over a thousand inhabitants; traders, merchants, and other businessmen who called it their home. In the last few years, a flood of Chinese migrants had come from the surrounding countryside as well as from Old Shanghai. The concession had agreed to take them in, in attempt to maintain relations with the Qing Empire.

"All the while making sure not to anger the rebels either."

"It seems like the foreigners are standing back and gambling on who will win," I remarked coolly.

I caught the flash of Wei Ming-fen's smile.

"We're trying to stay out of the fight," Burton insisted. "This is a matter between the Qing government and its own people."

"Unless something interferes with business," Miss Wei pointed out. "Then the warships come charging in."

Burton looked around the carriage at us and had to acknowledge he was outnumbered.

"In any case," he continued with forced cheer, "Wu's an interesting character. Apparently quite the businessman before being appointed as intendant. A dealmaker, I'd call him. He has connections to all sorts of people, foreigners included. That's likely how he was able to arrange an escape from Shanghai during the uprising."

"In Old Shanghai, Wu tried to pit rival gangs against one another," Miss Wei said. "Instead, they all banded together against him."

There was a trace of bitterness in the last part.

"Did any of those gangs come over to this side, to the foreign concession?" I was thinking of the wheel symbol I'd seen painted on the alleyway.

Both Burton and Wei Ming-fen fell silent.

JEANNIE LIN

"The Small Swords are notably against the foreign occupa-
tion," Miss Wei said stiffly.

"I wouldn't be so quick to dismiss the possibility," Burton
countered. "There are rumors they're associated with the
Triads."

I hadn't heard of that name.

"The Triad is what the foreigners call a shadowy secret
society that supposedly operates in Shanghai. Folktales," Miss
Wei sniffed, looking out the window of the carriage.

"It would be a mistake to just dismiss them as street gangs.
These groups are highly organized. Let us not forget that the
Small Swords rebels have met with consuls from the major
foreign powers in Shanghai to negotiate a truce." Burton
directed a pointed look at Chang-wei. "Something your
Emperor still refuses to do."

Instead of negotiating, the Emperor had sent us and his war
machines.

We had reached the riverfront where the oldest and grandest
of the foreigner's buildings stood. The area along the water was
well-lit with gas lamps and boasted a fair amount of evening
foot traffic. Tall brick structures faced the river, displaying to all
the wealth of the West.

The carriage rolled forward, emitting a hiss of steam as it came
to a stop before the steps of an opulent stone building that rose
eight stories high. Burton exited first, then turned around to offer
a hand to Miss Wei. Chang-wei took his hat in hand and gave me a
small nod of reassurance before following Burton's lead.

As Chang-wei took my hand to help me from the carriage,
he leaned in close. "You do look very pretty," he said in a low
tone, a bit rushed. "I should have said something earlier."

He set the black hat awkwardly on top of his head. It was a
tall contraption that added to his height.

I took his arm when he held it out and then stared at the

steps that led up to the building. How was I supposed to get this cage of clouds dress up to the door? Looking to Miss Wei for guidance, I gathered the skirt in my hand to raise the hem before beginning the climb.

Two attendants drew the doors open. I left the brackish waterfront behind and stepped into a glittering entrance hall. A chandelier made of intricate pieces of crystal strung together hung over the vast chamber. It looked like a radiant crown of light surrounded by sparkling jewels. I stared at it in wonderment until my neck hurt from tilting upward.

I'd seen the imperial palace with its grand halls and courtyards. The opulence of this building was of a different sort. It wasn't a place of kings, but rather an imitation where wealthy merchants and traders congregated pretending to be royalty.

We passed underneath the crown of lights to reach another set of stairs. Chang-wei and I followed Burton and Miss Wei upwards. After three flights, the staircase opened into a banquet room where guests had gathered.

Gas lamps lined the walls, flooding the room with a warm glow. Long cloth-covered tables laid with food were arranged along one side. A group of musicians assembled at the far end of the room. The space in front was crowded with pairs of dancers who whirled about with abandon. Watching the patterns left me dizzy.

This is what Ming-fen had meant about dancing.

The attendees who weren't engaged in the dance milled about in threes and fours around the room. Nearly every person was a foreigner.

"Would the two ladies care for some refreshment?" Burton asked.

"No," I replied.

"Yes, please," Miss Wei said.

"Yes, please," I amended.

Burton started off with Chang-wei beside him. I moved to follow before Miss Wei stopped me.

"It's part of the ritual," she explained. "They get to be gallant and use the excuse to roam the room and make important introductions."

"What do we do in this ritual?"

"Stand back and be seen."

"Be seen?"

"Be seen," she confirmed, snapping her fan open and waving it in a lazy rhythm as she surveyed the room.

I opened my fan without the same dramatic flair. I did, however, manage to draw Miss Wei's eye.

"That's quite an interesting piece."

Had she guessed the fan's hidden purpose? Chang-wei had given it to me, not as a gift but for protection. The fan was bladed with reinforced steel spines hidden beneath the silk. The edge was razor-sharp, capable of slicing through skin.

Ming-fen turned her attention back to the banquet with a sweeping glance. We were surrounded by pale skin and strange clothing. The only Chinese present were the servers and a group of young women who were there as to serve as dance partners. The buzz of conversation was unintelligible and the music had an unusual rhythm. The dancers moved in pairs around the floor, narrowly missing one another with each turn.

The current song came to an end and after a short pause, a new one started up. The couples resumed their dance, stepping and circling. It was fascinating to see men and woman paired together, practically in each other's arms. The dance wasn't a performance for an audience, but more of a public ritual.

"Do you know how to do that?" I asked Ming-fen.

"The steps don't take too long to learn. The music tells you what to do."

It all seemed so strange to me. This whole different world growing within our cities.

"Miss Wei," I began slowly.

"No need to be so formal, Little Sister," she said with a deceptively friendly smile.

Though we were visibly of the same age, she was adopting the position of elder sister. A not-so-subtle play to establish status.

"Mei-mei," she said sweetly.

"Jie-jie," I replied, politeness demanding I go along with it. "How did you learn so much about the Yingguoren? Their language? Their customs?"

"I spent several years at a missionary school run by foreigners." She looked out onto the dance floor as she spoke. "I grew up there after my parents disappeared."

"That must have been hard—"

"They're not dead," she added with a frown. "Just...lost."

I had so many questions. She'd lived in Old Shanghai before the insurrection. How did she end up here, working for someone like Dean Burton? I started to ask when she interrupted me again.

"It must be very painful, dancing like that."

I followed her gaze to a dancer with bound feet. She was dressed in Western clothing much like we were and managed to move with surprising grace across the floor on the tiny wedges of her feet which were wrapped in tight bands of cloth.

I'd attended to women in our village who continued to work the fields even after their feet were bound. Bound feet also required continual care. "The toes and the bridge of the foot often lose feeling after a time. I hear one gets used to it and simply endures."

"You're Manchurian aren't you, Mei-mei?" She was looking directly at me now.

"I am."

She made a sound of acknowledgment but said nothing more. By that time Burton and Chang-wei had finally returned. Chang-wei handed me a porcelain cup painted with a blue floral design. The drink inside was the color of Yunnan tea.

"What is this?" It smelled faintly of lemons.

"*Punch*," Burton replied, providing a cup to Wei Ming-fen.

I frowned at the odd name until Chang-wei explained, "It's liquor mixed with sugar."

I took a sip and coughed as the alcohol hit my throat.

Chang-wei met my eyes over the rim of his cup before he drank. "That's the captain of the municipal police force behind me."

I stole a glance at the tall Yingguoren with a thick mustache.

"There have been some recent altercations between his men and imperialist troops," Chang-wei continued with his voice lowered.

"But—" I forced my gaze away. "Aren't the troops outside of the settlement?"

"There's a debate over where exactly the boundaries lie," Burton explained. He held out his hand to Ming-fen. "Miss Wei, will you do me the honor of this dance?"

"Maybe."

He frowned. "Maybe?"

Ming-fen started off to the other side of the room with Burton dutifully following. I drank more of the sweetened liquor. It burned a trail down my throat to warm my stomach.

Chang-wei turned to face the room. We stood shoulder to shoulder to watch as the dancers swept by. I could feel the weight of the police captain's stare on us. My skin prickled as I waited for him to move on, and it felt like the start of the next dynasty before he did. Finally, I could breathe again.

"Did you find Taotai Wu?" I asked him.

"Not yet. Burton is asking Miss Wei to check with the hotel staff. Apparently, the staff will ignore him but will speak to her."

The police captain was circling back toward us, this time

with another man at his side. My heart raced as they looked directly at us.

"What do we do now?" I asked, my heart pounding.

Chang-wei finished his drink and then reached for my cup. I didn't realize how tightly I'd been gripping it.

"We dance," he said simply.

$\sim$

CHANG-WEI TOOK us away from the wall and onto the floor, just inside the edge. I watched helplessly as other pairs whirled by.

"Did you learn how to do this in London?" I asked him.

"Not well."

He took hold of my hand in his. His other arm circled around to rest lightly against my back.

I flushed warm at how close we were. "What happens if we run into someone? Or if they run into us?"

"Just follow me."

I didn't know what that meant.

Chang-wei began to move, guiding me along with the slightest pressure of his fingertips as his feet traced out a pattern. I stared at my own feet as I was helplessly tugged along. One moment, I would think I was close to learning the steps only to have my hopes dashed when I stumbled. If it weren't for Chang-wei's arms around me, I would have faltered.

A small laugh escaped my lips. "We must look like fools," I fretted.

"We look exactly like fools," he agreed. "That's what they'll think we are. The fool inventor with his wild schemes, dancing with his pretty wife. Trying to act like they fit in with the foreigners when they can't possibly do so."

I was taken aback that he had called me pretty. The rest barely registered.

My feet were moving one after the other. At the same time, I could hear the music in the background, but if one had anything to do with the other, I couldn't tell. I laughed at the absurdity of it and Chang-wei smiled back at me.

And then it suddenly did make sense in a different way. The circle of his arms and this almost embrace. This warm flush that filled me, first caused by embarrassment, but now taken over by something else. A rush of feeling lifted me from inside as I looked up at Chang-wei.

"He's here," he said.

I was so caught up in the wildness of the moment that Chang-wei had to repeat himself.

"Taotai Wu is here." He kept his gaze deliberately on me as he spoke. "It's time to go introduce ourselves."

CHANG-WEI BOWED to me when the music stopped, then took my hand and led me from the floor. I found the distinguished Taotai Wu immediately. Aside from us, Wu was the only Zhong-guoren in attendance. Wu wore his state uniform with an embroidered black silk jacket and official headdress. On either side of him stood several stern-faced gentlemen.

Burton intercepted us on our way to the intendant. "Taotai Wu," the American greeted. He exchanged a few pleasantries before starting in on introductions. "This is a good friend of mine, Mister John Chen and his wife."

Wu was a middle-aged man, of average height, average build and unassuming in every way. Hard to believe that he had been given authority over all of Shanghai. His gaze moved over Chang-wei with interest.

"Mister Chen lived for a time in London," Burton continued.

That sparked some interest among the men beside Wu. The conversation momentarily switched to Yingyu during which I tried to maintain a pleasant and patient expression despite having no idea what was being said. Both Chang-wei and Taotai Wu seemed to have no problem understanding or speaking the foreign tongue.

I finally understood the purpose of the Western clothing as well as having Chang-wei approach the intendant in this social, harmless way. These were all signs that were familiar to the foreigners. It made Chang-wei appear to fit into their world. If he dressed like them and spoke like them, then they could, of course, trust him.

Wu turned to me out of politeness. "London must have been exciting, Madame Chen."

"Sadly, I wasn't able to accompany my husband abroad. I remained in Peking to see to our household."

His eyes widened. "Peking. I haven't heard news from the capital in a long time."

"Perhaps I can share the latest news with you."

Our exchange had allowed us both to drop into the northern dialect of the capital. Like Burton, the traders who had any understanding of our language favored the Canton dialect. We still had to be careful about everything we said.

"What is it you do?" Taotai Wu asked Chang-wei.

Chang-wei made a show of puffing out his chest. "I'm an inventor."

"John makes the most clever machines," Burton insisted. "Machines that build other machines."

"Mister Burton is convinced there are many potential investors in Shanghai," Chang-wei replied. "This is my chance to, as they say, 'strike it rich.'"

That caused everyone in the close circle to burst into laughter.

The conversation continued in both Yingyu and Canton dialect, which left me with only half the meaning. These men made a lot of money in Shanghai and were happy about doing so, was the gist of it. That and how the women of Shanghai were very beautiful. One of the foreigners directed that comment at me, perhaps thinking it was a compliment.

"I'm not from Shanghai," I corrected.

An awkward silence ensued.

Chang-wei took my arm obligingly and spoke in northern dialect. "Taotai Wu, it has been an honor. If I may, I promised my wife I would take her to see the garden."

"Yes. It's a fine garden," Wu acknowledged, holding his gaze steady on Chang-wei as we took our leave.

"The garden?" I whispered once we were turned away.

"That's what Burton told me to say."

We returned to the grand staircase, but instead of heading down Chang-wei directed me upward. I felt like an empress ascending those gilded stairs, except an empress would be carried rather than be forced to walk. The sounds of the music grew faint as we climbed until we reached a set of double doors at the top.

A night breeze stirred the air as I stepped out onto the roof. To my surprise, we entered a deck arranged with greenery and carefully placed rock sculptures. The garden was illuminated by large hanging lanterns and the light of the moon. It looked like a courtyard one would find in a mansion. Yet instead of being a secluded sanctuary, I could see the riverfront and the dark water beyond.

"This place is so strange." I wasn't merely talking about the garden either. Shanghai was a strange island where castaways from disparate lands had drifted ashore.

Chang-wei stayed close as we explored the rooftop garden. There was a pond with large carp circling at the other end. Never mind that we were eight floors high.

I wandered to the edge of the terrace and set my hands onto ledge. The waterfront was dark and quiet in the night, with dark shapes floating in the water. Thin masts with furled sails rested. Beyond the river bend, I could see a cluster of faint lights.

"That's Old Shanghai," Chang-wei said. "Just a short sail down the river."

The lights were reflected in the inky darkness of the water. Inside, surrounded by the sounds of strange music and unfamiliar language, it was easy to imagine we were in a faraway place. Outside, I was reminded that Old Shanghai was under siege and that the walls were practically an arrow's flight away. Shanghai's fate could very well be the fate of any of our cities.

Beside me, Chang-wei was also gazing across the water, lost in thought.

"Did you dance with girls in London?" I asked.

He turned to look at me, surprised. "No. I was betrothed to be married."

To a child. I was young when Chang-wei was impressed onto the foreign ship. He'd been taken to distant lands and learned their customs to survive. He seemed comfortable wearing their clothing and speaking their language. He was even familiar with some more intimate details — my face grew hot at the memory of his hands pulling at the laces of the corset around my waist.

"You were in Yingguo for a long time," I remarked.

"There were times I thought I would never find my way home. That I would never see our country again. I thought of you."

I smiled wanly. "We'd never even met."

"But I knew you," he insisted. "Your father told me you were curious. And clever. That you liked frogs and sesame candy. And you were willful."

"Willful? You must have imagined me as a brat with a scowl on my face."

"The best scowl," he replied, then grew quiet. "I was kept on a steamship for months. They didn't even need to lock me up.

We were out at sea and there was nowhere for me to go. It was years before I received any news of Peking. I didn't find out about your father until much later."

How lonely it must have been for him to be stranded from everyone and everything he knew. Chang-wei had been taken against his will, yet he didn't seem to harbor any ill feeling toward the foreigners. Not like Yang Hanzhu

"I thought of you the entire time," Chang-wei confessed. "And of your father and mother."

Chang-wei had no other family. As for me, I'd barely had a thought for him at all. We had never met so the betrothal was just an idea to me. Everything else that was happening right in front of my eyes was very real. My brother had been only been a year old. A baby. Mother had fallen into a dark well of sadness and despair. If I thought of Chang-wei at all, it was only to conclude that he had abandoned us like everyone else.

He moved closer. "I vowed to return. To find you."

"It sounds like you only asked me to marry you because of past promises," I said sullenly. "Out of a sense of duty."

Chang-wei looked surprised. "Isn't it good to have a dutiful husband? One who keeps his promises?"

He placed his hand beside mine on the ledge. I could feel the warmth from his skin.

"W-well, maybe…" I struggled to put my thoughts together as I looked up at him. He really was handsome, his features clean-cut and well-formed. I'd never imagined my betrothed as someone handsome. He was just a formless shadow. A future and far-off thing.

"Maybe a woman wants to be sought after for irrational reasons as well."

He broke into a grin. "You want me to want you for irrational reasons?"

His hand brushed against mine. My heart thudded inside my chest and suddenly the corset felt too tight. Chang-wei's pupils darkened as he lowered his head toward me, but a voice cut through the evening air.

"Mister Chen."

I jumped at the intrusion. Chang-wei handled himself with much more grace, straightening his shoulders before turning to the newcomer. I hadn't heard the doors open or realized Taotai Wu had stepped out onto the rooftop. The intendant stood alone as he regarded us with an expectant look.

"You're here from Peking, Mister Chen," Wu said.

Chang-wei stepped forward. "Sent by the Emperor and the Grand Council."

"Finally." Wu let out a harsh sigh. *"Wáng yang bǔ láo,"* he quoted.

Now you'll mend the fence, after the sheep are already gone.

CHAPTER 20

The next morning, Burton arrived at the warehouse with a wagon packed with workmen. They had been selected by the taotai and loyal to the Qing government.

"They can be trusted," Wu had assured us the night before.

I had remained on the rooftop while Chang-wei and the intendant had coordinated their plans. This was why we were here, after all, and it was important to take back Shanghai from the rebel forces. I knew all of this, yet part of me was agitated Chang-wei and I were so rudely interrupted.

The irrational part of me.

As Burton had hinted, Taotai Wu was a wealthy businessman who had experience dealing with foreign trading houses in Canton before being appointed as the intendant of the Shanghai circuit. He'd been working to establish a foothold in the concession while waiting for reinforcements.

"The foreign devils smile with one side of their faces and condemn you with the other," Wu complained.

He was convinced foreign traders were supplying the Small

Swords rebels. Otherwise, how would they have managed to survive the siege for so long?

Wei Ming-fen was correct that the rebellion was putting more money into the foreign concession. Burton was apparently a small-time operator who didn't trade in arms or opium because he was able to profit simply by offering access. Taotai Wu was the one financing Burton's involvement.

As the work crews arrived, Wu was nowhere in sight. It was Burton and Miss Wei Ming-fen who were there to carry out the transaction.

"Anything you need," Mister Burton said to Chang-wei, putting on his hat. That was another oddity I wasn't accustomed to yet. The taking off and putting on of hats as a social ritual.

The workmen were arranged into teams which would be assigned specific tasks. It was the assembly line again, taken from Hubei to be recreated here. Kai had been folded into the work crew. He and I were ready for any injuries that might occur during assembly, but I imagined there would be few. The machines had already been built and only needed to be reassembled.

I expected Burton and Ming-fen would be on their way soon, but Ming-fen turned to address me.

"Where are you staying, Miss Jin?"

I explained about the office and Ming-fen made a show of looking horrified. "Oh, that must be so uncomfortable. And now with all these strangers, these men coming to stay. And you, a lone woman—"

I shot Chang-wei a warning look as she continued, but to my dismay he was looking on thoughtfully.

"It's not so bad," I insisted. "It's important that I remain close like I did in—"

I started to explain my function in Hubei, but we weren't supposed to speak of the Factories or what was being built there.

"Like I did in Peking," I amended, flustered. "In case anyone gets hurt…"

"It's improper, don't you think?" She turned to Burton for confirmation. He shrugged, already conceding her point.

"There's really no problem," I protested.

"You should come stay with me," Ming-fen invited warmly. "I have rooms above the store."

"Of course," Burton replied with his typical toothy smile. "You're more than welcome, Miss Jin."

"I can show you Shanghai," Ming-fen pressed. "The new Shanghai."

"This sounds like a reasonable arrangement," Chang-wei agreed. "Thank you for being so considerate."

I bit back a sound of exasperation. No one here actually cared about propriety. Ming-fen was just going to have her way no matter what anyone said.

I went to my temporary room to retrieve my things, more than a bit miffed at being suddenly evicted. Chang-wei appeared at the door as I tugged the ties of my pack closed.

"This might work out for us," he began. "You'll be able to keep in communication with Burton and Taotai Wu."

"Wei Ming-fen only has to lift her little finger around Burton," I warned him. "It's obvious she has some purpose and neither you, nor Burton have any idea what it is."

"So, find out what it is," Chang-wei suggested. "She lived in the Old City. She knows more about what we're going into than anyone else."

I let out a slow breath. The real reason I was upset was that I didn't want to leave Chang-wei or the rest of our crew. Mainly I didn't want to leave Chang-wei, but I couldn't admit that out loud.

I searched for something that I could find the courage to say. "I didn't find it unpleasant last night. Posing as your wife," I began, my voice sounding faint above the pounding of my heart.

Chang-wei went still before coming forward. He touched a hand to my shoulder, lightly with just the tips of his fingers. "You were good at it."

It had been a long time since his proposal, but maybe he was waiting for me to say something. Maybe it was his way of being respectfully proper.

"Afterward. After all this" —the words came with difficulty, scratching against my throat— "I wouldn't mind becoming your wife in actuality."

Chang-wei did smile then. Not a wide, overly flashy display of emotion, but a gentle, private show for us only. He bent closer and my skin heated. I wished there weren't so many strangers around.

"I would like that."

I could feel his words all along my spine. It was as if he had kissed me, even though his lips only hovered at my ear. Not touching skin, but near enough.

I was still flushed as I left the warehouse. Ming-fen greeted me with a slight raise of her eyebrows, but I kept my expression neutral and ignored her. Chang-wei helped me onto the wagon with a hand set against my waist, and I wished, all the more so, that we weren't going to be apart.

But there was the siege and this mission. A rebellion and our duties. Always, our duty.

I was only going to the other end of the American section. Only a carriage ride away. We'd been oceans apart before.

Ming-fen climbed onto the seat beside me. I watched Chang-wei through the window as we pulled away. He stood out in the street to see us off and I felt as if I'd just leapt off a very high cliff with nothing to catch me.

"I wish I knew what you were thinking of," Ming-fen murmured. "You seem happy. And terrified."

My smile faded. "Jie-jie."

"Mei-mei," she replied, her tone pleasant.

"Is there something you needed me for?"

For a moment, her expression remained neutral. Then she tilted her head to acknowledge that the charade was no longer necessary. "There is something."

WE REACHED Burton's shop around mid-day. The American and his assistant went off to discuss business matters while Ming-fen brought me past the shelves filled with goods and into the store room. From there, a set of stairs led up to the attic.

The upper floor was divided into several rooms, most of which were used for storage. One of the compartments had been cleared out and furnished with a low bed and end table on which a gas lamp was set.

"The room must be sparse compared to what you're used to in Peking," Ming-fen remarked.

"This is fine," I replied, voice tight. "Not all Manchurians are wealthy." Nor all of Peking.

"My mistake," she said with the air of someone who didn't have time to dwell on small social quibbles.

I stowed my pack in the corner while Ming-fen picked up a woven basket from beside the bed. I followed her back down-stairs where she headed directly for the stock shelves. Burton and his assistant only paused briefly before returning to the stack of papers on the counter.

Curious, I came up beside Ming-fen as she breezed along the shelves, retrieving this item and that. She paused before a collection of bottles. I stared at the inscriptions, wishing once again I was able to read the writing.

"Do you know what this is?" Ming-fen asked, handing me a bottle with a paper label. I pulled the stopper to smell the contents. The mixture smelled of licorice root and camphor mixed with alcohol.

I relayed the contents to Ming-fen. "Probably used for stomach problems," I surmised.

"Western medicine," she murmured, slipping it into the basket.

She retrieved several other bottles before taking everything to the counter where she noted the contents from the basket onto a slip of paper. When she was done, she walked over to Burton.

"We're going to Ironware Alley," she told him, holding out the list.

He took a cursory glance at it before tucking the paper into his pocket. "Be careful, Miss Wei. It's getting dangerous out there."

"It's different for foreigners than for natives," she said off-hand.

We left the shop together and fell into a leisurely pace down the street.

"You have an interesting relationship with the two of them," I remarked.

"They're too comfortable here in Shanghai," she said. "As if they were its masters."

I wondered about what she'd said to Burton about where we were going and asked her about it.

"The lilong neighborhoods have sprouted up very quickly. All of the dwellings are stacked and pressed together, with families living on multiple levels on top of one another in narrow alleyways. You'll see."

Ironwork Alley was one such section that had been built up around a cluster of forges and metal shops.

"They specialize in shipbuilding parts and other machinery," Ming-fen explained.

"Is this a dangerous place?" I was armed with a needle gun which could fire an opium dart, though I was only able to load one at a time. There was also the bladed fan. Both had proved

JEANNIE LIN

useful in the past.

"Burton would think it's dangerous. Everyone there looks like us, which is frightening." Then she grew serious. "There are always interlopers and con men roving about, searching for the vulnerable. I had to chase away a charlatan just a few weeks ago."

"Chase away?"

I could imagine Wei Ming-fen driving off the riffraff with her scathing tongue, but I had a suspicion there was more to it.

We'd come to a cluttered and cramped area. I was reminded of the slums that had cropped up in Changsha as the surrounding villagers fled from the advancing rebel army. Changsha was the closest gated city to our village. I'd found my mother and brother squatting in an alleyway with other refugees during a siege.

Here, the inhabitants were packed into tiny dwellings that were stacked two or three levels high on either side of a passage. The alley was wide enough to allow Ming-fen and I to move through side-by-side. We passed by open doors that were shops and homes at once. A barber had set out a stool where he attended to a customer with a straight razor. Commerce spilled out into the streets as vendors set out baskets of goods.

A group of children ran up to us. I panicked, thinking they were here to mob us and pick our pockets, but Ming-fen fetched a tin from her basket and handed it to the oldest child, a girl of around seven years.

"Everyone gets one," she instructed.

The little girl nodded. Prying the lid open with small fingers, the girl began passing out thin, square biscuits to the tiny, up-stretched hands all around her.

Ming-fen continued on. I ducked under a line of hanging laundry to follow and saw her come to a halt midway down the lane. A well of heat wafted into the alley from the open door.

222

"Uncle Chu!" she called out, shouting to be heard above the pounding of metal on metal.

The hammering stopped. A muffled voice from inside relayed her greeting and, moments later, an elderly man in a leather apron stepped out into the street. He wore a thick set of goggles, which he pulled up, leaving a pale outline around his eyes.

"The physician is here."

The man looked over to me, blinking curiously. His was of medium height with arms that were thick with muscle.

"Yishi," he greeted. Then proceeded to describe his ailments. Swollen and stiff joints that made it difficult to move. An ache in his bones that wouldn't go away.

A younger man with a family resemblance appeared. The son, I presumed. He brought out a bench so the blacksmith could sit as I felt his pulse and examined his hands where the pain was worst. I listened carefully, asking questions about how long he'd experienced the symptoms and were there times when the pain lessened or worsened?

It was likely gout. A hot compress soaked with ginger root over his joints would help for the pain and I promised to return with my acupuncture needles. As soon as our consultation was done, the lady across the alley had a young child with a cough. The blacksmith's son brought out tea and more neighbors gathered. Ming-fen distributed the supplies she had brought and the mood took on almost a festival atmosphere.

In a few cases, I was able to dispense the Western medicines. Essence of willow bark came in small pills. There were various oils and ointments that, between Ming-fen's ability to read Yingyu and my knowledge of remedies, we were able to decipher the uses for. For the common ailments, I tried to prescribe household treatments. There was no herbal shop within the settlement where people could go to purchase hard-to-find ingredients.

I was reminded of the days back in our village when I was Physician Lo's assistant. I'd travel from one end of the village to the other, out to the farthest plot of farmland, addressing all of the day-to-day aches and pains. Villagers complained of too little energy or, occasionally, too much, leading to restlessness and anxiety. Eat melon soup, I'd suggest, if one needed to cool the blood. Chicken with ginseng for warming.

At the Factories, I'd had to put all of that aside. Instead of cultivating overall health, there were torn bodies to mend. Bruises and broken bones and pain. No thought toward internal balance and long-term well-being.

"It's good you came," Ming-fen said once the inhabitants of Ironware Alley had had all their ailments addressed. "A couple of weeks ago there was someone selling snake wine as a cure-all and aphrodisiac. Before that there was a man claiming to be a Taoist sorcerer."

The children had gathered on one side of the alley to play a made-up game with the empty biscuit tin. Though the crowd had dissipated, a feeling of brightness remained in the air. Laughter sounded down the lane. A stream of friendly chatter floated from the doorways. Ironware Alley bid us farewell in good spirits.

"Jie-jie," I said, meaning it this time. "You have a sharp tongue but a kind heart."

"It's force of habit," she denied curtly. "In Old Shanghai, there were so many groups and gangs and bullies. It was my elder brother who believed in protecting the weak."

"Your brother?"

"His name was Ren." A look of sadness flickered across her eyes. "I haven't seen him since Shanghai fell."

It was the first time I'd heard her mention a brother. I started to ask her more about him, but was interrupted by a young boy of around ten years running toward us. His long skinny legs bounded forward like a cricket's and he was out of breath when he came to a stop at my feet.

"Are you the yishi?" His slender face made his eyes appear especially large as he stared up at me.

"I am," I replied.

"Please come!"

We followed him as he hurried out of Ironware Alley into another narrow lane several streets away.

"It's my father, Yishi," the boy said, pushing forward while checking back over his shoulder to make sure we were following. "My mother told me to go get you when she heard there was a physician who had come by."

Word traveled quickly through the lilong neighborhoods.

He brought me to a closed door. A heavy lock had been placed onto it.

"Is this where you live?"

"My father is inside. Mother had the lock attached two days ago," the boy explained.

Suddenly something crashed against the door from the other side. I jumped back, startled.

A wail came from down the alley. "He's gone mad. His mind is gone."

A middle-aged woman appeared. She pushed the hair away from her eyes, revealing dark circles beneath them. "We haven't been able to go inside. Does it look like mad dog sickness?"

A heavy weight thudded against the inside of the doors again, rattling the iron lock.

I backed a few steps away. "Was your husband bitten recently by a stray dog or any animal?"

"No," she insisted. "Never."

I'd seen something like this before. In Changsha, they had locked people who had become enraged due to an infection. Not knowing any better, the physicians had also diagnosed the condition as mad dog sickness.

"Does your husband use opium?" I asked the woman.

I could smell an opium pipe nearby. It was a deceptively sweet burn, like sugar left on the stove too long. I'd grown up with that smell in our house. I knew the moment Ming-fen recognized it as well. Her gaze moved to a shadowy doorway two hovels down.

Of course, there was opium in the lilong alleyways. Shanghai was the drug's primary gateway into the empire.

The woman started crying when there was another crash against the door, stronger than the last. And then another, as if an enraged animal was trapped on the other side. She forced an answer through her sobs.

"My husband smokes. He was trying to stop."

CHAPTER 21

There wasn't much that could be done for the man. His wife spoke of his addiction, the withdrawal symptoms he suffered whenever he tried to quit. The tremors, the sweats.

Hearing the woman's descriptions brought back those nights at our small house in Linhua where the walls were thin and I could hear my mother's every moan and cry. Tian would open a book and stare fixedly at the page, trying to distract himself from the wailing that came from the next room.

The rattle of the lock brought me back to the present. Missionaries had come to the lane the week before. They were foreigners who brought teachings of the Western God, the same God that the Taipings worshiped. They'd offered food and prayer.

Her husband had fallen into a deep sleep after the visit. He'd slept for a long time and when he woke up, something sinister had taken hold of him.

I told them to leave food and water and not open the door. I promised to come back in a few days to check on him, though I didn't know what I could do. This condition was beyond my experience.

The next day brought a visit to another neighborhood, called Seawall Alley due to its location by the river. Ming-fen appeared well-known there as well. She brought gossip from other neighborhoods, news about the workings of the foreign-run Municipal Council. Someone asked about the Old City and she grew quiet.

"No news from the old neighborhood," she murmured.

A municipal police patrol passed by while Ming-fen and I were sharing fried dumplings stuffed with fermented beans from a street seller. A momentary hush fell over the alley at the sight of the pale-skinned foreigners. Ming-fen leaned against the wall, tracking the patrol with her eyes.

"Those men aren't here to protect us," she remarked once the patrol had moved on. "The longer Old Shanghai remains under rebel control, the more powerful the foreign settlement becomes. Not that I particularly liked Taotai Wu's adminis-tration."

"It's a matter of balance," I conceded.

Ming-fen nodded slowly. "Balance."

"Did your brother help maintain balance?"

She hesitated before answering. "Ren always had such a strong sense of justice." Her face took on a wistful expression, just as it had the first time she'd mentioned him. "When our father and mother disappeared, I was taken in by the missionar-ies, but Ren was left on his own. He was too old for the orphan-age, too young to take care of a little sister. It was years before I would see him again. He came to the school, said he was family. They refused to let me go with him, vagabond that he was. So, I climbed out of the window in the middle of the night to join him."

"Is he still in Old Shanghai?" I asked.

She was taken aback by the question.

"You said you hadn't seen him since the city fell," I pressed. "I thought that meant you must have been together before it did."

"He's behind those walls now, I'm certain of it."

"Could you get a message to him? To let him know you're alright."

Her lips quirked. "It's complicated. There is more than a city wall between us."

Ming-fen had some business that afternoon to attend to with Burton and I had some supplies to deliver to the warehouse. I hailed a rickshaw and was surprised to see I recognized the puller from nearby Ironware Alley. We were able to exchange some minor gossip and I offered to bring him an ointment to help with his sore muscles the next time I came by.

That was when I thought of the opium addict who had been boarded up a few lanes away. There had been nothing I could offer to the poor family. They had cut a hole in the door to provide food and water, but the man was senseless and snarling when I'd tried to peer inside. His tongue was as black as ink.

The wife was unaware of whether he'd taken any opium cessation pills. There were no dispensaries that anyone knew of in the foreign concession or in Old Shanghai. Could it be possible the missionaries had brought him something thinking to help?

If this sickness was somehow connected to the cessation pills, then the cure was worse than the disease. I prayed my letter would reach my mother quickly to warn her.

The rickshaw reached the warehouse district by the wharf and the puller offered to wait so he could take me back. I rang the bell at the front door and it took some time before the door opened. Kai's face brightened when he saw me. His hands were stained with grease.

"Engineer Chen is putting you to work," I said.

"It's not so different from bone-setting," he said cheerfully.

Assembling the automatons involved connecting sockets and

joints and artificial limbs. If his bone-setting knowledge was of use, then all the better. The main warehouse floor was empty, which meant everyone was working underground. Kai held the trapdoor open and I tucked the delivery bundle beneath my arm before descending the stairs.

The hidden basement was far from empty now. The line was running in full force with workmen assigned to different stations. There were automatons in various states of assembly. Chang-wei walked among the stations to inspect the work. As soon as he saw me, he broke away.

"Soling."

From the distant look in his eyes, I could see his mind was still focused on his work, but I was accustomed to that. We retreated to the corner for some semblance of privacy.

"I have the supplies you needed," I began.

"You smell like camphor."

"Oh, that must be from...uh...muscle ointment," I explained, blushing. I didn't realize I smelled like a medicine cabinet.

"I don't mind it." His hand brushed mine as he took the wrapped bundle.

I froze as I looked over his shoulder. Standing there was one of the fully assembled automatons, the empty void of its face staring into nothingness. I didn't know if they would look more eerie with a face or not, but the sight of it looming over us, almost human, sent a shiver through me. The last time I'd seen one moving, it was rampaging in the citadel. It had crushed the skull of one of Chang-wei's engineers as if he were made of paper.

"Let's go upstairs," Chang-wei suggested, sensing my discomfort.

We went to the office where Chang-wei unwrapped the delivery. There was a mass of copper wire wrapped as delicately as if it were silk lace among various other boxes and tins.

Chang-wei's eyes darted to a tin decorated with blue flowers. His face brightened as he reached for it.

"It's been years," he said, prying off the lid to reveal a row of small golden-brown parcels wrapped in waxed paper.

"Is it candy?"

He nodded and held one out to me. I squeezed the parcel between my fingers. "What is it made of?"

"Cooked sugar." He thought for a moment. "And cream. It's called 'toffee.'"

I unwrapped the paper and took a bite. The candy was hard and sticky and incredibly sugary. Chang-wei popped the entire morsel into his mouth.

"It's good, isn't it?" he said, his words garbled.

I nodded gamely. My teeth were stuck together.

I was surprised when he dug back into the tin, but it wasn't to grab another candy. Chang-wei fished around until he pulled a paper out from the bottom. Instead of hiding away, he opened it in front of me. My chest swelled just a little. Chang-wei at least trusted me in this.

He moved the toffee to the other side of his mouth, sucking on it as he read the communication.

"From Taotai Wu," he said, his gaze still fixed on the note. "Can you get a map of Shanghai?"

I nodded. So, I was to be a go-between. Chang-wei didn't say anything else about what was on the paper, but we stayed together for a little longer as I recounted my trip to alley neighborhoods with Wei Ming-fen. I told him about the afflicted man who'd been shut away. Chang-wei hadn't seen as much of the mysterious opium disease as I'd had, but we'd been attacked once by a man suffering from that same sickness. He'd gone mad, tearing out someone's throat with his teeth before he was shot.

"This is why we have to win this war quickly against the

rebels," he said, jaw tight. "So we can address these other problems."

The scourge of opium. Losing our land to foreign devils. But the rebels weren't a single force, a single beast to be slain. There were so many factions who hated the Emperor and the Qing government and they would keep on coming for us.

"Have you learned anything more about the mysterious Miss Wei?" he asked.

"Everyone does know her. She seems to be a do-gooder."

"Like you," Chang-wei said softly. He reached out to smooth a strand of hair away from my face. It was enough to warm my skin to the very fingertips.

I didn't think of myself in such a way. Everything I'd ever done was to protect myself and the people I loved. I regarded Chang-wei now, looking silly with the candy bulging beneath his cheek, and realized he was one of those people. I loved him and wanted to be his wife.

Rationally and irrationally.

I WENT from the warehouse back to Ironware Alley. The rickshaw puller tried to refuse payment, but I insisted. We went back and forth the required number of times before he humbly accepted.

I'd brought my needles this time and went to call on the elderly blacksmith at his forge. He was grateful to see me and kept a steady expression, even though I could see how his hands were stiffer today than they'd been even the day before.

They allowed me into the narrow kitchen area to prepare the heated compress. I applied it to his arm outside, seated on the bench, with the heat of the furnaces at our backs. His son once again brought tea and we drank it while I waited for his muscles and joints to relax and loosen. Then I opened my case and started setting the needles into pressure points along his wrist and arm.

"Been working metal since I was a little boy," the blacksmith said. "Probably won't be able to much longer with these old hands. Do you know I fitted parts into the first steamships that came to dock here?"

"A long time ago," I murmured, focusing on the Waiguan pulse point at the left wrist. The needles were wire-thin, barely visible and produced hardly any physical sensation when inserted into the skin.

"Fifteen years. A long time ago," he echoed. "The Yangguizi, they're not so bad."

I bit back a smile. If they weren't so bad, I suppose he only called them foreign devils because everyone else did.

"Eastern. Western. What does it matter? Ships come and go. People come and go. Life goes on."

I treated both of his arms and left the needles to give time for the points to enervate and open. It was the end of the double-hour by the time I removed the needles. The sun had started to lower in the sky and it was time for me to return to Burton's shop.

After bidding farewell to the blacksmith and his sons, I remembered the wretched man whose family had locked him in not so far from here. There was enough time to check on him before sunset.

The walk there took less than half an hour and I felt accomplished being able to navigate the settlement so well on my own. As I approached the dwelling, I saw the son out in the alley.

"How is your father?" I inquired.

At first, I thought he didn't remember me. He regarded me fearfully before mumbling his response. "He's gone."

"Gone?"

He started toward the door. Just yesterday, his father had been locked inside, throwing his full weight against it as if deranged. Now the boy was able to open the door without incident.

"Where did your father go?"

The boy slipped inside as I moved toward him. "They came and took him," he said before pulling the door shut.

They?

Bewildered, I looked up and down the alley searching for someone who could answer questions. No one was about. I wandered to an open doorway, but no one came when I called. As luck would have it, I noticed movement at the end of the lane and decided to see if it was someone who could help. I went down there just in time to see Wei Ming-fen disappearing into a dark entranceway.

As I came near, I could smell the smoky perfume of burning incense. There was a shrine with a raised altar inside. Ming-fen stood before it, head bowed, three joss sticks of incense set between her fingers. Wisps of smoke rose from the smoldering sticks, and through the haze I could see a painting of a lotus flower on the wall.

The lotus was a sign commonly used by the followers of the enlightened Buddha. In the center of the petals was a circular design with a center hub and spokes radiating outward. I went shock-still, blinking at it.

It was the same design Little Guo had worn. The dharma wheel, a symbol representing the wheel of time.

Backing away, I stood in the alley and waited for Ming-fen to complete her prayer. A startled expression crossed her face when she saw me, but she composed herself quickly before coming forward.

"Mei-mei—"

I didn't have the patience for niceties at the moment. "Are you White Lotus?"

She turned and kept walking, her head high. "You make it sound like an accusation."

It *was* an accusation. "Gatherings of the White Lotus sect are outlawed."

"The Qing call anyone they don't like White Lotus."

Ming-fen pulled ahead and I watched as she left the narrow lane toward the main road. I considered leaving her and returning to the warehouse to tell Chang-wei of this, but what did I know really? I hurried to catch up with her.

"But you are White Lotus, aren't you?" I asked, in a calmer tone.

"If that's what you want to call it."

I knew a few details about the followers of the White Lotus. It was a Buddhist sect that worshiped a goddess they called the Eternal Mother. That in itself sounded harmless enough, but the White Lotus Society had its roots in rebellion. Long ago, the White Lotus sect had fought against the Mongols and the Yuan. Now the sect continued to oppose the Manchu and the Qing.

There had been an armed rebellion organized by the White Lotus Society about fifty years ago. After the sect was defeated, it had gone underground.

"You were sent to spy on us," I accused.

"*Sent,*" Ming-fen scoffed. "There's no dark shadowy overlord plotting to overthrow the Emperor. No one sent me to do anything."

"Then what is your business here?"

She stopped and turned to face me. "Mei-mei, we should find a more private place to talk."

"Like your secret shrine, Jie-jie?"

Her lips twitched. I wished Ming-fen wasn't so much taller than me. She gazed down at me now and, though neither of us wavered, she maintained the advantage.

"There are more opium dens in Shanghai than White Lotus shrines."

"What does that have to do with anything?"

"The White Lotus isn't what the Emperor needs to worry

about. Between the Small Swords and the Taiping, there are much more dangerous enemies."

I wasn't convinced. Jiang Wen and Little Guo had infiltrated the Five Factories to cause death and destruction. Weren't they also White Lotus?

We had reached the street that led to Burton's mercantile. Ming-fen sensed my hesitation.

"Whatever you may think of the White Lotus sect, I'm alone in the foreign settlement, cut off from my people in Old Shang-hai. We aren't an army with marching orders, Mei-mei."

"Your goals are fundamentally opposed to ours."

"And what are my goals?" she asked lightly. "What are yours?"

When I didn't answer, her tone shifted, becoming serious. "I think what I want is probably not so different from what you want. Come back to the store so we can speak in private. I swear on my family that no harm will come to you."

If I reported to Chang-wei that we had a spy in our midst, we would need to restrain Ming-fen somehow. We'd likely lose our ties to Burton and the entire mission would be in jeopardy. It was too much to risk on the slightest suspicion. I had to be certain of who she was.

"I know you have knives hidden beneath your sleeves," I told her.

I'd observed Ming-fen carefully the last time we'd been out together. She wore loose sleeves and kept her arms covered. It was more than just a sharp tongue that kept the charlatans and con men away.

"You have a poison dart gun," she replied casually. "And a bladed fan hidden on you. Come up for tea."

THE STORE HAD CLOSED, but Mister Lawrence remained inside straightening up and sweeping after the day's work. Ming-fen passed by him wordlessly on the way to the stairs while I bid him a hello, as it was one of the few things I knew to say.

Once upstairs, Ming-fen prepared tea and poured the steaming water into blue and white cups decorated with an elaborate pagoda design. "This style of porcelain is in high demand with foreigners," she explained.

We retreated to her room which had become my room as well.

"Jie-jie," I began.

"Mei-mei." She drank her tea slowly, regarding me over the rim.

"What is it you want from me?"

"Do you have family?"

I tensed. "I do."

"And you'd do anything to protect them?"

I didn't answer. For the last few days, Ming-fen had taken me around the settlement, making an effort to get close to me.

"My mother and father were imprisoned when I was very young," she revealed. "The Qing condemned them as rebels and marched them away, leaving me and my brother to fend for ourselves."

"Is that why you joined the White Lotus?" I asked carefully.

"The White Lotus has existed in some form for hundreds of years. One doesn't join, one just is through upbringing or circumstance. It's how we gather together and survive. It's not my aim to overthrow the Great Qing, if that's what you're worried about. What I want is the same thing you want."

"What do I want?"

"To protect the ones you love."

I hadn't told her anything about Tian or Mother, but I didn't have to. She was right that we both had people close to us we wanted to keep safe.

"I've known for a long time that Chen Chang-wei is a government agent. I know he's here to retake the Old City. I won't interfere with his plans," she said quickly. "In fact, I hope he does succeed in breaching the defensive wall."

Burton had said Ming-fen was dangerous in his half-joking manner, but he trusted her. On the other hand, I hardly trusted Burton.

"You have reason to resent the Qing government," I pointed out. "They tore your family apart."

A dull pang rose in my chest. In a way, hadn't the same thing happened to my family?

"I don't believe in revenge," Ming-fen said flatly. "And it was the Small Swords who tore my family apart."

I listened as she recounted the story of her brother and how they'd reunited when he came to find her at the mission. They had searched Shanghai and the surrounding areas in hopes of finding their parents.

"In Shanghai, everyone belongs to some sect or gang. The different factions tried for a long time to recruit my brother because he was trained in White Lotus fighting techniques. He'd gained a reputation as a street brawler. When the gangs came by the neighborhood to extort protection money, he was the one who chased them away."

I wondered whether she was deliberately leaving herself out of the story. Ming-fen also had a reputation for being a protector in the lilong neighborhoods.

"Ren is the only family I have left." Her voice grew quiet as it always did when she spoke of her brother. "On the day of the Small Swords uprising, Ren cut his hair and joined them. Work had been hard to come by and we'd gone for so long without any news of our mother and father. I think he'd come to the decision that they were truly gone and this was the only way to avenge them."

"How can you say, after all that's happened to your family, that you hope the Qing take back Shanghai?"

She claimed to be above vengeance, but it was clear we were on opposing sides. If one could even draw clear lines through it. I was Manchu. And Qing. My orders came ultimately from our Emperor.

Ming-fen glanced at me, her eyes hardening. "There is only one thing I want and that is to reach my brother. Just tell me when and where Taotai Wu is planning to attack the Old City. If the loyalists manage to breach the walls, then I should be able to get myself inside as well."

"How can you possibly do that?"

She stared back at me, unflinching, and I had no choice but to believe she could.

"If I can see my brother," she continued. "If I can just speak to him, I'll have one last chance to pull him away from the Small Swords."

This was preposterous. The plan wasn't yet established and, once it was, there was no way Chang-wei would give up that information to an outsider.

"I don't have any control over the assault," I replied neutrally.

"I think you can be very persuasive," she insisted. "And I think you understand that there's more at play here than red army versus green across a game board."

For once, Wei Ming-fen didn't sound haughty or overbearing. She seemed earnest, but I still didn't know if she could be trusted.

"With your past, with your feelings about the Qing government, why did you help Taotai Wu escape during the uprising?" I asked.

She looked surprised at the question. "To save a life."

"That's not what the White Lotus believes," I argued.

"It is."

"White Lotus rebels infiltrated the factory where I was

appointed. They sabotaged the facilities, set explosives that caused so many deaths."

Ming-fen grew quiet, considering everything I'd told her.

"I'm not those men," she said quietly. "They're not like me, but I know who you're talking about. They've come to Shanghai and I can lead you to them."

CHAPTER 22

Several days later, Ming-fen woke me in the middle of the night. I was still dressed — I'd been expecting something to happen this night, but it was still disorienting to be roused awake in the dark. We slipped out onto the empty street under the faint light of a crescent moon.

After some deliberation, I had decided to remain with Ming-fen in the rooms above the mercantile. Chang-wei and I agreed it was good to keep her close. If the information she'd promised us was merely a ploy, a lure, then it was a good one.

Ming-fen held a lantern with the light dimmed as we moved down the road. It was late enough that even Shanghai's night crowd had quieted. We went forth on foot toward what was supposed to be a secret meeting place.

There was a chill in the night air and I pulled the edges of the coat tighter around me. It was from Burton's inventory made of wool in the Western style. I was unaccustomed to the large buttons used to fasten it.

Halfway down the road, Ming-fen suddenly stopped. "Your beloved is following us."

Butterflies fluttered inside my stomach. At the same time, an embarrassed protest came to my lips and my cheeks burned. I was supposed to deny that he was my beloved, right?

None of that mattered. Ming-fen produced a small knife from somewhere and stood with it poised between two fingers, ready to throw.

"I told him not to come," I protested, then called out to him in the darkness.

Chang-wei emerged from a side lane wearing dark clothing with a black scarf wrapped over the lower half of his face. He unwound it as he approached.

"You're a dangerous woman, Wei Ming-fen. I couldn't let Soling go alone."

"I am dangerous," Ming-fen agreed lightly, tucking the tiny blade back into its sheath, which was hidden in the comb in her hair. "I intended to take Soling and only Soling to the meeting place."

"I have no interest in chasing down every member of the White Lotus," Chang-wei said. "I only came to find the men responsible for the sabotage."

Jiang Wen and Little Guo had managed to escape from Hubei and come to Shanghai.

"We need to go quickly," Ming-fen said, coming to a decision. "Before the meeting is over."

Chang-wei remained close to me as we traveled. Ming-fen took us through a maze of streets, down another alleyway, then to a structure on the corner that was larger than the usual lane house. There was an old buckled gate at the front and a stone pathway overgrown with weeds that led to the gathering place.

Ming-fen turned to us. "Nothing happens here tonight," she warned.

Chang-wei nodded grimly. His hand moved inside his jacket to rest at the line of his belt. We were not to take any action here. By waiting, we risked giving the perpetrators time to escape, but we had given Ming-fen our word. Still, Chang-wei had come armed as a precaution.

The building was dark and we stepped quietly through the gate. I could see light peeking through the slits in the doorway. As we moved closer, the faint scent of sandalwood and resin hung in the air. Muffled voices came from inside.

We followed Ming-fen to the side of the shrine room. A shard of light seeped through a window that had been boarded up. Chang-wei directed me toward the opening. At the Factories, I'd had the most contact with Jiang and Guo and would know them on sight.

There were about seven or eight individuals packed inside the shrine room, meeting by lantern light. I searched the assembly looking for a familiar face. I didn't recognize anyone. Part of me was relieved, but one person remained turned away with his face hidden from view. From the set of his stance and those broad shoulders—

All breath left me and I went completely still. Chang-wei sensed the change in me and moved in to take a look. I stepped aside with my heart pounding. I knew who that was. I prayed I was wrong, but I was certain without ever seeing his face.

Chang-wei recognized him as well. He looked at me for confirmation and I nodded, my hands clenching into fists.

His size. The towering height. It couldn't be anyone else but Kai.

TAOTAI WU CAME to the warehouse the next day with his brigade to apprehend Kai. I stood at the back of the room and Chang-wei looked on impassively as armed men entered the building.

I'd wanted to be there, but had said nothing to Kai that morning. It was hard for me to even look at him. I think Kai knew something was wrong because I was so distant, but he didn't try to run. He didn't even fight as they clamped iron manacles onto his wrists. He glanced back once at me before the men dragged him away.

"Yishi Jin," he said heavily and my throat constricted as I held back tears.

I half-hoped he would plead his innocence. Or, like Ming-fen had done, claim to be a religious follower of the Eternal Mother while not being part of the rebellion. He did none of that. Kai hung his head as he was marched toward the doors to the wagon outside. He stood head and shoulders above the brigade, but they outnumbered him. They were ready to shoot if he tried to escape.

"Where are you taking him?" I asked Taotai Wu.

He looked down his nose at me. His men weren't part of the municipal police force or constables of the Shanghai circuit. They were imperial loyalists, recruited by Wu, and disconnected from any source of authority other than brute force. Though he was still circuit intendant, Wu had no true authority in the foreign concession. All he had was the vague expectation that one day he would be restored to his appointed seat. It was enough to grant him a small measure of power.

It was enough power that Wu didn't feel obligated to give me an answer.

"We'll find out what this scum has revealed," Wu said, addressing only Chang-wei.

"What of the others?" Chang-wei indicated the other workmen that Wu had provided. They had come from all over, within the city as well as from outside. Any one of them could be a rebel.

"My people have been thoroughly scrutinized," Wu replied sharply, implying that ours weren't. "Pray that he hasn't revealed too much and our mission hasn't been compromised."

"We must assume that it is compromised," Chang-wei

warned. "We have to terminate the mission. Reassess—"

"That is not an option," Wu said sharply. "Be ready to proceed on my word."

He turned to leave. Only when the wagon was gone did I find my voice.

"They're going to interrogate him," I said weakly, my skin going cold. Interrogation meant torture. Kai was so strong, he would resist, which would only make it worse.

"He betrayed us, Soling. He was allowed all over the Five Factories. He was brought into the citadel and was able to convey the layout to his cronies."

I'd thought of Kai as my friend from the first time we'd met. He'd set bones and closed wounds. We had cared for the injured together. I tried to tell myself it was all a cover, but I couldn't forget how Kai had knelt over me on the deck of the war junk, with cannon and rifle fire all around us. He'd shielded me with his body without a thought.

And yet there was nothing I could do to help him now.

"Your mother was in that room when the explosive went off," Chang-wei reminded me grimly.

I nodded, feeling sick. "How can Taotai Wu continue? You have to assume the rebels know you're coming."

"Wu isn't risking his men," Chang-wei pointed out. "That was the advantage of our approach. We're only sacrificing heavy machinery. The loyalists will form their own assault once we've distracted the Small Swords. Taotai Wu will want to move even sooner now."

"What about Wei Ming-fen?" She was back at the mercantile, waiting for the aftermath of this morning's capture.

"We can't inform her of our plan. It would be too dangerous for us. And for her."

He was right, but we owed Ming-fen something. "She just wants to find her brother."

"Wei Ming-fen is not your friend," Chang-wei insisted.

"She's not on our side. She provided a potentially useful warning, or maybe she didn't. Maybe she wanted you to trust her and Kai was an easy sacrifice. It's best you have as little contact with her as possible. I've asked Burton to allow you to stay at his home until—" He paused, struggling for words. "Until this business is done."

Did it make it easier for him to think of it as just that? Business? Not a dangerous mission where he would be risking his life at the whim of the imperial court?

"You want me to stay with Burton?" I asked, incredulous.

"I want you to be somewhere safe and I don't trust Wei Ming-fen."

"But you trust the foreigner? He's more mercenary than businessman."

Chang-wei didn't have an answer for that.

"It won't be for long," he promised finally, which meant the attack would happen soon.

"Be careful, Chang-wei. Kai knows everything about the operation. You have to assume the rebels know everything too."

"Not everything," he replied cryptically.

DEAN BURTON DIDN'T LIVE in a house. He lived in a mansion the size of four houses. There was a footman, one of my countrymen, to open the door and an auntie of a housekeeper who sniffed when she saw me.

"So, it's true what they say," she said with a dour expression as she led me up the stairs. "This one he actually brings home."

The master of the house was nowhere to be seen and I was relieved. I didn't like the idea of imposing upon a stranger. Chang-wei seemed to think of Burton as a friend, while I still considered him an outsider. He was a foreigner, though, given the look of his business, this house, his connections — he had evidently made himself more welcome and comfortable in Shanghai than any of the native inhabitants. I looked around and around at the place, which was made up of large, expansive rooms with a handful of servants to tend to them.

And then there was me.

The housekeeper deposited me in a bedroom that was the closest to the stairs. The bed was higher than any I'd ever seen and the pillows looked like sewn sacks rather than the headrests I was accustomed to. Disbelieving, I sank my hand into one. It was soft, stuffed with feathers.

"Mister Burton is rich," I remarked. I'd been told he was a successful trader, but this was beyond the wealth of noblemen. Of aristocracy who'd owned land and kept it for generations.

The housekeeper sniffed again. "You must have known that before agreeing to this arrangement."

"I'm not his mistress," I said with a sigh, knowing I wouldn't be believed.

Did our customs even matter anymore? Shanghai had a way of shifting and subverting such morals. As did the upheaval of rebellion.

The housekeeper looked me up and down. "What are you then?" she asked, deciding that I indeed didn't look like any mistress.

"I'm a physician," I told her off-hand.

She had nothing more to say to that and left me to get settled in. I couldn't really be comfortable. My thoughts were consumed by Kai being held in chains while interrogators beat a confession out of him. And Chang-wei preparing to lead a contingent of machines into battle. Machines that could just as easily turn on him.

All of this was happening in the same city where I sat on a soft bed, walled away from any danger. I could see why it was so easy for the Westerners to claim neutrality. To turn and look the other way.

Dinner was brought to me on a lacquered tray. It was a salty dish of chicken and stir-fried bamboo with a bowl of steamed rice along with a pot of tea. I couldn't tell what region the dish had come from by the flavors. It was a non-descript meal with no time and place but Shanghai.

Afterward, I wandered to the library, but was disappointed to find that the books were in Yingyu. I browsed them anyway, searching for one that might at least have interesting pictures. While I was in there, the doorman and another servant came through to shutter all the windows and lock them.

"Is something the matter?" I asked.

"Routine, miss," the doorman answered, but I caught him speaking in lowered tones to the other servant.

I was in an odd place here, not mistress, not servant. Not the usual guest either, I supposed. I waited for Burton to return so I could inquire about what was happening outside, but he never arrived.

In the end, I retired to the guest room, my head sinking into the cloud soft pillows. I vowed to meet with Chang-wei tomorrow and ask about Kai. The bone-setter and I had worked side-by-side for nearly a year. Even if he hadn't been honest with me, we owed something to one another. I felt wretched for leaving him to the mercy of Taotai Wu and his men, even if he had revealed our secrets to the rebels.

I turned my head and the mound of feathers nearly smothered me. Tossing about, I changed positions but couldn't get comfortable. Kai must have had his reasons. Yang Hanzhu had his reasons to reject the Qing. I had my reasons to stay. We all had our reasons — even if they were all half-broken and poorly mended.

Finally, I fell asleep thinking of red and green armies.

I'd barely dozed off when I heard knocking. Startled, I opened my eyes to moonlight and a figure outside the window.

"*Mei-mei.*"

I jolted up, fully awake. "Jie-jie?"

Ming-fen tapped against the glass. "Open up."

I thought I had shuttered the window. I thought I had locked it. I turned up the gas lamp. "How did you get up here?"

She gave me a look and waved the question away. "I need to talk to you."

Still in shock, I reached for the window then paused, thinking of Chang-wei's warning. Wei Ming-fen was dangerous, but there wasn't a person here who wasn't dangerous. I didn't fear Ming-fen more than I feared Dean Burton or Taotai Wu.

As soon as I unlatched the window, Ming-fen climbed inside. She was dressed in the same tunic and trousers I'd first seen her in, the dark color blending in with the night.

"The big man, Kai, he's escaped," she reported.

"How?"

"The White Lotus. They freed him."

Part of me was relieved, but then I realized what it meant. "Are we in danger?" I asked.

"There are not enough members of the sect in the foreign settlement to be a threat, but they'll interfere with your advance on the Old City."

"I don't know when the attack is supposed to happen. Chang-wei is keeping the plan secret from me," I told her apologetically.

"I already know. It's this morning."

I stared at her. "Now?"

Behind her, the moon was lower in the sky than I originally had thought. I hadn't realized how close it was to morning.

"How do you know?"

"I know because the street knows. I know because the gutter knows," she replied urgently. "The Small Swords will know as well. It's a trap."

CHAPTER 23

We went to the carriage house where Ming-fen had me hold up the gas lamp while she fiddled the controls on the steam car.

"Do you know how to operate this?" I asked, directing the light back to Ming-fen.

"Easy enough. Water here. Coal here. If we wreck it, he has others."

A sweep of the room with the lamp revealed a collection of transports. Ming-fen seemed rather callous with Burton's property. I questioned whether the municipal police might consider this act stealing if they stopped us. Ming-fen had connections among Shanghai natives, but I doubted the Westerners would allow her such leeway.

"You would be surprised what one can get away with by speaking their language," was her reply.

I helped her open the doors and crank up the engine. Then we jumped in and were away.

"Fastest way is by water," she said.

The car picked up speed as steam gathered inside the boiler.

Soon I could feel the wind whipping over my face as the car rolled down the road.

"That's how I knew the garrison was moving. Activity down by the river is impossible to hide. They tried smuggling troops into large crates in the middle of the night. Those men must have stayed out on the water for hours before the boats set sail."

Garrison. Troops. Ming-fen was under the impression that we were smuggling Qing loyalists through the concession to march on the Old City.

"It's not a garrison inside those crates," I told her.

"Then what's inside?"

"Machines. Killing machines."

She paused, trying to process the new information. "Who's operating the machines?"

"No one."

Ming-fen frowned, not quite understanding. "Taotai Wu must be moving his forces at the same time," she continued, looking to me for confirmation.

I nodded slowly. For better or worse, I was in this with Ming-fen now.

"Are you sure you want to do this?" she asked as we neared the waterfront. It was a tributary which would eventually connect to the main part of the river.

"I need to warn Chang-wei. Are *you* sure you want to do this?"

She looked straight ahead. "I need to find my brother."

A skiff awaited in the water tied to a mooring. Ming-fen had carefully planned this run on the Old City. I had the disturbing sense that she was burning bridges behind us to get to her brother. Our only way lay forward.

We abandoned the steam car on the bank. Maybe Burton would recover it, maybe he wouldn't. Ming-fen was unconcerned.

"You know all of this has little to do with the likes of Burton," she said. "This business of cities falling, rebellion, and upheaval. He just sits back and profits, protected by rules that won't protect us."

The gunpowder engine on the skiff started with a few taps. The sky was beginning to lighten as we roared through the water. I hoped we were fast enough to reach the advance team. According to Ming-fen, they had launched hours ago on Taotai Wu's ships. We were smaller, faster — and we weren't relying on stealth.

"Tell me about these killing machines," Ming-fen said as she held the rudder steady, steering the boat through the waters.

I could have remained silent and kept what I knew secret, but the time for that was past. Ming-fen obviously wasn't in league with the Small Swords or even the faction of the White Lotus that had tried to sabotage us from the beginning. She was acting alone as I was.

"They're automatons. Like metal puppets," I began, though immediately knew how unfitting that description was. It had me thinking of traveling shows and dolls on strings. "Like walking warriors," I amended. "Suits of armor without anyone in them, capable of smashing and destroying."

"Mindless," Ming-fen murmured, contemplating what I had described. "Without fear. Without pain."

And they couldn't be reasoned with. Chang-wei could unleash a horde of the machines to break through the east wall, but once through, how would he keep them from rampaging through the city?

Maybe he never intended to, I realized with a chill down my spine. Maybe all the automatons were ever meant to do was stoke fear and destroy.

∼

"CHANG-WEI ISN'T BAD AT HEART."

It had been a while since we'd spoken. The skiff was speeding through the water toward the city and I was counting the seconds, hoping we weren't too late.

"He isn't vengeful. Or hungry for power. He just thinks—" I paused, trying to find the words to explain to her. "He thinks he can somehow engineer a solution that doesn't involve bloodshed and violence."

As if there was a way to cleanly design and plan and engineer a way out of this war.

"My brother isn't bad either," Ming-fen replied sadly. "He's come to the conclusion that bloodshed is the only solution."

The sun had risen by the time the warning gongs started to sound. The clanging came from the Old City and the sound carried far beyond the walls in the quiet morning.

I sat up straight in the skiff. "It's the assault on the East Gate."

We were still on the water, skimming past the docks that served the concession. As we neared Old Shanghai, the riverfront was in disarray. The sounding of the alarm had thrown what port authority remained into high alert. Ships were leaving port lest they be caught up in the attack.

"The waterway will take us directly to the city," Ming-fen shouted over the roar of the engine.

I could see the defensive wall now. The structure rose high, built of brick and stone, and was fortified by guard towers. The barrier circled the Old City, sheltering neighborhoods and the administrative center of Shanghai. The rebels had remained entrenched inside for over a year.

There was frantic activity up in the towers and then I saw where Chang-wei had breached the walls.

"They went through the smaller eastern gate," Ming-fen said. "It's less heavily guarded."

The heavy wooden gate had been broken down. Ming-fen moored the boat and we set foot on the bank at a run. There were bodies strewn just inside the gate and the battlements above had been abandoned. Another alarm sounded as we neared.

"The main assault," I muttered.

It would be a larger force led by the imperialist army camped outside the city. The rebels would have to divide their already thin defenses across two fronts.

"Heaven and Earth." Ming-fen stood over a metal carcass strewn beside the wall. It was an armored giant that had been mangled and heavily damaged. The helmet stared upward with its vacant eye socket. An arm had been torn off, exposing the tangle of wires inside. There was a large hole in the torso and the breastplate was warped outward as if something had blasted through the automaton.

I stared at the ruined gate. "The explosion came from inside the machine."

The scorch marks were unmistakable. Chang-wei's engineers had rigged the automatons with explosives, turning the machines into walking bombs.

Ming-fen unwound her sash revealing two daggers attached to it which she slipped into her hands. The sash connected the blades together. It was an unusual weapon, but Ming-fen seemed to know what to do with it. She wrapped the length of silk around her hand before walked toward the gate.

Warily, we crossed the threshold into the Old City. The area inside the wall was oddly deserted. Remnants of the defending force could be seen strewn about the road. Any surviving souls had fled.

I steeled myself against the sight of the dead. They lay in odd positions. Thrown. Crushed. A wave of nausea hit me and I faltered.

Ming-fen reached out to put a hand on my shoulder. The dizziness passed and I nodded gratefully at her.

Another fallen automaton lay among the rubble and carnage.

The metal frame looked surreal among the flesh and bone bodies. There was something wrong about it, the cold, sharp killing machine that looked human, but wasn't.

Something moved beside the machine. It was a person, injured. Unable to hold back, I went to him and my pulse thumped when I recognized him.

Little Guo looked up at me with blood pouring down the side of his face. He was trying to crawl out from underneath the metal hull.

"Yishi Jin?"

He was just as startled to see me. When I'd last seen him, Guo was recovering in the dormitory at the Five Factories. His leg had been amputated. I looked down now to see that it was a mechanical leg that had been trapped beneath the automaton.

It was much as it had been the first time we'd met when he was trapped beneath the wreckage of the factory explosion. An explosion that now I understood he'd likely caused. I searched around for something that could be used as a lever, but there was nothing but stone and splintered wood.

"Engineer Chen built an effective weapon," Guo said with a harsh laugh. "The Small Swords wouldn't believe me when I told them about it. Machines that moved like men. When they saw them, they tried to fight them as if they were men. But they're not. They don't have the same weaknesses. You have to treat them like machines—"

He was rambling.

"Do you need opium?" I asked, feeling hollow inside.

Little Guo shook his head. He looked over to another body lying nearby. "Is he dead?"

I didn't need to look, but I did anyway for his benefit then nodded slowly.

He closed his eyes. "Jiang Wen..."

The body was unrecognizable.

"You both came all this way after the Factories to continue this fight," I said dully.

"The Qing are ignorant tyrants. They executed your own father," he said with a tone of accusation.

Little Guo's father had to have been part of the Ministry of Science. He could be one of my father's men who was cast into exile — perhaps even escaping on the same airship that had carried Yang Hanzhu and Liu Yentai to safety. Guo had taken on all his father's knowledge to come back and seek retribution.

This youth, practically a boy, had dedicated himself to the cause of toppling the empire. And Chang-wei, my betrothed, had dedicated himself to preserving it. Chang-wei had caused this destruction and he would cause more.

"We need to go," Ming-fen said impatiently from behind me.

"Where did you set the explosives?" I demanded.

That was how Guo operated, wasn't it? If there was a trap inside, he would have been the one to build it. He had the knowledge and the background to do it.

I knelt down beside him. "I'm not your enemy, Guo."

The boy stared at Jiang Wen's body where it lay crushed in the dirt. When he turned back to me, Guo looked defeated. "The leadership of the Small Swords is stationed at Yu Gardens. The entire headquarter is rigged to explode."

MING-FEN KNEW the streets of the Old City. I followed her as we ran through them. The inhabitants remained shut away in their homes with doors and windows closed. This left the roads clear as we cut a path through them.

We encountered a patrol and Ming-fen gripped her knives, preparing to fight. I grabbed my needle gun from my belt, but the patrol ran past us without stopping.

"There's fighting at the North Gate," one of them yelled.

Our destination was also to the north, but Ming-fen veered away from the patrol. I heard shouting and the crack of firearms in the distance. The smell of smoke filled the air.

Ming-fen froze in the middle of street.

"What's wrong?" I asked.

"This is exactly what Old Shanghai looked like when I left," she mused darkly.

We continued on to an area with a pond and an ornate pavilion that appeared to be floating on water.

"The Gardens," I murmured.

The battle was already underway. The rebels wore red armbands and sashes to set themselves apart. They were clustered onto a wooden bridge with rifles aimed at two of the automatons. I could hear gunshots beyond the bridge, deeper into the grounds of the garden as well.

"Stay back," Ming-fen commanded and then proceeded to do the exact opposite. She ran into the fray.

I stared into the crush of bodies, the clouds of black smoke and rifle fire. The armored machines stomped among them thrashing and crushing. I strained for a glimpse of Chang-wei or anyone I recognized, but it was hopeless. With a prayer to the heavens, I pushed forward into the chaos.

A haze of smoke enveloped me, and the sound of gunfire rang through the air, accompanied by the ping of iron shot deflecting off metal armor. A nightmare slowness took hold of me as I tried to drag myself through the battle. It was like swimming through syrup.

An automaton smashed through a section of the wooden bridge. I found a clear though indirect route through the rocks that surrounded the lake. As I scrambled over the jagged formations, I could see Ming-fen had somehow managed to get past the bridge. An automaton loomed ahead, thrashing its arms and blocking the path. Rebel footmen shot at it in desperation, but each hit caused the machine to re-orient its attack and sweep its metal arm at them. The multiple inputs confused the logical wiring, but that didn't matter. A confused automaton was still a deadly one.

The machine swung its arm in a crushing sweep. Rather than jumping back, Ming-fen ducked and ran forward. Her sash shot forward like a whip to catch around the ankle joint of the automaton. She grabbed onto the tether with both hands, pulling back with all her might. The automaton toppled, falling headfirst into the water with a crackle of sparks.

I climbed down from the rocks. A jagged edge tore through my sleeve, scraping over my arm, but I ignored it. Finally on solid ground, I ran forward and encountered another automaton on the grassy terrace.

"How many are there?" Ming-fen came up beside me. She'd freed her knives from the sash and brandished one in each hand.

"I don't know."

They'd been disassembled in the crates. The containers were massively large.

Metal footsteps clanged toward us. Another automaton was coming to join the one on the grass, but this one looked different.

The riflemen divided into two teams to surround the second automaton. This one wasn't moving as wildly. It turned and revealed an entirely different design. Rather than the full-plated armor of the others, the front of the machine was a cage.

"There's someone inside!" a rebel shouted.

They'd finally realized one of the machines had an operator. The rifleman started targeting the cage. The operator was fitted with padded armor inside the cage, but still remained vulnerable to head shots. I gasped as a shot struck the man in the face. The armored suit he was encased in crashed backward onto the grass.

This was how Chang-wei had solved the problem. By putting a human mind at the controls.

Chang-wei had taken the design from the Japanese hitokiri assassins, creating an armored suit that was a hybrid of man and machine. His crew of engineers hadn't just come to build the machines — they were needed to operate the new design.

The armored operator positioned his killing machine at the entrance of the park to hold back the tide of people who were trying to flee. Not all of the rebels were armed with firearms. Many of them held nothing but long knives which were useless against the machines. Then again, the firearms weren't effective either. The rebels were running out of ammunition and falling back.

I ran to him. The bullet had shattered the operator's jaw and he lay still within the steel cage. Up close, I saw it was one of the engineers.

"Soling, watch out!"

I looked up at Ming-fen's cry. The automaton was still rampaging on the grass. I darted away as it came crashing through. Shots rang out all around me.

Dragging myself to my feet, I ran. I didn't know where I was going, but I needed to be clear of the fight. I caught sight of Ming-fen ahead of me in her dark tunic. I cut through the pavilion and ran after her.

We'd reached an ornate, palatial looking building. Red banners hung all around it. One of the armored hitokiri suits was fighting its way toward it.

"Stay away from the headquarters." I shouted as loud as I could, but the sounds of the fight drowned out my voice.

I tripped over something and fell. My hand hit against something hard. When I looked, it was into the glassy eyes of a rebel who not long ago had been alive. Shoving myself away, I squeezed my eyes shut but the image wouldn't go away.

Sick, scared, overwhelmed, I crawled through the grass.

Ahead of me, I could hear the creak and groan of the metal suit. The grand hall beyond had to be the rebel headquarter. The building that was rigged to explode. I had to warn Chang-wei, but the urge to hide away, to stay down and safe from danger paralyzed me.

"Ren!" I heard Ming-fen shouting through the darkness.

I opened my eyes again to the sight of a lone figure in the courtyard. It was a man, his hair loose and ragged, falling to his shoulders. He had a red sash wrapped around one arm and two sharp knives, both aimed at the center of the hitokiri cage.

That had to be Ren, Ming-fen's brother. They had the same long and lean look about them.

Ming-fen went to him, sheathing her own knives to take hold of his arm. Ren regarded her woodenly as they spoke. I couldn't hear her words, but I held my breath as his arm went around her shoulders in a rough embrace. Brother and sister.

Then he shoved her aside to run at the hulking armored frame at the steps of the hall. The thing lifted its meal arm to strike at him, but Ren dodged easily, snaking around to jump onto the back of the contraption. As the operator brought the machine around, I could finally see who the operator was. It was Chang-wei inside the cage with his hands gripped around a set of levers.

My heart pounded like thunder. I ran as close as I could. Out of the corner of my eye, I could see Ming-fen doing the same, weapons in hand as she searched for some opening to intervene.

"Chang-wei!" I shouted. "Get away, the building is going to explode!"

Inside the cage, he turned to look at me. At that moment, Ren climbed up higher and stabbed his knives into the gap in the metal armor beneath the helmet — where the back of a man's neck would be. The knife tore into the wires and a spark of electrical energy traveled up his arm. A loud snap emitted from the suit and the entire frame stumbled backward, carrying Ren on top of it.

Chang-wei was locked below within the steel frame. His eyes fixed onto mine before the entire headquarters burst into flame behind him.

CHAPTER 24

I fell to the ground and threw my arms over my head. A wave of heat tore over me. I was certain I was dead because there was suddenly silence. True silence amidst all the violence.

It was almost like peace. The only peace possible.

But I opened my eyes back to fire and destruction. Flames danced over the walls and columns of the hall before me as a high-pitched humming noise filled my ears. I could hear the cracking of the wood and the spit of the fire through the drone.

Chang-wei was no longer in front of me. Neither was Ming-fen or her brother, Ren. Pushing myself up with my arms, I searched the area frantically. There was an armored frame lying face up in the courtyard.

My knees wobbled when I stood, but I staggered over to the machine and found Chang-wei inside. His eyes were closed and he wasn't moving. I shouted his name and it sounded as if my voice had been removed from my body. I was shouting from the bottom of a deep well.

Chang-wei didn't respond. He was covered with ash. I couldn't tell if he was breathing.

With shaking fingers, I reached through the cage. I tried to feel for the pulse in his neck, but his armor was in the way. My hand brushed against his jaw and a lump formed in my throat. I bit back a sob and tried once again to reach for his pulse.

Suddenly his eyes fluttered open. His lips formed around my name.

"Soling."

When I asked him if he was in pain, he nodded weakly. His eyes started to close again. Frantically, I searched the cage for some kind of latch, but couldn't see anything. The structure was dented and the cage appeared to be jammed. I tugged at it, pulling with all my strength, but it wouldn't open.

I could see someone approaching at the edge of my vision. Standing up, I braced my foot against an armored plate and pulled so hard the metal bars dug into my palms.

Firm hands took hold of me by my shoulders to nudge me aside. Then a large, hulking figure grabbed onto the front of the cage and jerked it open with a loud creak.

I stared up into Kai's face. Half of it was covered with bruises. There was a gash down one side and his eye barely opened. He looked back at me for a moment that lasted forever. Then, without a word, he turned to go.

Then Chang-wei groaned with pain and Kai was forgotten. I knelt to help him out of the cage.

"My arm." He winced when I took hold of it. I quickly let go.

Moving slowly, he climbed out of the cage like a crab emerging soft and vulnerable from its shell. He cradled his arm against his side and said something that I couldn't hear. There was still a humming sound in my ears.

"It's not safe here," Chang-wei repeated as loud as he could, his breath wheezing with each word.

That was when I remembered Ming-fen. I searched the courtyard but didn't see any sign of her. There was a blackened figure laying on the ground not far away from us. A long knife rested just beyond his outstretched hand. Ming-fen's brother.

The courtyard was crawling with rebels with their red armbands. We needed to get out of there before they regrouped.

I draped Chang-wei's good arm over my shoulders so he could lean against me as we walked. Our progress was slow. I heard shots being fired, but I couldn't discern where the fighting was coming from. We were surrounded by it.

We left the gardens and trudged back into the streets. I couldn't remember the way to the East Gate, but at the moment all I cared about was getting away from the rebel stronghold.

"You...shouldn't have come..." Chang-wei gasped.

"Save your breath."

Alarm bells rang constantly now. There were people rushing through the streets amidst shouts of, "Invaders!" Among those cries, there were others that warned of foreign devils. No one knew who was attacking who.

"The imperial troops...should be...coming...from the North Gate," Chang-wei said.

I looked all around, searching for some place where we could take shelter. With Chang-wei's injuries, I couldn't risk moving too far. His ribs were likely broken and I feared he might puncture a lung — though for now it was promising that he could speak without coughing blood.

"Stop talking," I pleaded, trying to hold him steady.

That was when we saw them. A band of five armed soldiers without the red cloth that marked the Small Swords. The locals scattered in their wake, disappearing quickly into the nooks and corners that only they knew.

The men advanced on us.

"You!" the leader called.

Chang-wei held up his hand and tried to identify himself as aligned with the imperial army, but it didn't matter. The leader advanced with his rifle lifted to crack the butt of it across

Chang-wei's jaw. I screamed and fired my needle gun. The opium dart lodged into the soldier's neck and took effect almost immediately. He lurched forward before sinking to the ground.

Chang-wei was on hands and knees before me, still stunned by the blow. I tried to help him up, but the others were advancing. With a shaking hand, I reloaded and shot two more darts blindly into the closest ones, not knowing whether they hit or not. Rough hands grabbed at me and shoved me onto the ground. Through the blur of bodies, I could see Chang-wei lunge to try to pull them off of me.

I fought the tangle of arms around me. I couldn't see anything but dark shapes and cursed in despair that my ears were still ringing. Then I heard a gasp above me and the grip on my wrist fell away. There was another grunt, then a scream. I looked up to see the soldier reaching for his face. A silver dragon throwing knife protruded from one eye.

Blinking, I stared upward. Ming-fen stood over me like a statue.

The rest of the attackers had backed away. I pushed up from the ground. A soldier hovered over Chang-wei to the right of us, aiming a kick to his mid-section. Ming-fen was there in two strides, her hand lashing out. There was a flash of steel and then the soldier was clutching at his throat, blood seeping between his fingers.

I ran to Chang-wei and pulled him to his feet. The soldiers who remained were either unconscious from the darts or injured enough to leave off. Some had run away and I feared reinforcements.

Chang-wei leaned against me, his breathing ragged. I looked incredulously at Ming-fen whose face was covered in a smear of ash and blood.

"Mei-mei." Her eyes were black like stone. "We need to find a place to hide."

∾

WE FOUND a trapdoor in an abandoned dwelling that led down to a cellar. I gathered refuse over the door before stealing below.

There was little visibility inside. A small cut-out provided the only ventilation and looked out right below the ground floor of the building. Through it I could see the flurry of movement outside.

"The imperial forces are here," Ming-fen said grimly beside me. "Everyone who they decide is a rebel is a rebel. They won't care who they kill."

Chang-wei had collapsed onto a low bench in the corner. There were several bamboo mats laid out on the floor. A set of pipes had been left in the corner.

I recognized immediately what the hidden space must have been used for. It was an opium den.

For a long, long time we listened to the sounds of disorder outside. The sounds of a city falling to chaos.

Ming-fen sat back with her legs folded to her chest as she stared at the door at the top of the stairs. She had her arms wrapped around her knees. A knife remained in each hand.

When I finally dared to move again, I turned to Chang-wei. His arm was still cradled against his side.

"It's broken," he said through gritted teeth as I reached toward him.

Not only his arm was broken, but his hand as well. And a few ribs. I asked him to take a deep breath and he couldn't without pain.

"I can bind it."

I glanced over at Ming-fen and saw she hadn't moved. As much as I was grateful she'd come to our rescue, I couldn't forget that her brother and Chang-wei had been locked in battle before the explosion. She ignored Chang-wei now, as if he didn't exist. Which meant she remembered as well.

I turned to Chang-wei and undid his belt, helping him out of the padded armor that he wore. He winced as we freed his arm.

Coincidentally, I'd studied the skeletal structure of the hand and wrist quite a bit when I was younger. My father had lost his arm during an accident experimenting with gunpowder formulas. He'd had it replaced with a mechanical arm. The workings and comparisons of man and machine had become a fascination of mine.

I didn't know how much that knowledge would help here, but it was better than none. I cut and rolled up sections of the bamboo mat to form the splints. I also dismantled my bladed fan. The smaller metal pieces could be used to stabilize his fingers. The bindings I had to tear from our clothing.

"Here."

I took the strap of the belt and held it up for him.

Chang-wei bit down hard on it to keep from crying out. I would need to set the bones before splinting them and I'd used up all my opium darts to fend off the imperial soldiers.

"I'm not as knowledgeable about bone-setting as Kai."

Suddenly my chest hitched and my eyes flooded with tears. Chang-wei reached out with his good hand to touch his fingertips gently against my cheek. I couldn't bear to look up at him. Instead, I wiped impatiently at my eyes and set to work on his arm, trying to piece it back together like a broken puzzle.

I started to tell him not to move as he lifted his other arm to remove the leather.

"I did this," Chang-wei said gravely.

I stared downward, still unable to lift my head. My throat, my entire soul was clenched tight, struggling hard to hold too much inside. He flinched as I pulled a length of cloth around his wrist.

"I thought I could keep everything under control, Soling."

What was he speaking of? His own creations? The loyalist army? The Emperor?

"None of it was ever under your control, Chang-wei."

For once, I couldn't hide my anger. No one person was to blame for what was happening, but that didn't make Chang-wei blameless. I wasn't ready to absolve him — or myself.

"We shouldn't have come," I choked out.

"Someone else would have done the same. Or worse—"

"Worse?" I snapped. The Qing army, our side, was destroying the city they had claimed they were saving from the insurgents. "You can't keep on enslaving yourself to the will of the imperial court. You'll never be able to prove yourself."

I was met with nothing but silence. From the other side of the room, I heard a soft shuffling. Wei Ming-fen was looking away from us. I didn't know if she could hear our conversation, but it didn't matter if she could. These words had to be spoken. Finally.

Chang-wei gritted his teeth as he regarded me. His breath came in shallow gasps and he looked to the point of breaking. I was already broken. There was no knowing what form the pieces that were left would become.

"If we turn away from the Emperor, we'll be condemned. They'll come for us," he said gravely.

"No, they won't," I snapped. "Do you really think anyone cares about us? Do you think anyone will remember who we are?"

If we died in Shanghai, we'd be forgotten tomorrow. I was certain of it.

The Qing empire was in disarray. Its army scattered. They couldn't restore order against the foreign invaders or the rebel factions. Chang-wei was a fool to think he could save the empire — and I'd been a fool as well.

Blinking back tears, I returned to the task of trying to hold Chang-wei together. He swallowed a gasp as I secured the binding. Even as careful as I was, there was no helping the pain.

"Soling," he began, his voice strained.

I shook my head. There was no use arguing. He was loyal to the end, beyond reason because his loyalty gave him a reason. But my last tie to the Qing had snapped. For a moment, I was lost, but it wasn't hard for me to search out a new path. There was my mother. My brother. Liu Yentai and Yang Hanzhu.

"The only thing that matters is that we protect the ones we love," I said. "The people held deep in our hearts."

You and I, I wanted to tell him.

But the words wouldn't come.

NIGHT LEFT us surrounded by darkness. The sounds from outside had become louder. We could hear the stamp of foot-steps and raised voices then the long silences. Time stretched out for an eternity.

It was impossible to fall asleep. When I did nod off, it was a restless slumber. I lay down next to Chang-wei but was afraid to touch him due to his injuries. I woke up in the darkness with the fingers of his good hand lightly intertwined with mine.

When daylight finally came, Ming-fen was still crouched in the same position. We continued waiting, though for what, no one could say. Through the vent, we could see boots marching through the streets. There were cries, wails. In the distance, gunfire. I heard it all through the continued hum in my ears.

At one point, we heard footsteps overhead. I huddled close to Chang-wei and he circled his arm around me until the foot-steps receded.

"We need water," I said a long time later when the light through the crack began to fade.

We hadn't eaten or drunk anything in more than a day. I'd started ignoring hunger pangs long ago and I was certain Chang-wei and Ming-fen were doing the same. But hunger wasn't the worst of our worries. Without water we would continue to weaken and I wanted to find out what was happening outside while we still had the strength to fight — or flee.

"Anything nearby will have been sacked," Ming-fen said.

We'd seen the imperial troops marching up and down the street.

Chang-wei stood. "We'll go together."

Ming-fen climbed the stairs ahead of us and lifted the door a crack to peer out before turning back to indicate that it was clear. She then pushed the door open and climbed up. I followed and turned around to help Chang-wei up.

It was late in the afternoon with the daylight fading. The rooms of the small house were eerily empty as we walked through them, scouring for anything useful. We found some dregs of water at the bottom of a wash basin and shared it between us. It felt like barely enough to wet my tongue, entirely gone before I even swallowed.

We weren't bold enough to venture outside of our sanctuary. After peeking outside the windows into the empty lane, we retreated once more into the cellar.

The next day, we crept upside once more with thoughts of scavenging through the other buildings in the street. Instead, we ducked back as a band of soldiers dragged two men out into the street and cut their throats.

Anyone the imperial soldiers accused of being a rebel was irrefutably a rebel.

We hurried back into our hiding spot and stayed down despite the thirst and the hunger. I could feel myself growing lightheaded, my thoughts drifting without focus.

There was nothing but silence between us for most of the day. We were each lost in our own thoughts, but there was something I needed to say to Ming-fen.

"Your brother's death was a tragedy," I began.

Ming-fen didn't say anything. When I glanced at her, she was looking away.

"I'm sorry," I began, knowing the words sounded empty. "I'm sorry for everything."

We were in her debt. Ming-fen had saved our lives, but I realized she was within her right to turn around and take vengeance.

"I'm the one to blame," Chang-wei interjected.

"I do blame you, Chen Chang-wei," she said coldly. "Just as I blame the Small Swords. The Emperor. The foreign devils. I blame my brother for the choices he made."

She paused and only addressed me when she spoke again. "You don't need to worry about me seeking vengeance on your betrothed, Mei-mei," she said bitterly.

When the Small Swords had taken Old Shanghai, she had rescued Taotai Wu. Now she protected us while Qing loyalists tore the city apart. Ming-fen was White Lotus, but apparently adhered to a different set of principles than Kai or the saboteurs.

It was fire that eventually drove us out.

The imperial soldiers had looted what they could and were now burning the homes that remained.

We escaped the hovel before the fire traveled to us. From there, we huddled in dark corners and alleyways. Every time the sound of footsteps came near, we froze, barely breathing. Everyone, Qing or rebel, was a threat.

I'd fixed a sling around Chang-wei's arm and shoulder to immobilize it. If we were discovered, there was little we could do to fight back. We stayed in the shadows as Ming-fen scouted ahead. Eventually we hid away inside another abandoned residence.

"Why are they burning the houses?" I asked brokenly.

"Punishment," Ming-fen pronounced. "Because they won and the Old City lost."

Chang-wei swallowed with difficulty. We hadn't had anything to drink in over a day. "We need to get word to Taotai Wu. He needs to put a stop to this."

"Are you mad?" Ming-fen retorted. "What makes you think Taotai Wu has any authority here? How do you know this isn't exactly what he wants to happen?"

Chang-wei fell silent, but Ming-fen was far from done.

"Do you even see what's happening here?"

"I do see," Chang-wei said after a heavy pause. "I see what's happening."

My ears would not stop ringing.

THREE DAYS PASSED of looting and killing. I don't know why the violence finally stopped. Had the Qing loyalists satisfied their bloodlust? Was their nothing left worth burning? Had the last of the rebels been executed?

Taotai Wu was eventually reinstated to the circuit intendant seat. He attempted to restore order and allowed the displaced to leave Old Shanghai.

We crawled out of our hiding place and trudged toward the East Gate. The only water we could find was a in a muddy puddle by the roadside. Cupping our hands together, we drank from it greedily before dragging on.

Chang-wei leaned against me for balance. I leaned against him for strength. My body felt as if it were made of wooden sticks, ready to snap at the slightest touch.

Ming-fen stared as a wagon rolled past with a broken automaton loaded upon it. The steel parts lay in a pile.

Jiang Wen's body still lay where we had found it. He was hardly recognizable and the putrid smell of death filled the air. Little Guo, who we had last seen pinned beneath an automaton, was nowhere to be found.

We were in the middle of a line headed for the foreign concession when Dean Burton found us. He had come in his pressed suit, hat in hand. Ming-fen didn't say anything to him as she left the line to walk toward the tall foreigner.

I told him of Chang-wei's injuries and Burton ushered us toward a waiting steam carriage.

Ming-fen's spine remained straight as she entered the transport. Burton reached out a consoling hand to her, but she refused it, opting to stare out the side window. An invisible wall had formed between her and the rest of the world.

I helped Chang-wei into the carriage before climbing in myself. It was a silent ride back to the American section. Even Burton didn't find it fit to make idle conversation.

As I watched the pristine streets of the foreign concession roll by, I was stricken by the realization that the carnage of Old Shanghai had not reached the other side of the river at all. Business had continued in the foreign settlement, blissfully ignorant of the atrocities down the river.

It was as if the fires, the destruction, and the death had never happened. It all took place in some other place, far away.

Chang-wei's hand brushed against mine and my breath caught. He didn't try to take hold of me. He just laid his fingers alongside mine. Waiting. The engine hummed and we rolled past several streets before I had the courage to twine my fingers through his.

"Sī shǒu?" he asked softly.

"Together," I agreed as we held on to each other.

EPILOGUE

The expulsion of the Small Swords from Shanghai was hailed as a great triumph of the Qing state over a vicious rebel army. The three days of fire and death, murder and rape, at the hands of the loyalist forces were ignored. After a year of siege, the inhabitants of Old Shanghai, many who had their homes destroyed and looted, continued to flee into the foreign settlement. The lines between the old walled Chinese city and the foreign-controlled treaty port were forever blurred.

Wei Ming-fen left abruptly while we were recuperating at Burton's mansion. One morning, I heard the front door open and close downstairs, and she was gone.

I couldn't find Kai either. I tried to seek help through the White Lotus, but no one would speak to me, an outsider. The last I'd seen of him was when he'd helped me free Chang-wei from the cage of the mechanized suit. Even though he had betrayed the empire, Kai and I had once been friends. I wanted to believe he had made it out alive.

Months after Shanghai was recaptured from the Small Swords, the main army of the misnamed Heavenly Peace rebels made an assault on the port city of Ningpo by land and sea. They were repelled by the valiant efforts of an ignominious alliance of outcasts and ne'er-do-wells, including my good friend and Chang-wei's good enemy, Yang Hanzhu.

There were still bounties on his head in every port. In the meantime, he'd also received a commendation from the imperial navy for his heroic efforts at Ningpo. It was a strange world.

The Ministry of Science was commended after the victory, with Kuo Lishen granted an elevated title. The Chief Engineer then turned around to offer Chang-wei a promotion.

He respectfully declined.

"No more," Chang-wei told me privately. "I know where my loyalties lie from here on forward."

Chang-wei left the Ministry to take a post at the Academy, putting walls and more walls between him and the Emperor. It was easy to disappear into obscurity with so many others vying for access to the imperial court. We would continue to navigate the intricate web of politics in Peking, but we would do it together.

My mother also looked to becoming a teacher, though not in such an exalted location. She developed plans to open a smaller, private school that accepted all students, male and female. Chief Engineer Kuo continued to consult her. Apparently, his understanding of mathematics was quite poor, as he found frequent excuses to seek out her opinion.

The Emperor continued to refuse to meet with the Western delegations, instead sending his younger brother Prince Gong. The city of Nanking was still under rebel control. Western diplomats, no longer claiming neutrality, proposed a joint force to take out the remaining rebel strongholds. It would have allowed Western troops to march into our mainland.

The Emperor turned down their offer.

As for me, there was enough work in the neighborhoods of Peking for a physician to keep busy. In the traditional ways of a provincial yishi, those under my care only paid me when they were well. Once in a while, someone came to me hoping to be cured of opium addiction. For that, there was no cure.

I steered the addicted away from the cessation pills and kept my eyes on the opium refuges. In the meantime, I could only prescribe various extracts to ease the withdrawal symptoms along with a regiment of balance, rest, and perseverance. Like Hanzhu, I was looking for a solution to what seemed like an impossible problem. I was still searching.

Chang-wei and I were married in Peking within the year. Yang Hanzhu sent along a gift of a karakuri puppet that served tea. The scoundrel.

On our wedding night, Chang-wei took me finally into his arms.

"You're here," he whispered, his lips touching gently against my cheek, the soft skin of my throat. "I was always happy that you were there with me."

A wave of emotion swept over me. We had journeyed together across the empire, over land and sea.

I looked up into his face and pulled him closer. Chang-wei reached for the fastenings on the silk wedding dress with his clever hands.

We left the lanterns burning.

HISTORICAL NOTES

The Gunpowder Chronicles are closely tied to actual events in history surrounding the Opium War and the internal uprisings that plagued the Qing Dynasty at the same time.

The Rebellion Engines revolves around the very real Small Swords Rebellion when a group of insurgents took over the Old City, also called the Chinese City or Old Shanghai. As depicted in the story, many refugees from the Old City and from the surrounding areas flooded into what was previously considered the foreign concession. These events forever altered the landscape of the international settlement and created the melting pot of "East meets West" that ushered in Shanghai's glittering, lassez-faire reputation of the 1930s.

As shown in the book, when the Qing army recaptured Shanghai, they did execute the rebels as traitors, but they also rampaged through the Old City, looting, burning and raping for three days — an event that I was surprised I could only find mentioned in passing. Qing Dynasty depictions of the recapture predictably paint the Small Swords as rebel scum and the loyalists as liberators of Shanghai. The suffering of the civilians is glossed over.

Western records of the uprising from across the river were similarly obtuse about the human toll of the insurrection. The claims of being neutral while not quite neutral also ring true with historical accounts of rebel incursions on Shanghai and Ningpo.

Given recent events in the United States, I couldn't help but pay particular attention to factors that might cause such insurrections and the human and spiritual toll of them to be glossed over. The current day willful amnesia moved me to try to depict in some way the confusion and unrest of the Small Swords Rebellion and its aftermath. And then contrast the scale of the tragedy with the careless dismissal by British, American, and French interests within the same city who were profiting off of the downfall of the Qing Dynasty.

The White Lotus Society was first mentioned in Tales from the Gunpowder Chronicles and plays a role in the events of The Rebellion Engines. The White Lotus, frequently fictionalized in wuxia fiction, is a real group with a long history tracing back to the fall of the Yuan Dynasty. There were several major White Lotus rebellions against the Qing Dynasty as well.

As Ming-fen pointed out, there was a tendency to label any dissident faction as White Lotus. Gatherings of the White Lotus Society for worship and incense burning were branded as acts of rebellion and subsequently outlawed by the Qing government.

During the era of the Taiping Rebellion, there were actually many other ancillary uprisings, though the largest of them was the Taiping army, which numbered at its height in the hundreds of thousands. Many of the smaller rebel factions claimed allegiance with the Taiping Rebellion in "the enemy of my enemy is my friend" fashion. The Small Swords Rebellion is one such example. There were other factions throughout the country as opposition to the Qing rose from many different sides.

In the true historical account, the Qing government eventually needed to rely on support from outside, from foreign troops, to eventually put down the Taiping Rebellion. Also, in the actual history, another devastating loss in the second Opium War further erodes Qing rule and hastens the young Emperor's rapid decline.

The history of the Taiping Rebellion as well as the treaty ports and foreign-influence in China is a complex one and I know there are inevitably oversights and omissions in this alternative history.

In this re-imagined steampunk version of the Opium Wars, it was my view that a stronger empire would be able to hold off the devastation of a second Opium War. But there's a lot of drama still to deal with.

At one point, I worried that it would be impossible for the saga to resolve all problems and banish all evil. The Gunpowder world would remain a troubled place on the brink of war.

When living in tumultuous times, true peace can only be what you find and cultivate within yourself.

I realize this is a very Buddhist outlook at its core. Though some might find this hard to sit with, happiness while the world rages on, I find this thought comforting. Because don't we all live in tumultuous times?

And we all can hope to cultivate peace from within.

ACKNOWLEDGMENTS

A huge hug and thank you to my editor, Dayna Hart, who stuck with this series from start to finish. Thank you so much for your enthusiasm, your encouragement and your optimism about this odd little saga that took WAY longer than we originally thought to finish.

This book was many years in the making, through all sorts of ups and downs, stops and starts — the most recent hurdle being the COVID-19 pandemic. It was the constant online contact and encouragement from close friends — Shawntelle Madison, Sela Carson, Amanda Berry and Bria Quinlan that kept me from imploding. I can't wait for the day when we can all gather again in person so I can thank you all first hand for helping me keep it together.

I must give a special thanks to Elizabeth Essex and David Bridger who reviewed and provided guidance on the terminology and content of the chapters that involved sailing and nautical terms. Despite insisting on setting a huge portion of the story on a Chinese junk manned by pirates (or pirate-like characters), I know zero when it comes to sailing the great seas and they were brilliant in setting me on the correct course. Any errors that remain in the text are solely mine.

Finally, I want to thank the Authors of Asian Novels group. I remember when the group was a small ragtag band trying to write Asian-set commercial fiction. Now we're a large ragtag band and I can't stress enough how bolstering it is to know I'm not the only one out there, especially on those extra-hard self-doubt days. Thank you and may we continue to try to crack the code together.

ALSO BY JEANNIE LIN

Sign-up for Jeannie's mailing list at www.jeannielin.com to receive updates on new releases, appearances, and special giveaways.

ABOUT JEANNIE LIN

USA TODAY bestselling author Jeannie Lin started writing her first book while working as a high school science teacher in South Central Los Angeles. Her stories are inspired by a mix of historical research and wuxia adventure tales. Jeannie's groundbreaking historical romances set in Tang Dynasty China have received multiple awards, including the Golden Heart for her debut novel, *Butterfly Swords*. She also writes an Opium War steampunk series and a historical erotica series under the pen name Liliana Lee.

You can find her at:
Jeannie Lin's website
Newsletter

CPSIA information can be obtained
at www.ICGtesting.com
Printed in the USA
LVHW081135190322
713865LV00025B/508